CW00493457

Hot Flashes, Sorcery, & Soulmates

Menopause, Magick, & Mystery

JC BLAKE

Published by Redbegga Publishing, 2020.

HOT FLASHES, SORCERY, & SOULMATES

First edition. November 19, 2020.

Written by JC BLAKE.

For my family.

Chapter One

Strange as it seems, it began with an infestation of fairies.

Before you start thinking how charming that would be, let me tell you, fairies are a menace!

I'm sorry to ruin the fantasy, but fairies are devious little troublemakers and the worst kind of gossip. Add to that razor-sharp teeth and a short temper, and you've got nothing less than winged demons. So, when we had an infestation in the weeks after my initiation into the coven, life at Haligern Cottage turned upside down.

I had no idea that their presence was a portent of far worse to come.

Three weeks after the magical Solstice ceremony where I had become a witch of Haligern coven, I woke to a flash of light and tiny, high pitched giggles. At first, in my confused state, the voices seemed part of one of the bizarre, often troubled, dreams that had begun to inhabit my mind in the months before I turned fifty. I had put the dreams down to the hormonal chaos my poor body was being subject to, but since my initiation I had come to understand that they were from another source entirely. Disruptive hormones did, however, mess with just how many hours I dreamed.

Sleep was often difficult to slip into and remaining below the surface of consciousness throughout the night even more so. I would often rise to semi-consciousness, aware of an uncomfortable heat emanating from my body and the increasingly damp state of my pyjamas. Heart palpitating, the worst nights seemed to take forever, but just when I began to despair of ever sleeping soundly again, I would have a full and much deeper night of sleep and wake feeling recharged, reset, and ready to embrace this new era of life with all its chaos and beauty. Since my fiftieth, the menopause had moved on from its peri-menopausal learner phase; the training wheels were off, the safety switch disarmed, and the hormonal roller coaster was hurtling along at full speed. I was strapped in for the ride, and no amount of protestation would let me disembark.

As I sat up in bed with a jerk, one hand outstretched to fend off the blinding light, the other clutching the duvet beneath my chin, sweat trickling down my sternum, Lucifer, my acerbic familiar, yelped then hissed as he was bucked from the end of my bed.

"Do you mind?"

"There's something in the room!"

"Yes, you!"

"No, listen!"

Lucifer jumped back up onto my bed as the tiny voices became quarrelsome. Their squabbling was followed by the thud of an object dropping onto the carpet.

"Fairies," was Lucifer's nonchalant reply.

Felt as the displacement of air, and heard as fluttering, something whooshed above my head. A giggle followed. I sat petrified. This wasn't the first time in the past weeks that one of the tiny creatures had swooped above my head. In fact, tuned into my fear, they seemed to take delight in tormenting me.

Mice were my number one trigger to panic, and these winged demons slotted right into that category. There were other triggers of course, cannulas for example, and obviously rats, but rats were a whole other level of horrifying.

"Do something, Lucifer!" I demanded. "You're a cat. Aren't you supposed to catch them?"

By now my sight had returned and the grey early morning light was enough to discern Lucifer's form at the end of my bed. If his lips could purse, they would have. "Are you suggesting that I am a ... ratter!" He spat the last word and the eyes that glared at me flashed with anger.

"Yes! I mean no!" Another swooping demon brushed close to my head and I let out a yelp of fear. Lucifer remained passive at the end of my bed.

"Apologise!" he demanded. He made no effort to help as another beast joined the fun swooping low then disappearing into the shadows at lightning speed.

I pulled the duvet above my head. "Do something!" I begged from beneath the covers. "Please!"

The next moments were filled with squeals, hisses, and clattering objects as Lucifer chased the fairies from the room. At one point he jumped from my lap to my head parkour style, then used it as a springboard to attack the chittering demons. From beneath the duvet, I listened as books, my alarm clock, and a glass of water were all kicked from my bedside table and crashed to the floor. The curtain rings scraped along the pole and then the room grew quiet. Overheating and gasping for fresh air, I lowered the duvet and switched on the bedside light.

The room was a mess with my belongings scattered across the carpet. The curtains were flicked across the tottering bedside lamp. On my dressing table bottles of perfume and cleanser had been knocked over whilst the chair tucked beneath was wedged at an angle, its front legs raised. The contents of my makeup bag had spilled out, and powdered rouge lay in broken shards on the carpet.

There wasn't a fairy in sight.

I took a huge, relieved, breath.

"Thank you would be nice," quipped Lucifer.

"Thank you!" I said with an effort to keep exasperation out of my voice. I was genuinely thankful, but he hadn't given me any time to offer my thanks before demanding it.

Perched on the wedged chair he jumped to the floor, nimbly missing the shards of powdered rouge and strewn cases of eye shadow and lipstick. As he picked his way across the floor and jumped back onto the bed, my mobile rang. I scoured the room, searching for the phone as it continued to ring. Ordinarily, it was placed on my bedside table connected to the charging cable overnight, but now it rang from a hidden location. With the phone continuing to ring, and unable to see it, panic set in. Outside, the rising sun had pushed the dark back to grey. It was earliest morning. At this time of year that meant the time was around four am. Nobody called me at four am in the morning. It had to be an emergency.

The phone's ringing was insistent and even Lucifer uncurled from the foot of the bed to seek out the source of the demanding noise.

"Under the dresser," he said in his usual disinterested way.

Knowing that the phone would switch to voicemail at any moment, I crouched beside the dresser, and slid my fingers into the narrow gap at its base. Cold glass met my searching fin-

gertips, and I drew the mobile out. Of course, it stopped ringing just as I eased it out from under the drawers. Checking the
missed call log showed that the caller had been Pascal.

"Something's wrong, Lucifer. Pascal would never call me at
four in the morning."

"Hah! Perhaps poor little Toadie is feeling lonely." Lucifer's
tone was mocking and unsympathetic.

"Perhaps he is ... and don't call him Toadie, Lou."

"Well, he is a toad."

"*Was* a toad. He's not one anymore. The spell only lasted a
few days. I think the experience traumatised him."

"Well, he deserved it."

I didn't reply. Guilt oozed over me. Sure, Pascal's infidelity
had been devastating, but I had allowed my anger to boil over
into rage as I cast the spell that transformed him into an ugly
toad. Along with the guilt came fear. The power that had suffused every cell in my body had come from somewhere primal.
Yes, it was my voice when the spell was cast, but it hadn't
been me speaking. The knowledge came from some instinctive
source. I had been elated at the power coursing through my
veins, but terrified too. Now, in the knowledge that the power
wasn't entirely mine, I viewed it with a sense of awe and responsibility. I was channelling ancestral magic and, like the owner
of a Grade I listed building, merely the caretaker. I was also the
gatekeeper of a power only hinted at.

I stared at the screen, puffing a little as I caught my breath
after the exertion of jumping across the room and kneeling on
all fours to retrieve the phone. A series of beeps alerted me
to the voicemail. I ignored it and called Pascal direct. He answered within seconds.

"Liv!"

"Pascal!"

I expected an outpouring of words. When silence greeted me from the other end of the line, I feared the worst. Something terrible had happened. Someone we knew, perhaps a close relative, maybe his mother (I tried my best here not to get my hopes up – honest!) had died.

"What's happened?"

"Erm ... you called me."

"Yes, I know that, but I just missed *your* call."

"No. Yes. I know that." He was uncharacteristically flustered. "But you ... the video that you sent me earlier ... I kind of found it ... are you alright, Liv? I'm kind of confused."

He's confused! "I didn't call you earlier and I definitely didn't send you a video."

"You did!" He became defensive then. "About ten minutes ago."

"I was asleep ten minutes ago."

"Sure ... okay, but ... I thought it was over between us. After the – he coughed, obviously uncomfortable at the memory – after the toad incident ... I thought there was no way back."

After you called me by another woman's name, you mean! "It is over," I agreed, pain searing through me.

"Then why the video?"

"I don't know what video you're talking about."

"The one you just sent me ... ten minutes ago."

"I was asleep ten minutes ago!" We were going round in circles and the sense of his discomfort was making me squirm. What on earth was on the video? "Tell me about the video." I dreaded his response.

"Well, it's of you, in bed ..."

Oh, heck!

"... and you look to be asleep. Actually, you were snoring."

My cheeks began to burn.

"It's kind of weird ... sending your ex a video of you sleeping, or I guess pretending to sleep ... If you wanted me back, another kind of video might do the trick ..."

He left this suggestion to hang in the air and my jaw slackened to open. "Pascal," I took a stern voice. "I have no idea how you got that video, but rest assured I do not want you back and I would never send you ... suggestive videos of myself."

"Well ..."

"No! Listen. It's the middle of the night. Go back to sleep. I'll talk to you tomorrow. Okay?"

We ended the conversation and I immediately checked my phone. Sure enough, there were several photographs of me in bed along with one video. I watched the unflattering video. It showed a pudgy, pasty faced and middle-aged woman snorting in sleep. The flush of embarrassment as it stung my cheeks and crept into my hairline was intense. There was only one explanation—the fairies had videoed me and sent it to Pascal!

"That's it!" I exploded. "Those monsters have to go!"

Chapter Two

Despite the commotion, but sure that my room was now a fairy-free zone, I crawled back into bed and managed a few more dream-filled hours. The sense of oppression that inhabited my dreams was particularly dark that morning and I woke with a hammering heart and heaviness in my soul. No figures inhabited my dream this time, nothing discernible anyway, but I knew they were there—dancing in the shadows. The creatures undulated behind a wall of flame, dark shapes that writhed and twisted. Something entirely evil hid behind the fire and with each dream it seemed to grow closer, and more intimate.

Struggling to shake the creeping sense of coming doom, I showered, dressed, and made my way to the kitchen. It was surprisingly quiet though radiated chaos. Every surface was cluttered with glass bottles and vials of all shapes and various sizes. There were tall-necked rose-coloured ones, short angular green ones, bulbous clear ones, and a variety of squat cylindrical and square jars. The bottles were filled with elixirs and topped with corks. Some had been sealed with wax. The jars held tinctures, creams, and salves, each bearing a hand-written label in Aunt Thomasin's beautiful copperplate script. Over half the large and well-scrubbed pine kitchen table was covered in waxed paper laid out with slabs of sweet-smelling and hand-made soaps infused with honey, milk from Old Mawde, our goat, and petals from the garden. The kitchen smelled delicious but, in that moment, I would have exchanged it all for a waft of good coffee; despite the extra hours I'd managed in bed, my brain was fogged and my body ached with fatigue.

Before I had a chance to step to the stove and reach for the coffee grinder, Aunt Beatrice, ankle length red apron wrapped tightly around her waist, the bib reaching to just below the collar of her shirt, held up a tin bucket. I sighed. She didn't need to speak. I knew exactly what she wanted.

"Now?"

She nodded, the smile on her face mischievous. "Old Mawde will be just desperate. Serves the old hag right, but we need milk for your coffee."

Although her reference to Old Mawde's desperation as being deserved struck me as a little odd, my focus was on the caffeine. "I'll have it black," I offered without much hope.

"I'll grind the beans whilst you milk her." This last comment was made as a peace offering, but there was no room for discussion.

I glanced out of the window, looking for a final excuse not to tramp down the garden to the goat's enclosure, but quickly relented. The morning was already bright, the early summer sun hot. I had no excuse, felt a sense of responsibility to contribute to the smooth running of the household, and wanted to help, but I really wanted that coffee! I took the bucket from Aunt Beatrice's outstretched arm.

"Good girl!" she responded as though I were five years old again. The thought stopped me in my tracks. Old Mawde had been in residence at the cottage even then. "Aunt Bea," I said as I retrieved my wellingtons from the walk-in cupboard, "just how old is Old Mawde?"

Aunt Beatrice held the long-spouted teapot that she used to add drops of concentrated elixir to the bottles, mid-air. "Oh, not too old, Livitha."

"And why did you say that the 'old hag deserved it'?" My interest was now piqued. Was this a case similar to Lucifer's, where one cat had been replaced by another without my knowledge?

Beatrice appeared a little flustered. This was not unusual for my skittish aunt, but I was only asking about a goat. My curiosity roused, I pushed on. "So, I remember milking Old Mawde as a child. I'm fifty now. I didn't think goats could live that long. And even if they did, would a geriatric goat still be giving milk?" I left this hanging in the air as Aunt Beatrice returned to pouring the liquid into a group of newly filled bottles on the counter beside the sink. I knew that lying wasn't an activity my aunt indulged in. However, skirting around the issue was.

"No, generally they don't."

"Generally, they don't?"

"That's right. Generally, they don't."

She was being deliberately evasive, but my next question was interrupted by the chitter of tiny voices. After the trauma of last night, I was on instant alert. "Fairies!" I hissed and reached for the broom propped against the cupboard wall.

Turning to face the kitchen I stepped out of the cupboard, armed and ready to shoo the pesky vermin out of the room. The giggling chitter continued and, in one corner where a table was stacked with boxed soap and half-packed boxes of bottled potions, glass chinked.

"Over there!" I darted to the noise, surprised at my own bravery. Like mice, fairies set off my fight or flight reflex. But that morning, still appalled and humiliated by their video prank, I decided to fight. The giggling continued, glass chinked from another part of the kitchen, and then a bottle toppled beside the stove. I jumped to the clatter almost knocking Aunt Beatrice over in the process.

"Livitha! Calm down."

I heard Aunt Beatrice's voice but, still scorched by the knowledge that Pascal had thought I'd sent him some quirky – and to his mind, weirdly kinky – video, in an effort to get him back, I was possessed with my need to exact revenge. "I want them out of this house! They're nothing but interfering, trouble-making monsters!" I swatted at them across the bottles as several tiny creatures emerged. The chittering became annoyed and a bottle toppled, knocking two more over and spilling the contents onto the floor.

"My precious potion!" Aunt Beatrice gasped as more bottles wobbled. Liquid glugged from their open necks and poured onto the floor. One fell and shattered on the red clay tiles. Glass flew and skittered across the floor. "Now just stop this. All of you!" Aunt Beatrice scolded. With quick movements she stepped between me and the fairies and righted a teetering bottle.

I took a step back, appalled at the chaos and destruction my actions had caused. Once again, I had let my emotions take control of my actions. Just as with the toad incident, I had let anger rule my emotions and that was something I found difficult to reconcile. "I'm so sorry," I said, full of remorse. "I'll clean up, Aunt Bea. I'm so sorry."

"Don't fret, child," she soothed. "It's only a little mixture that is lost."

But I knew how much hard work and energy had gone into creating that mixture, knew too just how much she cherished each drop. I was acutely aware that each plant had taken an entire year to grow, was plucked at the exact moment when the moon or the sun was at its most beneficial, and its power invoked through ancient charms. For my aunts, creating the potions wasn't for fun, or commercial gain, it was a spiritual undertaking intricately woven with a deep love and appreciation for nature's bounty, a time when they channelled our ancestral magick.

I cleaned the mess of liquid and glass as Aunt Beatrice placated the little monsters. I found her methods fascinating. At first, she spoke to them in a soothing tone, then began to sing. The words were ancient, the melody undulating. The clinking of glass and wobbling of bottles stopped. After several minutes of singing the lullaby she retrieved a large, cloth-wrapped rectangular cheese from the pantry and cut a small chunk from one end. The cheese was of a soft and crumbly type, a little like a stilton with blue veins running throughout. It smelt like Pascal's socks in the days when he'd played rugby at the weekends, before he'd taken up potting a very different variety of 'hole' on his golf weekends. The cheese, with its odorous, stinky-feet whiff, was the one thing my aunts made that I didn't appreciate. After chopping a chunk off, she crumbled it into a saucer and then poured a little concentrated elixir over it before proceeding to mash the mess into a paste.

"Here, kitty, kitty," she called then made a kissing noise with her lips.

For a moment, as she placed the saucer on the floor, I presumed it must be for Lucifer or one of the other familiars that shared the cottage with us. "I don't think Lucifer-"

Before I had a chance to say another word, she turned to me with a determined voice and said, "Go and milk Old Mawde, Livitha, and I'll grind your coffee. Leave our guests to me."

At the hem of her long skirt a tiny face appeared. I realised then that the cheesy mess was for the fairies.

"There's one!"

"Livitha! Go and milk Old Mawde."

The tiny creature had the audacity to stick out its tongue before disappearing behind the long skirt. A ting of porcelain on fired clay followed and was joined by excited chittering.

"It calms them down," Aunt Beatrice explained.

"But they'll never leave if you feed them!" I complained.

"It's the best we can do ... until we find the right charm to rid the cottage of them. They're a pest, I admit, but this is the only way. Now," she said as the kitchen's energy returned to calm, "Go and milk Old Mawde—the old hag will only make my life a misery later if you don't."

Mystified and confused, I left the kitchen and made my way to the enclosure at the side of the house where Old Mawde had lived, and produced milk, my entire life.

Chapter Three

F ive minutes later I sat propped on a three-legged stool by the side of Old Mawde. Despite her swollen udder she had refused to allow me to milk her until a bunch of freshly picked dandelion leaves was offered. She stood chewing the leaves as I squirted the milk into the tin pail. I took the opportunity to check her over. She was a large goat with a coat of coarse off-white hair across her back, but her front haunches, neck, and head were varying degrees of dark brown. A large black stripe ran from her forehead to her nose. The ovals of her irises were a startling blue fading out to white which made the black lozenge of her pupil even more stark. She turned to eye me as I gave another pull, the mouthful of dandelion leaves already munched and swallowed. An irritated bleat followed, and I offered another handful of freshly pulled leaves. She took them greedily. It was then I noticed the old clay pipe on the stool in the corner of the stye and then the faint whiff of tobacco. I was shocked. One of my aunts had to be a pipe smoker! The idea was ridiculous. I knew that Uncle Raif detested tobacco but then so did my aunts.

With Old Mawde's udders relieved of their burden, I inspected the pipe. It was made of white clay and was discoloured with use. The rim of the bowl was blackened with smoke and tinged brown with nicotine. The mouthpiece too was stained and worn as though from years of use. Inside the bowl were the remains of tobacco. It even felt warm. A sniff at the bowl proved that it had been used quite recently with the odour being strong and fresh, not stale. I held it to the light. There were no signs of modern, assembly-line production. I had no idea if such objects were still made and it had all the hallmarks of being a relic of a past era. Perhaps an antique. I loved quirky pieces and decided to take it back to the house. Presenting it to the aunts would probably be enough to elicit a confession. If it was a relic, then it would make a nice addition to their collection of vintage pieces.

I placed the pipe in my jacket pocket and reached for the bucket of freshly collected milk. Pain spread through my buttocks and I shot forward, stumbling against the stye's wall. It took a couple of seconds to realise that Old Mawde had headbutted me. Startling blue eyes stared into mine as I scrambled to my feet and turned to my attacker. The goat was bearing down on me. She snapped at my hand, only narrowly missing chomping down on my fingers, then began to tug at my jacket.

With each tug she yanked me forward and made a low grunting noise. I knew that goats ate just about anything and that probably included my jacket. Unable to grasp more fresh dandelions, I shrugged off the jacket. Old Mawde whipped it to the far side of the enclosure and pawed at the fabric. She made no effort to eat it, and it became obvious that she was pawing at the opening of the pocket where I had placed the pipe.

I was staggered. Picking up the pipe had riled her!

"Do you want the pipe?" I asked as she continued to grunt and paw at the fabric. Taking a tentative step forward, I continued to speak in a soothing tone. She seemed to calm a little as I stepped closer, her pawing less frantic. "Just let me take the jacket. I'll get the pipe." Amazingly, she stepped back, her hind quarters pushing up against the wooden wall of the stye. I grasped the jacket and pulled it towards me. She grew a little skittish and I held up a hand in submission. "I'm just going to get the pipe and put it on the stool." Retrieving the pipe from my jacket pocket, I replaced the pipe on the stool and took slow steps away from the angry goat, collecting the pail of milk as I retreated. Old Mawde made no effort to follow me as I left the enclosure and locked the gate with a firm clack of the bolt. I strode back to the house, heart pounding, head reeling. A quick glance back at the enclosure as I reached the hardstanding behind the house showed Old Mawde with her head reaching over the top bar of the fence, clay pipe at an angle in her mouth.

I screwed my eyes tight shut, convinced that a trick of the light had caused the vision, but opening them showed the same scene. Aunt Mawde stared after me with a belligerent gaze, pipe firmly in the corner of her mouth. I was only thankful that smoke wasn't trailing from the bowl.

Back in the kitchen, the saucer of cheesy paste had been licked clean and Aunt Beatrice was corking the remaining bottles. The room was filled with the aroma of freshly ground and brewing coffee. I sat down with a thud at the table unable to explain what had happened. My aunt filled a daintily painted cup with coffee, placed it on a saucer then handed it to me. It took several sips before I had calmed down enough to relate the events that had taken place in the stye. There was something very off about the goat. My backside felt bruised; Old Mawde hadn't been playing around when she headbutted my buttocks.

"She attacked me!" I finally managed.

Aunt Beatrice only offered a mumbled acceptance as though it was expected.

"She headbutted me! It really hurt."

"Yes, she's fond of that."

"She's dangerous!"

"Well, only if you rile her. Generally, she's quite sane."

Sane? I was beginning to wonder if anything was sane at the cottage. "She could have hurt me," I complained.

"Normally she's quite placid ... well, normally she's not dangerous, but ... did you touch anything whilst you were there?"

This was said with an accusation of blame. "Well, I did notice a pipe-"

"There you have it. She's very attached to that pipe. It belonged to her mother."

My head began to swim. "Her mother smoked a pipe?"

"Yes, it was quite common in those days for women of a certain ilk to smoke pipes."

"Women?" My head buzzed. "But she's a goat!"

"She is."

"Oh, Aunt Bea! Will you please explain what's going on? We have a geriatric goat that smokes a pipe at the bottom of the garden, and fairies that are filming me in my sleep and sending the videos to my ex-husband. I feel as though I'm going mad!"

"Well, she's cursed darling."

"Cursed?"

"Yes, and the cursed do get rather tetchy after a while. Mind you, Mawde always was cantankerous—it's why she was cursed in the first place."

Cursed! There was that word again. My thoughts sprang to Garrett Blackwood. He was also cursed according to my aunts. For the past three weeks, since he had visited me in hospital after my torturous experience at the hands of the Witchfinder General, I had been waiting for his call. His words to me had been, 'Once this is all over, can I call you?' I had wanted clarification – did he want to call me on a police matter or for personal reasons? If personal just a catch-up or something else? – but knew that asking would make me look more than a little desperate and needy. Now, I just felt stupid for even thinking about asking if it were for personal reasons; there was no way that a gorgeous man like Garrett Blackwood would ask a middle-aged frump like me on a date. As if! The sting of embarrassment returned to my cheeks as my thoughts chewed over the scene in the hospital. I had been a fool.

"He's cursed too." Aunt Beatrice's voice cut through my thoughts.

"Aunt Bea!" I complained.

"I can't help it," she said as she drew out a chair to sit on the opposite side of the table. "You're so loud!" She said this with an exasperated sigh and reached for the pot of tea at the centre of the table.

"I'm so sorry," I quipped. "I'll have to try and think a little quieter."

"That would be nice dear." She said this with absolute sincerity and took a sip of tea, pulled a face, then sweetened it with a drizzle of honey.

In the next minutes Aunts Thomasin and Euphemia joined us at the table and the chatter turned to the summer fete at which they had booked a table. It would be their first time attending as 'vendors' and although Aunts Beatrice and Euphemia were excited at the prospect, citing it as good advertising for the shop they were to open before the autumnal equinox, Aunt Thomasin was a little more reserved though fully onboard with helping the project progress.

"And did you hear about the new doctor?" Aunt Euphemia said as Aunt Beatrice finished her update on the potions brewed and salves boxed ready for the village fete.

"What happened to the old one? I haven't heard that he retired."

"He disappeared. The word is that he was having an affair with one of his patients."

"I heard that Mrs. Rowbottom left her husband for a fancy man."

A communal 'ooh' filled the room as the aunts continued to gossip about Mrs. Rowbottom, the practice manager at the local doctors' surgery.

At that moment Aunt Loveday entered the room with uncharacteristic haste. "I know why we're all feeling so on edge," she blurted. "And just why those little devils have infested the cottage!" She stopped to catch her breath and all eyes turned to her, the extra-marital affairs of the local doctor and his practice manager forgotten. "Someone has stolen Arthur!"

A communal gasp of horror filled the room.

I had never heard of an Arthur.

"Are you sure he has not just been misplaced?"

"I've scoured the cottage and called for him. He's not here!"

"Who is Arthur?" I asked, now realising that yet another layer was being removed from the onion skins of their lives to reveal more secrets. Was Arthur some kind of house elf? Did my aunts have their own personal Dobby? It would answer the question of who helped keep the house maintained. Other than Mrs. Driscoll who came in three mornings a week to clean and do the laundry, I had never seen, or heard mention, of anyone else helping to make repairs. The only DIY my aunts had ever done was wallpapering my bedroom when I was a teenager, and that was still intact, although faded. The only other link the house had to modernity was the ancient heating system, installed before I was born but which managed to run without maintenance or repair. The existence of a house elf would explain that mystery. I became quite enthralled with the idea of our own personal Dobby, but the thought quickly turned to dread; what if he was like the fairies that my aunt insisted on feeding?

"Are you absolutely certain, Loveday?" Aunt Euphemia queried. "Perhaps Mrs. Driscoll has moved him?

"I've searched every nook and cranny of this house, Euphemia. I keep him under lock and key. He's just not here."

I was immediately appalled; our Dobby-elf imprisoned in the house! Locked away in a cupboard! "Perhaps he's run away then!" I blurted.

"Run away! Of course, he hasn't run away. He doesn't have legs."

The imagery in my head took a new and disturbing turn. This was becoming a horror story.

"Has no legs! Why on earth would you remove his legs?"

Aunt Loveday turned to me with confusion. "I didn't remove his legs."

Aunt Beatrice chuckled. "Calm yourself, Livitha. You're letting your imagination run away with you. Loveday, ignore her. Old Mawde showed her true colours this morning and she is rather upset about a video Pascal has of her in bed."

"Oh!" Aunt Loveday cast me a bewildered glance.

"Not that kind of video!"

"I'm not sure what kind you mean, Livitha, but I really do think it's time to move on. Put Pascal behind you, there are other fish in the sea."

"Or doctors in the village!" Thomasin nudged Aunt Beatrice.

"I thought the builder at the shop was rather nice."

"Sisters, if I can bring your attention back to Arthur."

"Please!" I said, exasperated and wishing I hadn't got out of bed that morning. "I *have* moved on from Pascal, but will you please tell me who on earth this Arthur is?"

Aunt Beatrice offered me a pitying smile. "Why, Loveday's book of spells of course. He's full of powerful magic and absolutely priceless."

"And dangerous in the wrong hands."

Muttered, doom-laden agreement filled the kitchen.

My relief was instant. I was also a touch ashamed that I had jumped to such grotesque conclusions. Sweat began to bead at my temple as a familiar hormonal heat began to swirl at my core. However, with this new information I was certain I knew who had taken Arthur. "Fairies," I blurted. "It has to be those pesky fairies. They're horrid little sneak thieves. Do you know

they actually filmed me whilst I was asleep! Can you even believe that they know how to use a mobile phone?"

All four pairs of eyes turned to me. "We must be careful
with the choice of our words, Livitha," Aunt Loveday said then
took a quick glance around the kitchen.

"Don't worry, Loveday. They've had their cheese this
morning."

Aunt Loveday visibly sagged. "Oh, thank goodness. If they
had heard Livitha's accusations, we would have a terrible time
of it later."

"Well," I said, now defensive, "it's time they went."

"It is, but without Arthur ..."

The energy in the room grew darker.

"Why don't you think the fairies took it ... him?" I asked in
a quieter voice.

Aunt Thomasin threw me a warning glance and placed a si-
lencing finger against her lips. It irked me that we were being
held to ransom by the tiny beasts in this way.

"They're not powerful enough. They do damage, but to
steal Arthur ... no."

"Then who? Was it one of the guests?" I gestured to the
garden where the witches had assembled for my Initiation
three weeks ago.

"Shh! Never say such a thing, Livitha."

"I'm sorry." My words had overstepped the mark. I continued with another possibility. "Then it has to be Mrs. Driscoll,"
I asserted. "She's the only other person who has access to the
house."

"Livitha!" Aunt Thomasin reprimanded. "How could
you?"

"Well-"

"No, I won't hear it. Mrs. Driscoll is the kindest, most honest woman there is. She is an absolute godsend around here."

A flush began to rise in my cheeks. "But who else then? No one else has been to the house."

"Blackwood has been here."

"Garrett?" I said with surprise, instantly riled to defend him. "You can't be serious!"

"He's a Blackwood. They are cursed! There's no knowing what they are capable of."

Cursed! That word again. "That's not fair. I don't believe it! There's absolutely no evidence to support that."

"No, he's definitely cursed."

"I meant the book. There's no evidence that he took it."

"She's blinded by love."

Thomasin's comment was irksome. "I am not!"

"I think you may be."

"That's absurd. I haven't seen him in weeks."

"Distance makes the heart grow fonder."

"Oh, for Thor's sake!" I said in exasperation.

"It's Freyja you need to invoke."

I ignored Thomasin's quip. "I'll prove that Arthur wasn't taken by Garrett. I'll find out exactly where the book is and who really took it."

Chapter Four

The investigation began right there. I had never seen Arthur, so quizzed the aunts. Loveday explained that Arthur was an ancient, leather-bound tome filled with quires of vellum. These were multiple sheets of prepared animal skin folded over and sewn together to form a booklet. There were over thirty of these ancient animal skin quires of different sizes, each one crammed with spells and ancestral custom stretching back through the centuries. Some of the booklets were made from calf skins, some from sheep, and a few smaller quires – when times had been difficult – were made of scraped and stretched squirrel and rabbit hide. Each quire was threaded with leather thongs and then sewn into the leather cover. Some later paper quires were sewn with hemp string. Tooled with intricate designs of intertwined and fantastical creatures and inscribed with runes, the cover was a wraparound style, closed halfway across the front of the book and secured with leather thongs. Several pieces of jewellery - inscribed silver beard rings from an early love - had been used as beads to decorate the ends of the thongs. Aunt Loveday stalled in her description, her mood descending to sadness. "They were his. My Erik." Her eyes glazed over. "Erik Guthfrithson ... Yfel ferhþlufu hêo. On ecnesse, Erik, on ecnesse."

Thomasin shook her head, although her smile was kindly. "He was special, Loveday, but Arthur ... we must focus on Arthur."

Loveday came to her senses. "Of course, ... Well, with so many pages, he is rather chunky and not neat in the modern sense – the vellum and paper were trimmed as precisely as I could, but I am a self-taught bookmaker," she smiled humbly.

"He's stunning, Loveday, for all his quirks."

"Well, he is unique and absolutely priceless—at least to us. He contains so much power, and so much of my knowledge; the essence of everything. There is so much of myself and our heritage within his covers." She grew quiet within a moment of introspection, then with sparkling, concerned-filled eyes said, "He's filled to the brim with our secrets! We must get him back." Although Aunt Loveday was attempting to remain calm, her aura grew visible as a shimmering violet halo. As it sparked, the aunts took a step away.

"You must stay calm Loveday," Aunt Euphemia soothed. "I'm sure Livitha can find him for us."

"She must! She really must."

Aunt Loveday became emotional at this point and it was painful to see tears in my beautiful aunt's eyes. The only other time I had seen her display that level of sadness was when she spoke of any decline in Uncle Raif's health. Despite the crackling energy, Aunt Thomasin slipped a comforting arm across her shoulders.

"We'll find him, Loveday. He'll call to us when he can."

At this Aunt Loveday gasped as some new realisation struck her. "It's worse than I thought sisters! Thomasin is right. He would call for us if he could. And he hasn't!" The pitch of her voice increased as panic rose. "Someone powerful has him! If he were merely lost, then he would be able to call. Whoever has him is blocking him." She paled and had to be helped to sit. "What will we do?" she whispered.

"It must be the Blackwoods," Aunt Thomasin insisted. "No others are so powerful in this area?"

"They are forbidden to practice."

"Being forbidden and following that directive are often not inclusive."

"The Council implemented safeguards."

"Which can always be overcome."

"I knew that they couldn't be reined in forever."

My head swam as they spoke about Garrett's family. There was so much I didn't know and every time I had tried to discover more, my efforts had been derailed. Energy sparked and crackled in the kitchen. My own anxiety began to fester.

"His disappearance does explain the fairies." Aunt Beatrice spoke this aloud but then turned away, muttering. She moved distractedly around the room seeming to check between the salves, soaps, and potions. Her aura sparked with bright violet flashes and Bess, her whippet familiar, pranced at her feet.

The energy in the room became fractious. I opened the door to let in the fresh air. Sunlight shone across the worn flagstones, motes danced and eddied in the warm rays, and I breathed in its peacefulness. Sunlight, and being closer to the natural world, always soothed me. I stepped out into the garden to gather my thoughts. Lucifer was instantly at my ankles, slinking between my legs. I bent to stroke his glossy fur and was immediately rewarded with loud purring. We walked together into the garden and the further from the stress of the kitchen I got, the calmer I felt.

The large lawn at the rear of the house was demarcated by a tall hedge with a gap at its middle, beyond this was the herb and vegetable garden and beyond that the orchard. I continued to the orchard, Lucifer at my side, the events since I had discovered my witchy powers, turning in my mind, searching for any clue as to who could have taken the book. Did its disappearance tie in with the infestation of fairies? Aunt Beatrice seemed to think so. If so, why? Aunt Loveday was certain that whoever had taken it was powerful. Were they holding it to ransom or just blocking its homing signal?

Sitting beneath the shade of a large apple tree, Lucifer on my lap purring loudly, I made a mental list of everyone who had been to the house. Given that my initiation had taken place at the time the fairies were discovered, it was an unusually long list. Although the guests were not encouraged to enter the cottage itself, a large marquee had been erected to one side of the lawn, I had witnessed several witches drinking one of Aunt Euphemia's famous aura enhancing cocktails in the kitchen—several of them had positively glowed! There had been deliveries made by the local caterers, pub/winery (a surprising amount!), and florists. A team had also erected the marquee. And yes, Garrett and his police partner had been invited into the cottage when they had turned up to question me about Selma's murder.

I sat for more than half an hour, ruminating on the problem, chewing over each part of the puzzle. I had only fragments of ideas and my mind kept returning to Garrett. In my aunt's mind, his involvement was probable, if not certain. It made no sense to me. I couldn't reconcile the adorable boy I had been so in love with, with their vision of a cursed man willing to steal the coven's most precious possession, but then, I was a novice, only recently initiated, and woefully lacking in knowledge even though the instinctive understanding of our ancestral magic was slowly waking within me. My gut instinct was to reject their hypothesis. I felt sure that Garrett was a good man, someone without bad influence, but then, I had thought that Pascal was a loyal husband! My head buzzed with contradictory thoughts, and I began to doubt everything. I checked in with my mental list and the imaginary bullet points. In no particular order the suspects were:

- Garrett Blackwood – 'cursed' and had access to the drawing room.
- Mrs Driscoll – saintly cleaner with unfettered access to the house and all its rooms.
- Florist – access to the kitchen
- Caterer – access to the kitchen
- Pub landlord – access to the kitchen
- Witches – Anne Whittle, Anne Redferne, Margaret Pringle, Bessie Yickar, Janet Horne – cocktails in the kitchen

That was the list, and it was obvious to me that the only person on that list who could have taken the book, which was kept in a private room at the back of the house, was Mrs. Driscoll, the saintly cleaner. I found it hard to reconcile the kindly cleaner who had been with my aunts for more than fifteen years with a despicable and sneaking book thief. I had nev-

er seen Arthur but, from Aunt Loveday's description, he was
a worn and shabby leather-bound, amateurishly constructed
book that held no real value to anyone other than my aunts. I
knew there were book collectors out there who paid enormous
sums for famous manuscripts, but they were inscribed works,
beautifully written and illustrated, usually by monk-scribes in
monasteries during the middle ages, their covers richly adorned
with gold filigree metalwork and jewels. If Mrs. Driscoll had
stolen it to sell on the medieval manuscript black market, then
she would be sadly disappointed. It made no sense; a cleaner
from a small village deep in the countryside, who rarely, if ever,
left the confines of the county, and whose favourite television
programme was 'Love Island', was unlikely to have the kind of
connections with art dealers and millionaires necessary to enter that trade. I sighed as my head began to throb, my thoughts
too fanciful to have any bearing on reality and pulled myself
back to common sense.

No one on the list was a realistic suspect. None had access
to the house beyond the kitchen, or drawing room, apart from
Mrs. Driscoll and theft on her part would be the end of her em-
ployment, so unlikely from that point of view too. It had to be
an intruder. Someone who knew about the book, and its value,
and who had the audacity to break into the cottage and steal it
under the cloak of night.

With that conclusion reached, dappled light warming me,
apple leaves shading me from the bright sunshine, and Lucifer
on my lap, I fell into a light sleep, and dreamed of Garrett and
an old house in the woods. A woman, an old crone, twigs and
branches gathered in her arms, shuffled to a fire where a soot-
covered cauldron hung from a blackened tripod. Sparks flew

and embers glowed as she threw the logs onto the fire. Steam rose from the cauldron, and Garrett, unseen in my dream, slipped his hand into mine.

Chapter Five

T he next thing I was aware of was Bess' paws digging into my belly and a sharp yelp in my ear. I woke with a jolt, the echo of my voice being called, and a disconcerting feeling of being watched. Above me, Benny, Aunt Thomasin's raven familiar, squawked. One beady eye stared directly at me.

"Liv!" my aunt called again.

Lucifer hissed as Bess caught his tail beneath her paw then sprang away as she turned on him with all the excitement of a young child at Christmas. It didn't seem to matter how offensive he was to her, she always wanted to play. It always amazed me to see the feline turn from nonchalant cynicism to playful pet. He seemed to forget his carefully crafted attitude of caustic reserve when she tagged him. They bounded off as Aunt Beatrice called me again and Benny took flight, swooping low to circle the pair. Bess yelped as he took a peck at her rump.

With the familiars at play, I made my way to the cottage and stepped back into the kitchen with a deep breath against the chaotic energy that had overtaken it this morning. Calm had returned, however, and Aunt Beatrice was busy placing bottles and jars into a box. Two other boxes were sealed and stacked on the sideboard by the door.

"Those are for the fete," she said as I entered. "This is the last one." She folded the cardboard box flaps to closed then signalled for me to place it on the sideboard.

"When is the fete again, Aunt Bea?"

"Oh, Livitha! As if you don't know. It's the day after tomorrow."

I did know when the fete was, at least I should know, but despite it being a continuous topic of conversation in the house since the aunts had agreed to book a table to showcase their wares, the date hadn't sunk into my brain. Sometimes facts just didn't seem to stick! I wasn't sure if it was menopausal hormones, the lack of unbroken sleep, or that my mind was so full of everything that was opening up to me that caused it. There was so much family history to learn, and unlearn, so much coven knowledge too. I also had to master the energies that my initiation had unleashed and, given that they seemed so intimately linked with the hormonal roller coaster ride of my menopause, I wasn't sure quite how I was going to manage that feat. I often wondered, in those early days, if other women struggled with 'the change' as I did, or if my suffering was peculiar to me because I was a witch. It seemed at the least provocation that my fingers would fizz and tingle, then heat would rise from deep within my core, and sparks fly from the tips. On the worst mornings I'd wake to the definite smell of singeing bed sheets, sure that the only reason I hadn't gone up in flames overnight was the night sweat dampened bedclothes entwined with my arms and legs. I had hoped that becoming a witch would lessen the purgatorial symptoms, instead it had only seemed to make them worse!

"Now, Livitha, you have remembered what I asked of you yesterday, haven't you?" Aunt Beatrice asked as though it were me in my dotage. I made a desperate search through the fug of my mind. She sighed before I had a chance to reply. "I don't know how you manage to breath sometimes."

"Excuse me!"

"Well, it's all so foggy up there, isn't it."

It wasn't like her to be so acerbic. "Well-"

"No need to explain, darling. I remember it well. I often wondered quite how I managed it too."

I relaxed a little then. She wasn't being critical, just empathetic. "It's such a ... oh, fudge, what on earth is the word ..."

"Like your mind is swimming through treacle?"

"Exactly that!" I laughed. "You're right. I'm not sure how I remember to breath sometimes either."

"It will pass, you know. It's worse for us Haligern women, we have so much more to contend with. Instead of thinking of your brain disintegrating, think of it in terms of growth. You're passing into a new phase of being, Livitha. Embrace it, your power is only just growing."

"Thank you! You know, it has felt like a kind of deterioration – my brain, that is – as if my faculties are declining ..."

"I understand. But it is a metamorphosis, darling. Your brain is on a new path, struggling to link new synapses. Once it's over, you'll be amazed at how clear and lucid your thinking is." Her eyes twinkled as she spoke, and golden particles shimmered in violet irises. "Now!" she said with determination. "Do you remember what I asked of you yesterday?"

"Erm ..."

"The shop?" she prompted.

I remembered instantly. "Yes! Yes, I do," I said triumphant. "You want me to help you at the shop."

"I want you to come and meet the builder." Here she raised her brows. "Just to help me explain how I want the shop to look."

"I thought you'd already had the initial meetings."

"Oh, we have, but I'd like you there too, Livitha. Afterall, you're going to be running the show."

This was news to me although I had secretly hoped to be able to play a role and thought that I could be the bridge between my aunts and this new world. "I am?"

"It's what you want, isn't it?"

"I guess you already know that!" I said with a shake of my head. Aunt Beatrice was notorious for reading other people's minds.

"You know that I can't help it," she said. "And you are so loud sometimes, Livitha."

"Well, perhaps you should turn your hearing aid down!" I couldn't help that snip, but Aunt Beatrice only laughed.

"That's a nice way of putting it, Livitha. I think you're right, perhaps I should. Now, if you will, I'd very much like to go to the shop."

"I'm ready when you are."

"I'll change into my outdoor wear and then I shall be ready."

Aunt Beatrice left the kitchen and returned ten minutes later in her 'outdoor wear'. She looked quite lovely. Her red pinafore and full-length dress had been replaced by a fitted two piece of Harris tweed in the softest natural greens. The skirt ended at mid-calf – rather daring for my aunt – and the jacket was superbly fitted and accentuated her tiny waist. A hat of rus-set felt, with pheasant's feather secured by a jewelled broach to the side, completed the ensemble. The emeralds in the broach glinted in the sun. She reminded me of a very sprightly and youthful looking Miss Marple.

"You don't think I look a little too autumnal for this time of year, do you dear?"

"No! You look absolutely perfect, Aunt Bea." It was true, with her creamy complexion, violet eyes ringed by dark lashes and snow-white hair secured in a chignon at the nape of her neck, she not only looked elegant in her outfit, but quite ex-quisite. A tiny pang of envy was quickly squashed; I could never hope to look as beautiful as my aunt, but I admired her im-mensely.

"Thank you!"

There was a hint of relief in her voice and it occurred to me that perhaps she was feeling a little anxious. Taking on the shop was a huge undertaking for my reclusive aunts, as was attend-ing the fete. Leaving the cottage was a rare event, particularly for Aunt Beatrice who was the real homebody of the family. I offered another smile. "It's true, Aunt Bea. You look beautiful."

A slight flush rose to her cheeks and her eyes sparkled. "Come along, then. I'm excited to see the shop again. The builder has been busy by all accounts."

At the door she stopped and glanced to the stairs. "I do hope that Raif is feeling better soon. I was quite concerned when Loveday called in the doctor, but it is a relief to know that he is receiving proper medical care. There's only so much our potions and lotions can do." She sighed as though the weight of the world were on her shoulders then opened the front door and stepped out into the sunshine.

"The doctor came here?" I asked in surprise. This was the first time his visit had been mentioned in my hearing.

"Oh, yes, it was a couple of weeks ago, not long after your Initiation."

"And nobody told me?"

"Well, Loveday didn't want to worry you; she knows how much you fret about Raif."

"I don't fret about Uncle Raif!"

"Perhaps fret is the wrong word. You worry. We all do."

"Of course. Uncle Raif is such a special man. He's been like a father to me. I couldn't bear it if ..."

"Exactly. You fret. Now, come along, the builder will be waiting."

"But Aunt Bea, if Dr. O'Halloran came here ... to Haligern, then he is a suspect too!"

"Pssht! What would a doctor want with a witch's grimoire, Livitha? And besides, it wasn't Dr. O'Halloran, it was the new doctor. I don't quite recall his name ... Oh, yes, of course. Dr. Cotton. That was it. Plus, he was under surveillance the entirety of his time in the house. Your aunts were far too interested in him to let him out of their sight."

"Oh?"

"Yes. It's not often we have visitors and he certainly was a curiosity; a proper old-fashioned doctor and he treated Raif as the gentleman he is."

"Oh." I could see the doctor in my mind's eye: portly, bespectacled, wearied and drained by an endless procession of patients all in need of help. Despite my aunt's protestations as to his innocence, I decided that the doctor would go to the top of my list of suspects.

It had been quite some time since I had last driven one of my aunts, but I had not forgotten the etiquette. Aunt Beatrice stood beside the car waiting for me to open the door. Once open, she sat on the seat and then swung her legs in. 'It's how a lady should enter a car, Livitha,' she had reproved after I'd made comment as a teenager. Sitting upright, the seatbelt clicked into place, Aunt Beatrice waited for the engine to start.

"Hah! I'll never get tired of hearing the engine start. It's magical," she laughed. Quite amazing how a mechanical carriage can come to life, and without the aid of magick too."

"They've been around a while now."

"Indeed, Livitha, but I have been around a far sight longer, and the longer I live, the more ingenious man's ingenuity becomes. He is harnessing a kind of magic, not our kind, but another kind."

"Yes, physics."

"Yes, physics," she agreed.

"And chemistry."

"Quite."

The drive to the village was filled with random talk, one subject leading on to another. As we reached the top of another hill the village came into view and beyond it the Black Woods. Dark clouds filled the sky above the woodland casting it in black shadow.

"There's a storm brewing," I said as I admired the view; the sun shining on the village seemed particularly bright against the dark clouds beyond. The road was clear of traffic and I pushed the car over the speed limit, enjoying the sense of freedom it gave as the road twisted and turned, rose, and fell. Aunt Beatrice made no indication that she disapproved but began to mutter about the weather as we hurtled towards the village. The clouds hovering over the Black Woods lit up as lightning erupted within them.

"Black clouds. Lightning. It doesn't move." She continued to talk as though thinking aloud. "Static. It is in stasis." Lightning flared again. "Hmm. Black clouds over the Black Wood. I haven't seen that for quite some time." Her lips pursed as she stared at the cloud. Her eyes narrowed.

A face appeared at the window!

I squealed and the car veered towards the middle of the road.

Impossibly, a figure, some bizarre creature, was running beside the car. Its arms pumped rhythmically whilst it stared at my aunt. Fangs were revealed as it licked its lips then left its tongue to dangle, dog-like, as it ran. Short horns protruded from long and lank yellow hair. It seemed excited, as though enormously happy. It was the strangest thing I had seen in my life. It was also naked, at least from the waist up which was the only part of its body I could see.

It caught my gaze and, startled as it locked its eyes to mine, I swerved, crossed the road then frantically tried to straighten the car, only narrowly avoiding crashing into the ditch. Aunt Beatrice made a yelp of fright as an oncoming car came into view. I turned the wheel and manoeuvred the car back onto the correct side of the road and checked the rear-view mirror for the creature. It was nowhere to be seen. I slowed to a stop and allowed the car to idle as I caught my breath. My hands trembled as adrenaline shot through my veins.

"Whatever happened, Livitha? You nearly got us killed."

She hadn't seen the creature! I gripped the steering wheel unsure what to say. Aunt Beatrice was already on edge about going into town, telling her that a bizarre creature had been running at seventy miles an hour beside our car, staring directly at her, would make her anxiety worse. I took a breath. "I think I hit a pothole."

She scanned the road. "Perhaps we should take it a little more slowly for the rest of the journey, Livitha?"

Chapter Six

We arrived outside the shop to a gaggle of children peering into the window.

"Pests!" Aunt Beatrice said as I pulled up to the kerb.

The tone of her voice surprised me.

"Just park behind the shop, Livitha."

"But there are spaces in front."

"Yes, but park behind please."

There was an edge to her voice and, as I pulled away from the kerb, one of the teenagers turned to stare, following our progress down the road. Aunt Beatrice bristled beside me. I parked behind the shop as requested. She removed her seat belt with pursed lips as the engine died, then waited in silence for me to open the door. As we crossed the road together, her arm hooked through mine, movement caught my attention.

At the end of the road, peering from behind a road sign, was the creature that had run beside the car. Only its head and claw-like hands were visible; the rest of its body was impossibly hidden by the narrow pole. It had to be an illusion! Someone was playing tricks on me! With a quickened step, I hurried Aunt Beatrice across the road and into the yard at the back of the shop, closing the gate behind us, unsure of quite what I had seen, but sure that it was some sort of bizarre hoax, or my mind playing tricks on me.

On entering the shop, Aunt Beatrice sniffed in a disapproving fashion as the children's chatter became audible.

"Aunt Beatrice, are you alright?"

"Perfectly fine."

"You're obviously not."

"Well, if you must know ... those children ... have become a bit of a nuisance."

We made our way down the narrow corridor, past a small cloakroom to the left and a larger storage room to the right. A door opened to another antechamber which then led to the shop itself. I opened the door. At the shop's front five faces pushed up against the glass.

"See!"

Each face was pushed up against an individual pane, some squashed to form a pig-like snout. Snot smeared against the glass. In one pane, a boy's fat tongue slid like a grotesque pink slug. A girl tapped on the window, acrylic fingernails clinking on the vintage glass.

"You a witch?" Her voice, audible through the window, was mocking.

"Hey witchy, got any toads?"

I riled instantly, mortification for my aunt spreading through me like quickfire. How dare they mock her! "How do they know you're a witch?" I asked as the continued to peer through the glass.

"They don't. I'm just different. It's what they do—what they've always done to us, Livitha. They sense it in us, know that there's something a little unusual, and then the persecution begins."

A quiver in her voice became a tremble, and I slipped an arm around her slender shoulders, wanting to wrap my arms around her to protect her from their poisonous energy. How could they be filled with so much spite at such a young age?

"It's not the first time. I don't suppose it will be the last."

"They're just silly kids," I placated although I knew her pain went much deeper and she wasn't really talking about the children. "But I'm shocked at how mean they are. The villagers love us, don't they?"

"They do, but these are new children, from the new estate built on old farmer Borril's field."

A boy tried to open the door, and when it didn't budge, he shook it. Aunt Beatrice trembled beneath my arm.

"I'll deal with them. Don't worry."

"I wish they had never built those houses!" she blurted as the boy continued to yank at the handle.

A chittering giggle came from the back of the shop and I turned expecting to see a fairy skittering among the ceiling's beams or scurrying on a worktop. Instead, a door opened, and a man walked through.

"I'll sort the little buggers out!" Unnoticed, the builder and his mate had entered the shop. The larger man opened the front door, then spent the next minutes berating the teenagers.

"This village is going downhill since those townies arrived," the smaller man quipped. "Take no notice of them, they're just kids. They'll soon learn our ways."

This mollified my aunt a little and she relaxed enough to offer him a smile of thanks.

"I thought that only a few houses had been sold," I said as the builder stepped back into the shop. The children had dispersed and now the street was quiet apart from an elderly gentleman making his way slowly along the path.

"Aye, there's only a few sold, but if this is what the incomers are gonna be like, the village won't know what's hit it."

"Ahh, give them a few months," the smaller man returned. "I reckon they'll settle in."

Chapter Seven

Throughout the afternoon my thoughts had churned over the suspects in Arthur's theft, and, more than Garrett Blackwood, the name of Dr. John Cotton returned to my mind. I determined to discover what I could about the doctor and pay him a visit.

The information I had gleaned from Aunt Beatrice was that during my sleuthing efforts to uncover the true murderer of my husband's mistress, Uncle Raif had experienced a couple of 'funny turns'. He had become momentarily disorientated and his memory had 'shifted to a different plane'. It became clear that, for those few minutes, Uncle Raif had believed himself to be his younger self living back at home in Tudor Staffordshire. Only being led by Aunt Loveday to the portrait on the gallery landing had placated him. Beside herself with worry, but unfamiliar and wary of hospitals, she had at last consented to calling the local doctor. He had been kind enough to make a house call and examined Uncle Raif then made a follow-up visit the next day. Uncle Raif, in his professional opinion, had perhaps suffered a 'Transient Ischemic Attack' caused by a restriction of blood flow to the brain. Loveday was beside herself with worry, but I hadn't been told of the events as she believed clearing my name of murder and going through my initiation was enough to contend with. Plus, Uncle Raif had made a remarkably good recovery and hadn't suffered since.

Deeply concerned for Uncle Raif, and toying with the idea that the theft, invasion of fairies, and my uncle's 'funny turns' were perhaps connected, I returned my aunt to the cottage then made my way to the doctor's office.

The office was situated at the end of the village in one of the older houses, a double fronted Georgian property of narrow bricks painted white with new uPVC sash windows. A single storey extension, that had once been a row of outbuildings, had been converted to the surgery, reception, and waiting area. Without a front garden, the house sat on the street, its front door opening onto the path, but the surgery was set back to the side of the house behind a high brick wall and was fronted by a block-paved parking area. I walked through the open iron gates, noting the immaculately polished two-door Porsche cabriolet in the small carpark. Silver bodywork glinted in the warm afternoon sun. It was another car Pascal had always hankered after, so I knew they weren't cheap. The car was immaculate, the surgery was not.

A ramp led up to the door painted in a now faded red. Paintwork on the windows was peeling, the putty holding the glass in-situ cracked and in places dislodged. Moss grew in the corners, and the windowsill beside the downpipe had rotted. Posters on the door and slatted blinds on the windows blocked the view directly into the building and when I tried the handle the door was locked. I stood back to view the building as though that would miraculously unlock the door, then checked my watch. It was five-thirty-five. Opening hours were nine until five-thirty. I peered through the glass between the posters. All I could see through the dinge was a heavy-duty red carpet and a row of plastic chairs that served as the waiting area. The whole place had a rundown air about it which I found surprising. Apart from one or two notable exceptions, the village was pretty, and well-kept. Given the expensive car parked beside the house, perhaps the new doctor would invest in refurbishment. It was obvious that Doctor O'Halloran hadn't spent money maintaining the property for some time, but then he was in his dotage, retiring decades after the recommended age which made his affair with the much younger practice manager all the more surprising and scandalous.

The lowering sun warmed my back as I continued to stare at the locked door. I tried the handle once more just in case it was sticky rather than locked.

"G'day! Can I help you?"

Startled, I yelped, and turned to a blond man leaning out of a downstairs window in the main house. Golden hair shone around a tanned face. White teeth gleamed. Blue eyes dazzled. He was also shirtless! I stood mute. There was something familiar about him. He threw me a dazzling smile then said, "Sorry! I didn't mean to startle you!"

Fractured senses knitted together—after a fashion. "No!" I blurted. "No, you didn't." *Obviously, a lie*! "I've come to see the doctor. Doctor Cotton."

"Dr. Cotta," the bronzed god corrected. "Well, you've come to the right place then," he beamed.

I continued to stare and I suddenly realised why he looked so familiar. "Thor!" I blurted

"Sorry?"

Was it really Thor, or rather, Chris Hemsworth? He even had an Australian accent. Uber-white teeth dazzled against sun-kissed, honey-toned skin.

"Dr. Thor?" Blue eyes sparkled with mirth. I was the joke! *Mother Earth! Open up and swallow me whole!* "Nope, it's Dr. Cotta. Surgery is closed though."

Before I had a chance to reply, the man drew back, and the sash window dropped down with a clack as wood thudded against wood. The window vibrated and I was in an agony of unease; had I annoyed him?

I turned to leave.

The door to the house opened.

"Can I help you? I'm Doctor Cotta." The god-like man stepped out onto the block paving and stood beside the gleaming Porsche.

Doctor Cotta was nothing like I had imagined. Not at all. In any way.

Six foot four of bronzed, broad-shouldered male stood before me. Sparkling blue eyes shone from honey-toned skin and perfectly white teeth gleamed through a broad smile. Blonde, sun-kissed hair greying at the temples, completed a picture of a slightly older Chris Hemsworth. An Australian Adonis!

"Thor!" I breathed, then instantly realised I had said the word aloud. My cheeks burned, the flush sweeping up my neck to my cheeks within the second.

He chuckled.

He got the reference! Oh, for the love of Odin please let the ground swallow me now. "Pleased to make your acquaintance, Doctor Cotta." *What the hell was I saying?*

He held out his hand. "Likewise, and you are?"

"Liv. Livitha. Livitha Carlton. Well, not anymore. Pascal, he cheated on me, so, so now I'm Livitha Erikson, again. That was my maiden name anyway ..." I shut my mouth tight. I was rambling. My pulse throbbed at the base of my throat as the doctor continued to look at me with a slightly quizzical frown, then smiled kindly. *Pull yourself together, Livitha!* I took a breath to calm myself as I returned Dr. Cotta's smile. There was no way I would be registering at this surgery whilst he was in residence, the awkwardness of explaining my ailments to this outrageously handsome man would be far too excruciating for me to cope with. I sincerely hoped that my witchy powers meant I would be immune to illness and never have to visit a doctor again!

"Well Livitha Erikson, how can I help you?"

I stalled. I'd come to investigate him, but on what pretext? I scrambled for words. "My uncle Raif - Mr. Wolfreston - you came out to the cottage to see my uncle."

"Ah." His eyes narrowed and he looked at me as though inspecting an insect. "Haligern Cottage. How is he? Not worse, I hope?"

"No, not worse, but obviously, I'm very worried."

"You know I can't discuss his case with you."

I knew that. "Oh. No?"

"No."

Determined to find out more, I had to keep him talking. I scrambled again for words. The sun seemed particularly hot, and my fingers began to fizz. I staggered slightly and he caught my elbow. "Are you alright?"

My core was beginning to overheat. There was something about Dr. Cotta, apart from his exceptional good looks and testosterone infused virility. Intense purple sat at the innermost edge of his aura. I didn't know what that signified, but there was a depth to him I felt drawn to explore. He offered me the opportunity I needed without me having to ask. "Come inside and sit for a moment. I'll get you a glass of water. You've become very pale."

This surprised me; with the heat coursing through my body, and particularly in my face, I expected to be glowing like a puce Belisha beacon.

Stepping through the door into the main house was like stepping back in time. In that respect, it reminded me of Haligern. The floor was laid with black and white encaustic tiles that looked original to the property, and so did the foot-tall skirting, and shoulder-level wainscoting. An impressive staircase with carved baluster and handrail that ended in an elegant curl led upstairs. Light filled the hallway from a glass panel above the heavy front door.

As Dr. Cotta led me through to the kitchen at the back of the house, we passed a room with its door wide open. A blackout blind was pulled halfway down the window but there was enough light to see that it was filled with books. In the seconds it took me to pass, I noticed at least two bookcases filled from top to bottom. A table at the centre of the room was set up as a desk and books were piled either side of a lamp. Beneath the lamp, a book lay open, its spine resting on a cushion. It was obviously old, and the doctor was treating it with care. Although I had only managed a glimpse into the room, I had noticed that many of the books had worn bindings, and some were bound in leather.

As Dr. Cotta ushered me through to the kitchen, my mind remained with the books. I had to find a way of exploring the room.

In the kitchen, the table was set for dinner for two. A bottle of red, a 2014 Rioja Reserva, stood open on the countertop. A large casserole dish sat on the stove. The room had an air of neglect. The kitchen units were of 1970s brown Formica. An Aga sat within an old chimney breast. A glass of water was handed to me, and I took a sip whilst gathering my thoughts and the doctor filled a kettle with water. As the kettle boiled, and I considered the room filled with old books, Dr. Cotta rose to the top of my list of suspects—with an asterisk next to his name.

I wanted to know who was coming to dinner, perhaps an accomplice, or a love interest—maybe they were both, but asking outright would have been too rude, so I plumped for digging about the books. "So," I ventured as clouds of steam billowed from the kettle. "You collect books." I made an effort to sound natural although in my mind the handsome doctor had become a masked invader, albeit in the Zorro/highwayman style, climbing through the window at Haligern and grabbing Arthur. The array of books in the library, particularly those older books, was evidence that he either collected antique books, or traded in them. Perhaps he had connections with the black-market trade in priceless manuscripts. I was certain I had discovered the thief and watched him carefully as he replied.

"Yes, I do," he said without hesitation and a large smile. "You noticed my study then?" He gestured to the room full of books.

"Yes," I agreed. "You seem to have an awful lot, and I noticed that they were quite old, so thought that perhaps you collected them." *A brilliant deduction, Livitha!* I gritted my teeth. Even to myself, I sounded lame.

"Coffee?"

"No, thanks. So ... what kind of books do you collect?" *Grimoires by any chance?*

"Oh, I see! You really are interested in them."

I felt my cheeks begin to burn. There was that smile again, as though he were laughing at me.

I tried to play my interest down. "Erm, well ... kind of." Under his gaze, I began to panic, my thoughts scattering. "My ex, Pascal, he liked books, but ... architecture, that's what he liked." He raised an amused brow as I spoke. He made no effort to talk about his books and I didn't want to arouse his suspicion by digging anymore, so turned my attention to the house. "You have a lovely house, Dr. Cotta."

"Thank you, although I can't take any credit for it. There's a heck of a lot of work to be done, but I do love a challenge."

"You're renovating?"

"If I stay long enough."

"Oh? Aren't you planning on that?"

"It depends. If the village takes to me or not."

How could they not? "Oh, I'm sure they will."

"We'll see. I'm here for the short term though. I wanted to experience England for myself. My family are full of tales of the old country. We originate from Coventry, apparently."

"Oh, that's a lovely part of the country."

"Yeah, my great, great ... well, grandfather from way back, was a doctor too. I followed in his footsteps I guess, although he was kind of famous. You may have heard of him. John Cotta."

"But that's you!"

He laughed then. "It is, but it was also him."

"I'm sorry, but I haven't heard of him," I admitted.

"No worries. I guess he's a bit obscure, really. Lived way back in the 1600s. Wrote some bonza books on medicine. Cutting edge stuff at the time. He was a Galenist."

"Oh?" I had no idea what he meant.

"Yeah, he published a book about quack doctors and argued that medicine had to be learned. He pushed for doctors to be trained at uni. He was a real forward-thinking bloke." I merely nodded at this information not quite knowing what to say. "That's one of the reasons I'm here, to do a bit of family research. And yeah, some of the old books in my room are the ones he wrote, and you're right, I am collecting them." He offered me a broad smile. "He was an inspiration, and I intend to follow in his footsteps."

"Well, that's very ... commendable!" I managed as my belly flipped. My pulse was galloping. Dr. Cotta's smile was overwhelming, and I began to wonder if one of the aunts had slipped *me* a love potion this time.

"So, your Uncle, Mr. Wolfreston, he's doing okay now?" There was genuine concern in his voice.

"Yes, he's much better, thank you."

Silence fell between us and I glimpsed back through the door to the pile of books on the study table.

Dr. Cotta caught my glance. "Some of my ancestor's books."

I wanted to question him further, but only came back with a pathetic, "They look really old."

"They are. Some date back to 1612."

"Nothing older?" *Like a leather-bound manuscript filled with animal hide quires dating back to the Viking invasions and crammed with Haligern coven knowledge?*

"I've got older ones too-"

Here we go! "Oh?"

"But they're back at home ... in Oz"

"Oh ... You mean Australia?"

"Yeah, Oz. I'm from Queensland."

"The books ... do you think I could have a look? I'd love to know more about your ancestor."

He shot a glance through to the study. "Well, another time perhaps." He motioned to the kitchen table, "I'm expecting a guest for supper." He checked his watch. "And they should be here at any moment."

As though summoned, a series of short knocks at the back door was followed by a man's voice. 'Hello! Dr. Cotta?'

Dr. Cotta raised an amused brow. "Well, talk of the devil!"

"And he shall appear," I finished.

"He does."

Realising my time with the doctor was at an end, I followed him out through the house. Waiting at the back door was the doctor's guest, a tall and slender man with prematurely thinning hair and pale green eyes hidden behind dark-rimmed spectacles. He held a flan dish in one hand and a book in the other. Like the books in Dr. Cotta's study, this too was an ancient tome with frayed binding.

"Cheesecake!" he said by way of greeting, holding up the circular flan dish.

As he held up the cheesecake, I scanned the book. It was smaller than many modern-day books and had a hardback binding. Along the spine, part of the title was visible: 'Ignorant Pr ... Physicke'.

"And look what arrived today!" This time he held up the book. "It's a facsimile of the original."

Dr. Cotta noticed my interest. "It's by John Cotta, my ancestor," he explained. "It's a facsimile of one of the books I was telling you about." He held out his hand for the volume then read the title. "'A short discovery of the unobserved dangers of several sorts of ignorant and unconsiderate Practisers of Physicke in England'. It goes on, but I'll stop there. It gives you an idea of what it's about."

I stared back uncomprehending.

"It's his book about quack doctors! See ..." He pointed to the bottom of the book. "By John Cotta, Doctor of Physicke. My great, great, great and a few more greats, grandfather!" He beamed.

I understood. "Oh!"

"I have the original, but it's too fragile to work with, so Reverend Parsival very kindly sourced a more recent copy.

"This one's from the 1970s," the reverend explained. "The original was written in 1612."

"Oh, of course. Way too old to read."

"Exactly." Dr. Cotta turned his attention to the reverend. "Dominic, there's a bottle of red in the kitchen. Help yourself whilst I show Livitha out."

"Will do!"

As the reverend stepped forward and I moved towards the door, he caught my glimpse of curiosity and returned it with a piercing gaze. I hadn't met him before, but a time would come when I would be unable to forget those cold green eyes.

Back in the warmth of the afternoon sun, I thanked Dr. Cotta for the water, and he apologised for not being able to discuss my uncle and then asked me a question that turned my world upside down.

"Liv, your uncle's my patient, but you're not ... I know it's ... that we've only just met, but ... can we ... I'd like to get to know you. Would you like to go out for a coffee sometime?"

I could only answer with a breathy, shellshocked, 'Yes!'

Chapter Eight

I started my car with trembling fingers, pulled out into the road and instantly slammed on my brakes. Just ahead, on the opposite side of the road was a black dog. It looked identical to the dog that had crossed my path in town. It had appeared on the bridge and harassed Matthew Hopkins, the Witchfinder General. It had appeared on my road just before I was abducted by him. And it had appeared at the abandoned swimming baths as he tortured me. A shiver ran down my spine; did it mean that the Witchfinder was tracking me down again? I scanned the road, path, and shops as I twisted the key in the ignition, searching for any sign of the malevolent man. The engine thrummed into life and I continued along the road. The black dog trotted down the path, casting a quick glance my way before disappearing down an alleyway.

I decided to follow it.

The alleyway came out on the other side of a row of houses and led to the local church. I took a left then drove to where the dog should be. I scanned the area, but there was no sign of the dog and, after waiting for several minutes, decided to give up and return home. Just as I began to make a three-point turn and continue my journey to Haligern, a figure appeared from the alleyway. Breath caught in my throat; it was Garrett.

The car stalled, jolting me forward. "Wait!" I shouted through the windscreen as he crossed the road and took the path beside the church. Overhung with trees, the path was narrow and hemmed in by a garden wall on one side and the ancient stone wall of the churchyard on the other. It was a pretty pathway, often used by walkers and villagers taking an evening stroll. Oblivious to me, Garrett strode down the path, disappearing into its shadows. "Garrett!" The call came out as a whimper as I realised making a spectacle of myself wasn't the best way to gain his attention. I'd wanted our next meeting to be casual, an 'Oh! fancy seeing you here.' kind of thing. *That's right, Liv, casual. Remember?* My efforts to chase after him came to an immediate halt; he would consider me ridiculous, perhaps even a little deranged, if I chased him through the village shouting his name. It definitely wouldn't come across as casual. Plus, I was bound to catch up to him out of breath, red-faced and sweaty—not exactly the image of casual elegance I wanted to portray. *Hah! Casual elegance! Who was I kidding?* I was overweight and over fifty. Why would he even look at me twice? Deflated by my inner monologue, I returned to the car, now unsure whether the man had even been Garrett. And the dog? The dog couldn't be the one from town—that was just a ridiculous assumption to make!

Having talked myself into believing I was close to making an idiot of myself, and was probably losing the plot, I returned to my car and drove through the village, unable to push thoughts of Garrett and the black dog out of my mind. They pushed against new thoughts of Dr. Cotta and I churned with conflicting emotions. Dr. Cotta was gorgeous, and he had asked me out, but the man I really yearned for was Garrett.

Ridiculous! We had had one or two conversations during the investigation into the murder of my husband's mistress and, despite promising to call, he hadn't. *Move on, Liv! Move on.* "Oh, I will," I said aloud as the car rolled over the village boundary and into the countryside. "I will. I'll go for coffee with Dr. Cotta. That will show detective Garrett Blackwood I'm not waiting for him to call!"

My face flushed as the terrifying thought of sitting opposite the gorgeous doctor set adrenaline racing through my body. "What if I make an utter fool of myself?"

"Well, you're used to that, Livitha, so it shouldn't be a problem."

I slammed on the brakes and once more the car stalled.

"Ouf!"

Lucifer shot off the back seat and into the footwell.

"You are a terrible driver!"

"Lucifer! What are you doing here? You scared me half to death."

"Just doing my job."

"Doing your job?"

"Yes, you recall, I am sure, that one of my duties is to be your spy."

My brow furrowed. "Yes! But you're not supposed to spy on *me*!"

"Pah! Semantics."

"Lucifer! You have! You have been spying on me."

"Well, if you were to be unkind, you could call it that. Others might say I was taking a healthy interest in your welfare!" He jumped back up onto the seat. "The doctor is certainly attractive – I think you're definitely punching above your weight on that one! – but go for coffee. It will be very entertaining."

"Lou ..." I wanted to throw something acerbic back at him, but after the morning I'd had, my reserves were low and all I wanted now was to get back to Haligern and relax, at least relax as far as was possible whilst the house was infested by tiny, chaotic, and extremely mischievous fairies. I needed Lucifer on my side, so instead I said, "I've saved a lovely thick slice of roast beef for your tea. Let's go home."

Lucifer jumped onto the front seat then curled up in the footwell and began to purr whilst I focused on the road, my mind seesawing between thoughts of Garrett Blackwood and Dr. Cotta.

Chapter Nine

The following morning, I woke to the memory of Garrett Blackwood and a strong desire to see him before I went for coffee with Dr. Cotta. It was ridiculous, but I wanted to give Garrett a last chance to ask me out, I guess to rule out the possibility that he did want a 'friendship' between us.

In the kitchen a pot of coffee had been set to brew. I helped myself to a cup and sat warily at the table. The room was uncharacteristically quiet with no sign of my aunts, or the fairies.

I relaxed a little but had only managed half a cup of coffee before a bottle clinked in the corner of the room. "Fairies!" I hissed.

Another bottle clinked, this time from the pantry, and then soot sprinkled from the chimney. A scurrying noise came from within the cupboard of the welsh dresser that dominated one wall. I resisted the temptation to react. My last efforts had caused chaos and damage so, instead, I searched the pantry for the smelly cheese. Behind me fairies began to chitter, and I felt that distinctive displacement of air as they flew about. There had to be more than three of them in the kitchen and they were obviously growing excited by the prospect of Aunt Bea's soothing concoction of cheesy elixir. The familiar stirrings of panic began to rise, but I made my best efforts to quelle them. As I found the cheese and took it from the shelf the noise and fluttering died down, Aunt Beatrice appeared, and I stepped back into the kitchen with relief.

"Good morning, darling," she said taking her long red pinafore from its hook behind the kitchen door.

Before I had a chance to reply, she spotted the cheese. "Have they been playing up again?"

I nodded. "They were becoming irritable. I thought I'd try your cheesy mix to quieten them."

"Quite right, but how will we quiet you?"

"Pardon?"

"Well, all this turmoil, it gives one quite a headache, Livitha."

I placed the cheese on the side and unwrapped it. A waft of smelly feet rose to fill my nostrils. "Ugh! I'm not sure what you mean, but this cheese gives me a headache."

"You seem a little distracted this morning, Livitha."

"You've only just walked into the kitchen, we've barely spoken. How can you tell?"

"Well, your top is on inside out and back to front for a start."

I dropped the knife and inspected my top. A white label printed with the size of my top for all to see sat along the neckline. "I dressed in a hurry. I thought there was a fairy in my bedroom."

I could tell she wasn't buying my explanation.

Chittering erupted in the pantry.

"They're argumentative this morning!"

"They are every morning!"

"I thought I heard them in the rafters above my bedroom last night," Aunt Beatrice said. "They seem to be in every nook and cranny of the house, although I don't believe there are any more than seven here, at least, I haven't seen more than seven at any one time."

I shuddered at the thought of seven fairies scurrying around the house.

I chopped a chunk of cheese from the smelly block.

"Aunt Bea?" I had her on my own and determined to ask her the question that had been burning into me for weeks. "Why are the Blackwoods cursed?"

"Blackwood, Blackwood, Blackwood! It's all you ever think about, Livitha!"

"Oh! I don't!" I mashed the cheese into a saucer.

Aunt Beatrice added drops of elixir.

"I just wanted to know why they're cursed. Do they even live at Black Wood Manor? I don't think that Garrett can do. I imagine he lives in town, closer to work."

"Well, you have his telephone number ..."

I wasn't sure if this was encouragement or an accusation. "How do you know that?" As I asked the question, she gave me an exasperated look. "Okay, yes, I have his number, but I haven't used it," I added quickly.

"I didn't need to read your mind to know that one, Livitha! But what you are dabbling with? They're cursed!"

"Yes, you've said – on numerous occasions – but ... Anyway, I'm not dabbling with anything. I haven't seen or heard from him in weeks – not since the hospital."

"No, but you've thought of him."

Daily. Hourly. "Well, perhaps a bit. Maybe sometimes ..."

"Oh, Livitha ..."

She didn't say another word – her silence said it all – she knew that my thoughts were infused with the man. There wasn't an hour that went by when a memory of his face, from our early romance to our meetings last month, didn't pop up. More than that, the shockwave that had spread to every cell in my body as our hands touched when I'd slipped past him on the steps under Loveday's invisibility spell, seemed to live within me. But it all made me feel like a fool; he hadn't called as promised.

As I continued to mash the cheese and elixir, squashing out all the lumps as instructed, Aunts Loveday and Thomasin joined us in the kitchen.

"They've not eaten yet, then?" Aunt Thomasin said as she noticed me at work. "In that case, I'll milk Olde Mawde and take my breakfast later."

Glass chinked and more soot fell from the chimney.

"What are they doing up there?" Aunt Loveday asked as black particles sprinkled on the hearth.

"They were in the rafters above my bedroom last night!"

"And beneath my floorboards!" Aunt Thomasin added.

"They're everywhere!" I said in exasperation.

Movement above caught my eye and one of the vintage plates displayed on the dresser wobbled and then we all turned to a crash from the pantry.

As Aunt Beatrice disappeared to inspect the damage, Mrs Driscoll stepped into the room. "Good morning, Ladies." She said this without her usual smile. Generally, Mrs. Driscoll would join us for a cup of tea once she arrived before beginning the chores. All the aunts helped with the work, and they would all take a break for a cup of tea and a biscuit a couple of hours later, sitting around the table to chat and catch up on gossip. This morning concerned glances were exchanged; Mrs. Driscoll didn't seem her usual self.

Bottles clinked in the corner. I wanted to shush the creatures but didn't want to draw attention to their presence; so far Mrs. Driscoll was unaware of them. The saucer of cheesy elixir sat on the counter. I couldn't put it down for the fairies now.

After a round of lacklustre greetings, Mrs. Driscoll made straight for the Welsh dresser, damp cloth in hand. Bottles chinked again in the corner and this time she turned to the noise. Irritated chittering grew and a vintage platter moved on the dresser. A fairy fluttered close to my head. I felt something tangle in my hair. Unable to control my fright, I squealed. The vintage platter began to slip. Startled by my squeal, Mrs. Driscoll yelped in fright, noticed the wobbling plate just as she twisted to me, and twirled back to stop the plate falling. The plate fell, slipped through Mrs. Driscoll's fingers, and crashed to the floor, shattering across the tiles. Bottles chinked and the noise of scurrying feet was audible.

"There's something in here!" she gasped scanning the corners of the room. "You've got rats!"

"No, Mrs. Driscoll. They're fair-"

Aunt Loveday's warning glare stopped me in my tracks.

"Perhaps a mouse?"

"You were going to say fairies!"

"No, of course not. I was going to say ... field mouse. I hate mice. They set me off in a panic and the mere thought of saying that word ..."

"Mice?"

"Yes ... mice, stopped me. At least the field ... variety are a little cuter than most," I waffled. "The house variety ... ugh!" I managed a shudder for dramatic effect. Mrs Driscoll watched my hammy performance with deepening confusion.

"Dormice are the sweetest little things, don't you agree?" Aunt Beatrice added. "They're my favourite."

As Aunt Beatrice continued to talk, Aunt Thomasin moved in the direction of the rocking bottles, muttering a charm beneath her breath. The words, as usual, were spoken in the language of our people and I realised it was less of a struggle to understand. As she moved across the kitchen, her words stilled the bottles, and the chink of glass grew quiet. It wasn't that she had soothed the fairies, far from it – as she approached, one had risen above the potions in clear view whilst another clambered up a bottle's neck – but the area around them became still, the fairy held aloft by an invisible force, the creature climbing the bottle now clinging as though in a still from a film. Waves of energy shimmered like heat rising from the surface of a road in high summer as the fairies were caught in an aspic of magick. Mrs. Driscoll made no indication that she was aware of the fairy held in freeze-frame scrambling over the bottle tops. The charm must have cast an invisibility cloak around them too. I badly wanted to inspect the little beasts whilst they were in such a harmless state, and then Mrs. Driscoll dropped a bombshell.

"My Agnes has one."

"A mouse?"

"Oh, a dormouse? How sweet, although I do hope she'll return it to the wild."

"No. Not a mouse. Agnes has a fairy. She keeps it in the vivarium at home."

All four aunts exchanged surprised glances.

"Agnes has a fairy?"

"Yes, at least that's what she calls it, but I think it must be some sort of exotic foreign animal. Obviously, there's no such thing as fairies."

"Of course not."

"Preposterous idea."

"Just fantasy!"

"Oh, I love the ideas of fairies ... believed I had seen one as a child, but of course if you begin to tell people that, they think you're mad and the grownups hush you ... It was in the old sweetshop ..."

As she continued to reminisce, the source of the infestation became clear—the old sweetshop which was being renovated to become my aunts' apothecary shop. The troublesome sprites must have followed my aunts home after their first inspection of the property.

"But this creature she had in the jar, well I guess in a poor light, if it was in flight, although its wings are far too stubby, you would say that it could be mistaken for a fairy, but it really was rather ugly and such sharp teeth. It bit her finger, you know, made a terrible mess and I had to take her to the doctor's. She wouldn't listen to him either."

"And where did she find this ugly creature?"

At this question, Mrs. Driscoll grew quiet.

"Mrs. Driscoll?"

The colour drained from her cheeks and she shrank a little from our gaze, guilt oozing from her in waves. "Well, she said she found it here."

What had Agnes been doing at Haligern Cottage?

"I'm so sorry, I should have mentioned that she-"

Mrs. Driscoll's words came to a stuttering stop as Aunt Loveday muttered a rapid succession of words. She waved a hand through the air as though spreading an invisible liquid over Mrs. Driscoll. The woman became as still as a wax dummy.

"Cild ælfen!" Aunt Loveday hissed and visibly quivered.

Aunt Euphemia gave Mrs. Driscoll a tentative prod. When this elicited no reaction, Aunt Loveday repeated, "Cild ælfen. A fairy child; the larval stage."

"Larval?"

"Yes!" Aunt Loveday's eyes glittered. "Mrs. Driscoll described the larvae of a fairy. That is why they are so ... so out of sorts with themselves."

Larvae! My imagination immediately went to maggots and my revulsion of the creatures grew.

"They remind me very much of ladybirds or dragonflies," Aunt Loveday continued. "The larval stage of those creatures, as with fairies, is quite hideous, and it is only once they go through their metamorphosis that they emerge as beautiful creatures."

"It makes absolute sense why they're behaving so badly these days."

"Yes, it most certainly does."

"Are you saying that Agnes has kidnapped one of their children?" Aunt Thomasin asked.

"She took their babies!" Aunt Beatrice threw Mrs. Driscoll a disapproving frown. "How could she do that?"

"Well, technically it is an insect, isn't it?" I added. "Or an amphibian? But if she has it in a vivarium, does that mean it's a kind of – my stomach curdled – reptile?"

"No, Liv, of course not. It is a fairy. A fae, an ælfen. And a larval fairy is just as precious to the fairies as a baby is to us, even if it is rather-" She glanced at the fairies trapped in their aspic of magic. "... rather unattractive."

The pain of barrenness pricked at me. Although we had tried, even resorting to IVF, Pascal and I had never conceived. I had sought solace in my garden, Pascal in golf and then other women!

Aunt Loveday immediately picked up on my pain. "Oh, darling girl. I didn't mean to be so insensitive."

I felt her aura surge with pity. "Please, don't apologise. I know absolutely that you didn't mean to hurt me. I'm okay. I've had a long time to ... grieve not having my own child and given how things have turned out between me and Pascal, I'm glad we never had one.

"Oh, Liv, don't say that."

"Well, it's true. I've been happy."

"It's never too late, you know," Aunt Beatrice added.

I laughed at this through my pain. "Oh, Aunt Bea! I'm going through the menopause, of course it's too late."

"Darling girl, have you never read Thumbelina?"

My head began to buzz as it so often did in conversation with Aunt Beatrice.

"Sisters, we need to get back to the problem in hand. I think it makes sense to conclude that Agnes Driscoll has captured one of the fairy's children and taken it home."

"Where she's keeping it in a jar!"

"A vivarium isn't quite a jar."

"It's made of glass, so the same thing."

"Oh, the poor darling!"

"Its poor mother must be frantic."

"Yes, and that's probably what all the commotion is about. They're checking every nook and cranny in the cottage to find it."

"Well, we know where it is, so it should be easy to get it back. I'm sure if we speak to the girl, she will return it."

"Yes, I'm sure she will."

"And if she doesn't?"

"She has to!"

"Well, we can't inform the police ..."

"I'm sure that we can convince her to return it, sisters. It is nothing a little magic can't fix. But one thing is certain, we need to make sure she has no recollection of the little creature. I only hope that she hasn't told anyone."

"I would be very surprised at that. From my conversations with Mrs. Driscoll about the girl, and her friends, teenagers these days want instant gratification. I imagine she has placed an image of it on Snaptock, or Twatter."

"Twitter," I corrected.

"Well, whatever it's called, they photograph everything from the shoes they are wearing to the food they are eating and then wait for public reaction."

"Terribly narcistic."

"Just so."

"I have no idea how we will fix that faux pas if it has occurred."

Muttering agreement passed from aunt to aunt.

"Liv, you must talk to the girl."

"I will. Although I'll have to keep the … creature in its jar until I return."

"You must. They are terribly wayward at that stage and quite destructive when apart from their parents."

I shuddered at the thought of the insect-like larvae, amazed that Agnes would want to keep it. Even more surprising was that she had recognised the larvae as a fairy. "Have you had experience in the past—of fairies?"

"Once or twice and I have it all documented in Arthur for future reference. That is how I discovered he was missing. I have been observing the little creatures, for research purposes, and wanted to add my findings to his pages. They've evolved over the years, you know."

"They are certainly far more unruly these days," Aunt Euphemia added.

During this conversation Mrs. Driscoll had remained inanimate. "Sisters, we are agreed then. Livitha will accompany Mrs. Driscoll to her home and retrieve the fairy child?" Again, a series of yesses were accompanied by nodded affirmations, and Aunt Loveday released the spell. Mrs. Driscoll's flow of words continued as though without interruption.

"… It was quite hideous, but she assured me that it was a fairy. She even had an old book with a picture of it drawn in violet ink."

Aunt Loveday hissed again, and a flicker of anger sparkled in her eyes. "A book?"

"Yes, an old book full of writing and drawings. I couldn't understand a word, but she assured me that it was English with a bit of ... now what was it? Yes! That's it. She called it Old Norse. It's what the Vikings used to speak," she said with satisfaction. "But I tell you, if we went back in time, there's no way we'd understand a word of what they said. It wasn't written in any kind of English I know. And some of it was just symbols, runes Agnes said they were, although I couldn't make head nor tail of them."

"What did the book look like Mrs. Driscoll?" The aunts stood mute as they reigned in their anger.

"Well ... it was really old, I'd say at least ... oh, I don't know. I'm not an expert, but it had these thick yellowish pages that felt a bit like plastic. Which makes me wonder if it's not some Chinese knock-off of an old book-"

"The book's cover, Mrs. Driscoll. What did that look like?" Aunt Loveday pressed.

"Oh, quite rough. Old leather – or at least imitation leather. They can make anything look old these days. It had patterns on the front. Like ropes all twisted together and what looked a bit like dragons. And it was a fold-over cover, like a wrap, and held closed by leather strings with silver beads at the end. I'm not sure how the Professor could have let her take it home—if it was valuable."

"The professor?"

"Oh," Mrs Driscoll beamed. "She's been on a history taster course at college and one of the teachers is local." Mrs. Driscoll beamed. "She wants to go to university! Obviously, I try to encourage her, but I did challenge her about the book. She said the professor had bought it from a shop in the village that sold antiques and vintage knick-knacks to the tourists. You know the one, Muriel Acaster's shop."

I knew of the shop, and the woman's reputation for dealing in antiques, but it was obvious that the girl was lying to her mother. Agnes had taken the book. My aunts exchanged worried looks. They didn't need to speak for me to understand their concerns. Agnes had discovered Aunt Loveday's Grimoire and used it to identify the larval fairy, possibly taking it to the Professor for help with translation. Haligern's secret identity as a coven of ancient witches was at enormous risk of being revealed.

I had to discover every detail of Agnes' visits and rectify the situation before it became a disaster. "Mrs. Driscoll, when did Agnes come here last?"

"Why just before the big party," she said referring to the Solstice gathering. "The Saturday before. There was so much to do, and I just couldn't get it all done in time. I had her up here to clean the garden furniture. A lot of it needed a good brush down—lots of spiderwebs."

"Mrs. Driscoll, I'd like to talk to Agnes."

Chapter Ten

We arrived at Mrs. Driscoll's house just before lunch. I'd known her since she began working for my aunts but other than on the few occasions when I'd been at the cottage for elevenses – when all four aunts joined Mrs. Driscoll for a mid-morning break with tea and biscuits – I hadn't had much contact with the woman. In recent weeks she had seemed a little subdued and, on a couple of occasions a little irritated, particularly with Bess, Aunt Beatrice's overly excited whippet familiar. On one occasion Lucifer had refused to move as she tried to clean, and she had eventually had to physically unpick his claws from the fabric of the chair she was trying to hoover. I'd watched the scene with amusement as Mrs. Driscoll went from polite request to frustration as Lucifer refused to vacate the seat. When she did try to pick him up his claws had sunk deep into the lavender velvet fabric. 'Naughty cat!' she had scolded as Lucifer's legs stretched, his claws piercing the fabric. I swear he smirked as she huffed and complained. 'Just my way of getting through the day,' he had admitted later over his saucer of port. Even Benny, Aunt Thomasin's glossy, ink-black raven hadn't been spared and she'd shooed him from the kitchen muttering about dirty birds. Thankfully, Aunt Thomasin hadn't been around to hear, and I didn't stir the pot by mentioning anything. The reason for her behaviour became clear that morning.

The house wasn't what I had expected but was exactly what I should have expected. I had imagined a small terrace but Mrs. Driscoll lived in an immaculately presented dormer bungalow on a corner plot complete with mock-Georgian bow windows, an ornamental bird bath at the centre of the lawn and a front door flanked by two concrete whippets remarkably like Bess. The lawn was edged by vibrant bedding plants, standard fuchsias, and symmetrically placed and carefully clipped box topiary. It was an attractive house, much like Mrs. Driscoll; clean and tidy and on the verge of being twee.

"I bought them because they looked like her," she said as I stepped up to the front door. For a moment I was taken aback, imagining that, like Aunt Beatrice, Mrs. Driscoll could read my mind until I realised that she had noticed me looking at them.

The interior of the house was as immaculate as the outside, not Selma Maybrook immaculate with its minimalist uninhabitable-unless-you-cover-yourself-in-clingwrap chic, but pristine in a colour coded everything in its place kind of way. A pale blue hallway with white painted woodwork staircase led through to a bright kitchen of cream and blue. A cream and blue teapot sat beside a trio of cream cannisters containing tea, coffee, and sugar. On the shelves were pretty cups and saucers, again following the cream and blue seaside theme. It was a pretty kitchen, and the house had a nice vibe. My ability to sense energies had become more sensitive since my initiation and I picked up on the particles of a volatile energy. The energy had a stale scent to it rather like a house that has been left empty for a few days. Whoever the energy belonged to was no longer in the house. "Is Agnes out, Mrs. Driscoll?"

Mrs. Driscoll turned to me then, her eyes brimming with tears. "She didn't come home last night."

This explained the staleness of the energy and I sensed friction between the women. "Why didn't you say?"

"I didn't want to worry your aunts. It's not the first time she's done this, or even the second, but usually she's back by morning."

"How old is she Mrs. Driscoll?"

"Eighteen."

I had friends whose teenage children would sometimes come home in the early hours and one who seemed intent on worrying her father to death by staying out all night and not calling home. "So old enough ..."

"Yes, but I still worry. She used to be such a good girl, but these days, since she got friendly with some new kids, she's been different ..."

"Do you know where she is?"

"No!" Her voice cracked. "And when I tried to call her mobile, she just rejected the call." I should have had that tracker put on her phone ..."

"She's technically an adult, Mrs. Driscoll."

"She's still a child!" Mrs. Driscoll appeared horrified. "She's all I've got!" she wailed. Mrs. Driscoll's pain was obviously far deeper than difficulty with an uncommunicative and wayward teenager, albeit one on the cusp of adulthood. "Since Patrick died ..." At this she broke into sobs.

I remembered the story of her husband, Patrick. His death had been a complete shock to the whole village. The man was a keen cyclist and runner, the very last candidate for a heart attack, but he had suffered a massive coronary as he manoeuvred a forklift of pallets at the local garden centre and crashed into a display of garden gnomes, spearing the mound of earth they had been stood on. Heads had separated from bodies and jolly faces with blushing cheeks had stared dumbly as they hurtled through the air. Patrick was dead before the last head rolled to a stop beside the forklift.

"I'll put the kettle on, shall I?" I offered, feeling awkward as she continued to sob, and remembering the image of shattered, dirt-covered gnomes in the local paper.

"It was hereditary ... the heart defect, and undetected until the autopsy."

I offered platitudes and boiled the kettle.

Only after we had shared a cup of tea and a biscuit did her spirits rally. I took the opportunity to continue my questions about Agnes. Her father had died several years ago and she hadn't slipped down the slippery slope of delinquency then, so it intrigued me as to why she would go off the rails at this time in her life – she was nearly an adult, at an age at which parents take off the brakes. As we continued to talk, it became obvious that Mrs. Driscoll was something of a helicopter parent and had gone into overdrive once her husband had died. Agnes' decline in behaviour – or loosening of the shackles – had been incremental, but since a group of young adult holidaymakers had decided to stay in the area for the summer, she had taken a saw to chop the shackles off. The argument about the fairy, the 'disgusting, smelly creature' she was keeping in her bedroom had been the last straw and Agnes had stropped out of the house, rucksack packed, and sworn to go and live with people who actually appreciated her. Mrs. Driscoll assured me these 'people' had to be the newcomers in the village as Agnes didn't mix much with the local teens.

"They're either a fair bit older, or a lot younger, and the only other child within a five-mile radius is a 'dweeb' according to Agnes. That's the problem with living in a small village—there's not much choice when it comes to friends. I did always try of course – ballet lessons, taekwondo, kick boxing – all in town. The vicar's Tuesday night scripture classes didn't appeal." Here she raised a brow.

It was obvious that Agnes was something of a loner, or at least lonely, which is perhaps why this new group held such interest for her. "Mrs. Driscoll, do you think that we can take a look in her bedroom? Perhaps there may be clues there, or even – I barely dared to hope – the creature she claims is a 'fairy.'"

My reasoning was that if Agnes had left in a strop, she was unlikely to have packed the book or left with the vivarium and I could take them both with the promise of returning the book to the professor and setting the creature free in a local field.

Mrs. Driscoll raised her brows, and a horrified look came over her face. "If you dare! Agnes isn't the tidiest of girls."

Mrs. Driscoll led the way upstairs and as soon as the bedroom door opened, I realised just what the look on her face had signalled. It was mortification. Agnes' bedroom was the antithesis to the rest of the house. Where the house was light and sun-filled, the bedroom, with its black walls and drawn curtains, was dark. Only a thin sliver of strong morning sun cast any light. Turning on the light made little difference – the shade was black too. Mrs. Driscoll strode to the windows, drew the curtains, and pushed the dinge back to the corners of the room. The bedroom was a mess and had the fuggy odour of unwashed bedding and stale air.

"I'm so sorry ... about the smell!" She opened the windows and the breeze caught at the papers on the bed causing them to flutter. One slipped to the floor. "No need to apologise. I'm sure lots of teens are like this ..."

"Well ... that's kind of you."

As she continued to apologise and fluster about the mess and begin to tidy up, I searched the room for any sign of Arthur or the fairy. On the desk, littered with more papers, and mostly hidden beneath a denim jacket, was the vivarium.

"That's her 'fairy'." Mrs. Driscoll clarified as I removed the jacket. I had never seen the larval form, so wasn't sure what to expect. I peered into the vivarium. It had been lined with cloth, a small bowl had been set in one corner and a pile of wilted leaves in another, but there was no sign of the creature. I worried then that it had starved to death!

"I think it's empty," I said, unwilling to remove the lid. If the larvae were still alive, and anything like the adults, then it could be vicious.

Mrs. Driscoll peered in "Maybe hidden in the cloth?"

I made no effort to find out and when Mrs. Driscoll reached for the lid, I took a step back. Heart beating, and that familiar mouse-phobia-induced panic rising, I watched as she tentatively moved the fabric.

"It's empty. She must have taken it with her."

My relief was immense as she replaced the lid, but I was also disappointed; I had banked on the fairy being left behind. I couldn't tolerate another video incident. I had hoped that in reuniting it with its parents, there would peace at the house tonight and I'd become a hero of sorts, imagining they'd leave me alone out of respect and awe, or at least be grateful!

With the lid finally in place, and my heart rate slowing, I turned my attention to the books and papers piled and strewn around the room. Among several books on Anglo Saxon history were a variety of books on witchcraft—mostly the dross I'd passed over whilst searching the online bookstores when I'd discovered that I was descended from a long line of witches, or 'cunning folk' as my aunts preferred. I picked up a volume entitled, 'Satanism: A Complete Beginners Guide.'

"What's that?"

I passed the book over to Mrs. Driscoll and turned my attention to the papers as she groaned and mumbled her discontent. "Oh, dear!" she exclaimed in low tones. "Oh, dear, oh, dear."

Among the papers were notes on witchcraft, some spells, and pages of Agnes' name written in runes, along with various doodles of pentagrams and other sacred symbols.

"She was obviously interested in witchcraft," I said as I leafed through the papers.

"She's a silly girl!"

"It's probably just a teenage thing," I soothed. However, I was concerned. Many of the spells and notes Agnes had made veered to the darker side of magick. And now, after a fruitless search of the bedroom, I was certain that she had taken Arthur and the fairy with her. I was also increasingly concerned; if what Aunt Loveday said was true, Arthur, in the wrong hands, was a serious problem indeed. I had to find Agnes and the book. "Where do Agnes' friends live?"

"Up in the Black Woods. They've got a campsite close to the old Blackwood house."

Dread washed through me.

Chapter Eleven

The mid-afternoon sun shone with an intensity that matched my need to find the campers as I motored away from the village. Inside the car the air was stuffy, and I began to sweat. The air-conditioning had failed several months ago and having continually put off taking the car to the garage to get it fixed, I now sat with perspiration beading on my top lip unable to tell whether the heat infusing my body was from the summer sun or a wave of hormonal hijacking. I opened the window to allow fresh air to cool me and instantly regretted it as the car filled with an odour of pig manure so strong that it seemed to stick to the hairs in my nose. Arable farmland stretched over the rolling hills between the village and the next town, the stench part of the yearly cycle of production. Closing the window would be futile; the car was filled with the smell, the air re-cycling system no match for the stink. With the ripe particles of eau-de cochon filling my mouth and nose, I accelerated in the hope of finding clean air soon.

The Black Woods were several miles outside of the village, in the opposite direction of Haligern Cottage, and the road be-came winding and steep as it cut through the rolling hills of the Wolds. As I reached the highest point, the Black Woods came into view. Beginning half-way down the hill they spread across the landscape and engulfed the surrounding hillsides. The sight was impressive, and the thick canopy was only broken by a cluster of buildings at the base of one hill and, in the far distance, by a clearing that surrounded a turreted mansion. It had to be Blackwood Manor, Garett's ancestral home.

Mrs. Deacon had said that the campers were situated between the tenant cottages and the mansion. I presumed the tenant cottages to be the cluster of buildings at the bottom of the hill and followed the road into the woods, only noticing an ancient and carved standing stone as I passed over the threshold. With my focus on finding Agnes I made a mental note to come back to the stone and read its inscription on my way back. Bright sunshine became dappled light. Flanked by trees, the earth was held back by ancient moss and lichen covered drystone walls. Tall fronds of bright green bracken sat still, without breeze. The road turned and twisted as it made its way downwards. At one point the trees thinned enough for me to see the tops of the cottages and then the view disappeared as the car was once again engulfed by woodland.

The road diverged into three narrow lanes. To the left would take me back up the hill and into the woodlands whilst the right would take me downwards. The centre lane was nothing more than a track overhung by trees. I took the right lane, presuming it would take me down to the cottages. The lane curved downwards at a steep angle and then opened to a clearing with three cottages and a small lake beyond. The lake boundary was also hedged by trees but, from my position on the slope, I could see the golden fields of farmland beyond.

I slowed to a stop, then left the car, hoping to find someone home. The cottages were picturesque. Each was built from red brick with sash windows painted white. High-pitched rooves tiled with dark slate had gable ends decorated with a prettily scalloped and pierced bargeboard painted white and topped by a carved finial. Each house had a storm porch with matching decorative bargeboard. Low stone walls and a wooden gated archway marked the front of the properties. Each archway was covered by abundantly flowering roses. The image was of bucolic perfection as beautiful as any William Affleck painting. I half expected a young woman, pinafore neatly tied over a full-length skirt, wicker basket in arms and filled with flowers, to step through one of the rose-drenched archways. Instead, a stout and balding man dressed in sage green trousers and dog-tooth brown and cream shirt appeared from the side of a house.

"How do?" he called as he strode forward. The trousers were bagged around the knees and seat. The shirt, which had a small tear in one sleeve, was rolled up to his elbows to reveal hairy forearms. He was a man used to hard work. To compliment his outfit, he wore a pair of mud-smeared wellingtons. String dangled at the front of his trousers from his waist and, as he approached, I realised it was being used to hold his trousers up. I noticed then the air of decay about the houses beneath the beauty of the flowers. Paint was peeling from the sash windows and beautifully carved bargeboards. The rooves undulated as their lathes weakened, weathered by the seasons. The tenant cottages were being neglected and it crossed my mind that perhaps the Blackwood family fortunes were in decline.

Hands on hips beneath an overhanging belly, the man stood outside his house to face me. "Can I help you?" His tone was wary rather than unfriendly. I was a stranger, and he treated me with a hint of suspicion. This gave me hope. If there were a group of people camping in the woods, he would be aware of them.

"Hi, yes. Sorry to bother you." He nodded his acceptance. "I'm looking for some people who are camping in the woods."

"Pah!"

I waited for him to continue. He didn't.

"I ... there are some campers-"

"I wouldn't call them that!"

"So, you know where they are?"

"I do."

"And? ... Could you tell me, please? It's very important that I find them. A girl has gone missing, and I'm hoping they know where she is."

He glanced at the woodlands behind the cottages just as a cloud passed overhead casting us both in shadow. It deepened the frown lines on his face.

"A girl?"

"Yes, from the village. You may know her – Agnes Driscoll."

"Never heard of her."

I searched in my bag and pulled out the photograph Mrs. Driscoll had allowed me to take. "Have you seen the campers? Do you think you would recognise them again?" I held up the photograph. "This is Agnes Driscoll."

He peered at the schoolgirl photograph of Agnes smiling shyly at the camera. Mrs. Driscoll assured me it was a good likeness.

"This was taken a few years ago, so she may look a little older."

"Aye."

"So, you recognise her?"

"No."

"Oh. Were there any young blonde women with the group?"

"Aye."

"Do you think she was one of them?"

He shrugged his shoulders. "Dunno."

It was obvious that my efforts to gain information were not going to be fruitful. "Well, thanks for your help," I said without letting my frustration show. "Could you point me in the right direction of the campsite, please?"

"Squat you mean."

"Yes, squat. If you know where it is, I can talk to them.

"Aye, they call thersens travellers but they're nothing but squatters. A bunch of idle layabouts. They're not gypsies—gypsies have their traditions—they work. These are just poor little rich kids sloping off and mekkin' a nuisance of thersens!

"Still, I need to talk to them. They may know where Agnes is. She could even be with them. Her mother is beside herself with worry ..."

"Aye. Kids'll do that to you," he said with an edge of cynicism. "You'll need to go along yonder track – you'll see it when you go back up the road. Follow it. They're about a quarter mile down, but there's not many as is left."

My hope faded but I left the man and the cottages with renewed determination to find the remnants of the group and question them about Agnes.

Chapter Twelve

I arrived twenty minutes later after a bumpy ride over pot-holes and deeply rutted forest track. At several points, the track was submerged beneath water, and I worried that my small car would get stuck in the wet earth; it definitely wasn't up to off-roading.

It became obvious that vehicles had used the track recently and I hoped it wasn't evidence of an exodus from the campsite. If it was empty, my enquiries would come to a dead end. About a quarter of a mile down the track I spotted them through the trees. Two vehicles, a Volvo estate, and a Volkswagen Tourer, were parked up and several people were moving about the site. Only flattened grass and rutted tracks remained as evidence that the group had been larger.

I pulled into the clearing, parking in a vacated spot, and scanned the figures, searching for Agnes, but the only people I could see were two men in their mid-twenties and a young woman of a similar age. They appeared to be packing. The taller man with a long beard and shoulder-length hair finished stuffing a tent into its sack and threw it into the back of the Volkswagen. The young woman, a gaudy addition to the forest in dark purple harem pants and a fuchsia shoelace top grabbed a holdall and swung it beside the tent. With long black hair in fishtail plaits hanging over her shoulders and numerous bangles and pendants dangling on leather thongs from her neck and wrists, she was every inch the new-age hippy, or at least my idea of one.

The second man paused his work and turned to greet me with a questioning frown. With Agnes' photograph in hand, I smiled and introduced myself.

"Hi, sorry to interrupt, but I'm looking for a young woman." I thrust the photograph towards him and watched his reaction.

"Agnes, yeah, she was here." He bent to pick up a sleeping bag and stuffed it into the boot of the Volvo. It was filled with camping equipment and even a portable loo; they were obviously campers who weren't keen on 'roughing it'.

The long-bearded man and hippy-style girl joined us. I picked up on their anxious energy. It was misplaced in the forest.

"Do you know where she is now?"

As I asked the question a rumble shook the forest and the ground vibrated beneath my feet. The girl gasped and grasped her boyfriend's arm. From somewhere within the woods came another loud rumble and then the light began to dim. Above us the blue sky with its cottonwool clouds, had grown to a haze of twilight purple. The space around me continued to darken and the girl whimpered.

"It's just a thunderstorm," I soothed.

"No!" The girl blurted. "It's not a thunderstorm."

"Shh!" the tall man chided. "Stay quiet."

"What's going on?" I asked as the light continued to seep away. A thunderstorm was the logical explanation, but the purple haze that had replaced the blue summer sky was bizarre, and the way the dark was encroaching on the campsite, unnerving.

Ignoring me, the trio returned to packing, throwing their remaining possessions into the cars.

"Hurry!" the girl hissed as she jumped into the passenger seat and pulled the door shut. She gave the bank of trees a terrified glance and pulled at her seat belt.

The last of the light seeped away and her scared eyes disappeared. Heart pounding, I fumbled in my pocket for my torch.

"Get out of here, lady!" A voice hissed from the darkness. Car doors slammed, engines burst into life, and headlights shone against the pitch black.

Torchlight on, it illuminated the driver in the Volvo. I hammered on his window, but he headed for the track out of the clearing. The second car followed, but this time the driver stopped, rolling down his window a fraction.

"I'm looking for Agnes Driscoll." I thrust the photograph at him. "Where is she?"

My voice didn't carry. It seemed to be swallowed by the dark as though I were speaking through a thick cloth. "Where is she?" I shouted.

"At the house!" He shouted back and the window began to slide up. "She went to the house. She didn't come back. None of them come back." The window closed to shut and the van lurched forward. Brake lights shone red against the dark as he stopped and, opening the door, he shouted, "There's something in the woods. You have to get out!"

The hairs on my neck stood on end and a chill washed over me. He was right. Something had entered the forest. I felt it all around me, stroking at my skin, and it was toxic.

The van's taillights were swallowed by the darkness and only the small circle of torchlight helped me find my car. Within seconds a flash of chrome and metallic paint revealed it but, before I had a chance to open the door, the darkness began to fade. I jumped in, locked the doors, and started the engine, watching as the dark receded and the abandoned campsite reappeared. As I shunted the gears into first, the darkness cleared, and late afternoon sun broke through the forest canopy as dappled light. The toxic energy that had enveloped me also evaporated. I made a quick three-point turn and followed the campers, catching up with them as we reached the forest boundary. After several hoots of my horn they pulled over, parking on the verge. With Agnes' photo clutched in my hand, I approached with a confident stride, determined to get as much information from the group as possible. Was the house he referred to Blackwood Manor? And what did he mean 'none of them come back'? The search for Agnes and Arthur had taken a sinister turn!

We stood beside the standing stone that marked the Blackwood estate boundary. The girl gripped her companion's arm, her eyes flicking from the forest entrance to me. It was obvious she wanted to get back in the car and the passenger door remained open. I held the photograph up. "So, you know Agnes?"

The girl nodded but remained mute.

"Back in the forest, you said she had been with you."

"She was, until the day before yesterday," the bearded man replied

"That's all we know." The girl tugged at her boyfriend's sleeve. "Can we go now?"

Agnes had been missing longer than Mrs. Driscoll had admitted! "Please! Just wait a minute." There was so much more I needed to know. I made an effort to appear professional. "Agnes has been reported as missing and may have important information about an ongoing investigation-"

"Are you a police officer?" the taller man asked, throwing me a quizzical frown after a barely hidden scan of my figure. Disbelief flickered in his eyes.

"She could be one of them undercover cops."

"What 'ongoing investigation'?"

"Has Agnes done something wrong?"

"She could be one of them detectives like 'Vera,'" the girl said. "My mum watches that programme. She's a bit fat too and doesn't wear a police uniform. Are you a DCI?"

As my cheeks stung with the comparison to the overweight and shabby detective of the famous television crime drama, I scrabbled for something to say. I couldn't tell the truth, so I lied. "I'm a private investigator working on behalf of Agnes' mother and another client whose identity I'm not at liberty to reveal."

All three goggled at me, each instantly wary.

The girl tugged at her boyfriend's sleeve once more.

"Hang on a minute, Ruth. We should tell her what we know."

Now we're getting somewhere! "If you could, please." The man nodded and I took this as my cue to continue. "When Agnes was with you, did she have anything ... unusual with her?"

The girl's eyes widened. I had hit the mark.

"When you say 'unusual' what do you mean?"

I didn't want to accuse Agnes of being a thief and bring their defensive walls up, so smoothed the situation. "Well, Agnes may have borrowed a book. It's rather old and unique, and the owner would like it back."

"I told you she was lying," the taller man said. "No one leaves an old book like that just lying around." He turned to me then. "She stole it, didn't she!"

"Is it worth a lot?"

"Well, we prefer 'borrowed', and it's only valuable for sentimental reasons."

"It looked really old. I could tell from the pages that it was old. They're vellum, right? Made from animal skin?"

I didn't want to give any information away, so just said. "I do believe it is rather old."

"It's a devil book!" the girl blurted. "It was full of old writing and symbols. Agnes said it was full of spells."

"Shut up, Ruth!" The man snapped and glanced back into the woods.

"It's true! It's her fault about the others and that thing in the woods!" This was said as a hissed whisper to the man.

He stepped back to the car. "It's time we left."

"No!" I blurted, the import of her words sinking in. "I mean, please! I haven't finished asking my questions. It's important that I find Agnes. She may be in trouble."

"She caused trouble!" Ruth's face had paled, but she was defiant. "If she hadn't read that book-"

"What did she read, Ruth? What did she do?"

"Ruth!" The man barked. "Get back in the car."

"What did she read, Ruth?" I tried again. The man took a step to block Ruth from my view and she got into the car. The door closed with a thud.

"Don't you care about your friend?"

"Listen ..." His lips pursed. He obviously didn't want to talk to me. "If you want to talk to Agnes, she's up at the house."

"Which house?" I shouted as he slammed the car door shut.

The window rolled down a fraction. "Blackwood Manor."

Chapter Thirteen

The vehicles left the verge and lurched onto the road, disappearing over the hill at speed. I turned back to the woods, stunned; Agnes, and Arthur, were at Blackwood Manor and something terrible had happened. Was Garrett involved? Dread churned in my belly, but I had to discover exactly what was going on at the house.

This time, where the roads diverged, I took the left fork. The direction took me up and through the woods along a winding and narrow road overhung with trees. Against the backdrop of the darker woodland, dappled light fell upon the roadside verge, illuminating the fronds of elegant ferns to a brilliant emerald green and the spires of heavily flowered foxgloves to a vibrant purple. The ancient voice that spoke to me, and that I was learning to accept and understand, whispered 'foxesglófa' as we passed a particularly large cluster illuminated by a break in the canopy. Foxgloves were among my favourite flowers, and we had a large collection at Haligern where they filled the cottage garden borders and grew wild in our ancient woodlands. It intrigued me that foxgloves were as deadly as they were beautiful, but it was a little disconcerting, that with their ability to kill or cure, they were also called dead men's bells, or witches' gloves.

Either side of the road the trees were undergrown with shrubs which blocked the view into the woods. On the occasions they thinned out, the steep fall of the bank down to a trickling brook became clear. Any error on my part could see me veer off the road and fall into the ravine. I gripped the steering wheel a little tighter, and focused on staying central to the narrow road, hoping that I wouldn't meet any oncoming traffic. At this point in the road, with a high bank to my left as the hill continued to climb, and a steep drop to the other, either I, or the oncoming vehicle would have to reverse. It wasn't a manoeuvre I felt confident in achieving!

My concerns were unfounded and, as the road began another descent, a break in the woodlands showed the cleared grounds of Blackwood Manor, although the house itself could only be glimpsed rising above the canopy. I motored forward and within five minutes passed the opening to the driveway. I reversed and hesitated. The driveway was narrow, really nothing more than a muddy track, and I decided to park the car and walk to the house; if there were locked gates at the end, reversing all the way back to the road would be a nightmare.

I stepped out of the car to a gust of ice-cold wind. My fingers sparked as a current of energy so strong that it made my arms spasm shot through me. Bright light from my hands illuminated the forest. I dropped my keys. The pain, a sensation of being electrocuted, was intense, my fingers twitched, and sparks shot through the air. Smoke rose in twining columns from the forest floor where my keyring lay. The silver 'L', a forty-ninth birthday gift from Pascal, was tinged black. Damp leaves smoked beneath it. "What on earth?" I whispered in disbelief, unsure of quite what had happened. The ice-cold wind had hit me like a blast, but the trees were unnaturally still, their branches and leaves unmoving. I retrieved the bunch of scorched keys with a twig and held them up to the light for inspection. Now tinged black, heat emanated from the metal, but they didn't appear damaged.

Unsettled, I scanned the trees. All was still, and the driveway was clear. Taking a breath to fortify myself, I locked the car, thankful that being electrocuted hadn't damaged the fob, slipped the keys into my pocket, then made my way towards the house.

The driveway curved through the trees keeping the house hidden, and my anticipation grew. During our time together, Garrett had always found an excuse not to take me to his home, so I had never been inside or even seen the house. So, it was with trepidation, and some excitement, that I walked the last few steps before the house was revealed.

The air around me vibrated and a rumbling thunder rolled in my ears.

As before, a twilight haze descended and within seconds the light had been obliterated from the forest. I stood on the woodland track in complete darkness, the noise of rushing, tumbling wind loud in my ears. Disorientated I twirled on my toes, searching out any chink of light.

There was none.

Somewhere within the wind, a howl rose.

Remembering the torchlight in my pocket, I grasped it with trembling hands and clicked it on. For a small torch, it had a powerful beam, and cut through the darkness to illuminate the trees.

A pair of red eyes stared straight at me.

I yelped.

The eyes blinked and a creature, both grotesque and familiar, stepped away from the light.

It snickered.

Its thick tail swished.

Gnarled and enormous hands at the end of sinewy arms clutched the trees, its talons sinking into the bark. It held one leg aloft, and then the other. It seemed to be stamping or doing some strange kind of excited dance. With its hairy body, cow-like ears, and mouth full of sharp teeth it reminded me of the imps carved in stone and on a pair of candlesticks owned by my friend Jenny. A medievalist, Jenny collected art from the period but although the candlesticks were Victorian, they depicted the famous Lincoln Imp, a fourteenth century grotesque carved into the walls at Lincoln Cathedral. Images of the imp, pre-dating the grotesque at the cathedral, could be found across England. The legend was that two imps had turned up to cause mischief and even tripped up the Bishop before being turned to stone by an angel. In the flesh, with its bulbous belly covered in thin hair and skin glistening beneath, the creature was far more hideous than the carvings. Unlike the story, the energy leaking from this imp wasn't at all mischievous; it was malevolent.

It took a step towards me.

Chapter Fourteen

I stood, unsure whether to run or to stand my ground, as the hideous creature took another step forward and uttered a snickering chuckle. Wind howled but the forest was still. The imp swished its tail, its tip barbed and bulbous like a cat-o-nine-tails. Heart pounding, I knew the thing would pounce on me as soon as my back was turned. I was paralysed. So far, my lessons in magic hadn't covered how to deal with this kind of creature.

'You vanquished the Witchfinder.'

'You dealt him a blow, Livitha.'

'Look within.'

Voices swam in my head and despite the terror coursing through my veins I began to recite the words I had thrown at Matthew Hopkins, the Witchfinder General.

Fiend, fiend, mortal enemy. "Feond, feond, ferhþgeníðla."

Shrivel like a turd. "Scring þu alswa scerne awage."

The creature stopped in its tracks, cocked its head, and stared at me, much like a curious dog. My fingers sparked and I felt my energy grow. I winced at the pain but continued with the spell.

Become as nought "Naþiht geþurþe."

Go north, to a far town "Ac þu scealt north eonene to þan nihgan berhge."

Shrivel like a turd! "Scring þu alswa scerne awage!"

The light in my hands grew and the creature cringed. It did seem smaller. Encouraged by the change in the monster, I began to recite with renewed confidence.

Shrink as the coal upon the hearth! "Clinge þu alspa col on heorþe."

It began to shrink.

Become as nought "Napiht gepurþe."

Shrivel like a turd! "Scring þu alspa scerne apage!"

Although the creature had visibly shrunk, it remained between the trees, tapping its tail in an annoyed fashion. The reduced version of the imp took another step forward. Miniaturised, it was still ugly, and its cackling laugh made my flesh creep. Worse, the double row of yellowed and sharply pointed teeth could still give me a nasty bite and I was certain its bite would be poisonous.

May you become as little as a linseed grain. "Spa litel þu gepurþe alspa linsetcorn,"

And much smaller, likewise, than a hand-worm's hipbone! "And miccli lesse alspa anes handpurmes hupeban."

As it stepped forward, I took a step back. The light surrounding my hands ebbed.

'No, Livitha. Carry this burden. You must fight! Feohtan, Livitha! Feohtan!'

Pushed on by the voices, I continued.

And even so small may you become, that you become as nought. "And alspa litel þu gepurþe þet þu napiht gepurþe.

Shrivel like a turd "Scring þu alspa scerne apage."

Become as nought "Napiht gepurþe."

I had reached the end of the spell, and though much shrunk, the creature was still advancing, its snickering malevolence as strong as ever. No amount of me yelling at it to 'shrivel like a turd' was going to work.

"Go away!" I shouted as it continued to stare. I decided my best line of defence was retreat—straight to my car. I took a step back. The howling of the non-existent wind had dropped although the blackness in the forest hadn't decreased, and I stood with the torchlight trained on the hideous beast desperately trying to locate my car in my mind. I failed.

I tried a different tactic. If my spell-craft wasn't yet strong enough to extinguish the beast, then perhaps the raw energy that had electrocuted me as I stepped out of the car would.

I focused on my core, distilling my fear into the roiling heat in my belly. As the heat increased, the painful, tingling sensation of pins and needles worked down my arms to my fingers. Sparks crackled around their tips. As I raised my hands to throw out the magical force, the creature followed them much like a dog watches a ball about to be thrown.

As the electrical charge grew, I recited a charm in the language of my ancestors. The sensation of prickling and heat grew stronger. My hands sparked. The imp-like creature watched mesmerised. Green sparks of pure energy crackled and then the power exploded from my fingertips, shooting to the ground beside the creature.

"Rats!" I blurted as the startled creature jumped back knocking into a nearby tree. "Missed!" The creature righted itself, hopped from foot to foot, stamping harder with each angry step like some demented Rumpelstiltskin figure, and then had the audacity to snicker. The horrible creature was laughing at me!

I tried again.

Heat rose, my fingers crackled, and pure energy shot towards the monster. Now alert, it knew what was coming and, with impressive agility, jumped out of the way. The effort of summoning my magical energy was enormous, and I began to tire but, faced with the horrible beast, I tried once more. Again, the creature managed to evade my strike. Fatigue infused my muscles.

The beast snickered at my failure then chuntered something unintelligible and animalistic. The words, if it was speaking, weren't in any kind of language I had ever heard. As it continued to growl, yip, and yap, it reminded me once again of a dog. Remembering how the creature had followed the light created by my magick, I shone torchlight on the forest floor. It followed the beam. I reached for a broken branch at my feet. If it wanted to play, then I would let it play!

From deep in the woods came a howl.

I froze.

Another howl. Closer this time.

The imp disappeared into the dark.

Heart pounding, I scanned the forest, shining my torch among the trees. Instinct told me I was being watched.

I turned full circle, illuminating the space between thick trunks and, as I returned to my starting position, red eyes stared at me from within the dark, far closer than before.

I suppressed a scream. "Playing games with me, are you?" I shouted. "Well, how about this!" I waived the stick in the air and threw it over the creature's head. It landed with a thud against a tree. To my amazement, the imp yelped, turned tail, and disappeared into the dark. It had worked! The horrible creature was playing fetch. With precious seconds gained, I sprinted to the car.

In an instant, pounding feet were dangerously close. Twigs snapped. Breath rasped.

As I continued to run, stitch beginning to stab at my sides, my car appeared in the beam of the torchlight. In the next second the creature was running beside me, its arms pumping in unison with mine, its hairs brushing against my sleeve!

There was no way I could make it to safety.

It yipped and chittered with excitement as it stroked my hair then gave it a tug. I screamed and lost sight of the car.

In an instant, the pounding feet and heavy breathing of the beast stopped, and I was alone again.

It was then that I realised the creature was playing with me like a cat plays with a mouse. If the malicious imp played with its food the way Lucifer played with the birds and mice that he caught, then it would spend hours torturing me until it took its final death-bringing bite. My only saving grace would be to blackout with shock, just as the birds and mice often did!

Thoughts of Lucifer gave me an idea. Like any cat, Lucifer enjoyed hunting at night. The imp, I presumed, had created the night in order to hunt. The creature had reacted to my torchlight, keeping out of its beam. Could it be that, with its red eyes, like albinos, it was sensitive to light?

I decided to blind the hideous creature.

It was my only hope.

When the pounding feet and heavy breathing returned seconds later, I fumbled in my pocket for my mobile phone, and swiped it on. "Please work! Please work!" I whispered. The beast was close as I turned and held my mobile up to its face.

The flash was intense.

The creature squealed and covered its eyes.

I ran.

With my senses in overdrive, acutely aware of the squealing, yelping, then chittering anger, I sprinted through the woods, lighting my way with the torch, intensely aware that at any second the beast would be on me.

Ahead, my car came into view.

Behind me fallen branches cracked and snapped as the creature thundered through the undergrowth. It was coming and this time it was angry!

I fumbled with my car keys, pressing the buttons on the fob. The indicators flashed orange, and the car clicked to locked.

"No!"

Hot breath blew against my neck. I screamed and turned. Towering above me, returned to its full size, the beast stood only inches away. Fetid breath filled the space between us. I will never forget that smell, or the look of insane pleasure and triumph, that gloated in its eyes. With every ounce of effort remaining, I drew on my inner force. Light radiated from trembling hands and dazzled the creature—and me. Barely able to see, it squealed and gibbered then stepped back. Its fetid breath no longer brushing my skin, I clicked the car to open, fumbled for the door handle, then scrambled inside, slamming the passenger door closed behind me. As I scrabbled across to the driver's side, the car rocked. Heavy thuds came from above my head; it was on the roof.

I started the engine.

Headlights illuminated the forest and I screamed.

The beast was staring straight at me through the windshield, watching me with glaring eyes as it straddled the bonnet. It leant forward, squashing its nose and mouth against the glass and left a slimy trail of mucous and saliva—taunting me again. In the next moment, its face thudded against the windshield and its fangs, revealed as its lips were forced back, scraped across the glass. For less than a second, a huge mass of dark fur replaced the imp before it too fell off the bonnet and disappeared.

Startled, my mind unable to process the scene, I slammed the car into reverse. As I swung the car around, my headlights illuminated a scene from a horror movie. A massive wolf-like creature straddled the monstrous imp, and its huge jaws were wrapped around the creature's throat.

Heart pounding, and head buzzing with the surreal scene, I drove the car like a rally driver, hurtling through the winding and hilly roads until I reached the forest boundary. Even then, I barely slowed down, and didn't stop until I reached Haligern Cottage.

Chapter Fifteen

"I have never been so afraid!" I blurted as my aunts gathered around the kitchen table. Four pairs of eyes stared at me with intense concern. "It was monstrous! And ... and I knew that it wanted to harm me. It was evil, Aunt Loveday! Purely evil."

Aunt Thomasin clutched me a little tighter. "There, there, Liv. It's alright now. You're safe."

I leant my head against her shoulder, a child again, and instantly soothed. The kindness was too much, and tears welled. A tissue was thrust at me and a cup of tea clinked in its saucer as Aunt Beatrice placed it on the table.

"Take your time, Liv. We need all the details."

"Drink your tea, child," Aunt Beatrice urged. "I've put a little something in to help you along."

Obedient, I took a sip of tea and grimaced. "What's in it?" I asked as the bitter concoction slid down my throat. "It's bitter."

"Brandy! It's supposed to be good for shock. I can add sugar if you like?"

"No, it's fine." I wasn't sure if I believed that there was only brandy in the tea, but I swallowed the bitter mixture. As a sensation of calm began to flood my veins, I became certain brandy wasn't the only additive. Several minutes passed and I felt slightly cloud-like and experienced a sensation of floating.

"Hold her down!"

"What did you put in that mixture, Beatrice?"

"My special brandy, that's all."

"Then why is she levitating?"

"The tea must have allowed some of her defences down."

"A leakage then?"

"Hmm, yes, I guess so."

"She's inebriated!"

"Beatrice, be honest, what did you put in that drink?"

"Oh, just a little something, as you say, to let her defences down. She was in such shock, it would have blocked her clarity, and she must recount her ordeal with exact recall. Even I couldn't access her thoughts—they were so jumbled."

"True, she was blathering on about monsters and imps and Lincoln. Quite unintelligible."

"And a furry monster with fangs."

"The tea will calm her."

"Well, if it calms her much more, we'll have to peel her from the ceiling."

My aunts' voices faded as I closed my eyes and enjoyed the sensation of freedom. The fear that had coursed through me in the woods and settled as panic as I drove home began to ebb. Time passed and then the fogginess that had enveloped me and wrapped around my fractured thoughts cleared. The past few hours began to run like a movie, each scene presented with perfect clarity and brightness. Aunt Euphemia held my chin in her hand.

"Look at me, Liv."

I opened my eyes.

"She's ready."

Aunt Euphemia stepped aside and was replaced by Aunt Loveday. "Now, Livitha, you must recall the events in the woods. We need every detail, however small."

With the scenes playing out in my mind being so clear, recounting exactly what had happened was easy. I explained about finding the campers and exactly what they had said about Agnes reading the book and blaming her for the 'thing in the woods' and then I recounted my ordeal with the imp-like monster.

Aunt Loveday's face was grave as I finished. "Livitha, darling, tell me again what the youngsters said about Agnes and the book, please."

"The girl, the one with purple harem trousers said that Agnes had brought a book along that was full of old writing and symbols. She called it a devil's book and blamed Agnes for the 'thing in the woods' which must have been the monster which attacked me."

"Hmm!" Aunt Loveday sat back in her chair then, with a glance at my aunts said, "I think that what Liv encountered in the forest was a wælgæst."

"Yes, I think you're right," Aunt Euphemia agreed. "Nasty creatures."

The frown on Aunt Loveday's face deepened. "I can't understand how a young girl without any magical knowledge could conjure such a beast though."

"Perhaps she had help?"

"She was on the Blackwood estate after all."

"What's a wælgæst?" I asked mustering a modicum of interest; the tea had done a wonderful job of making me feel relaxed but also dulled my curiosity.

"A murderous imp, darling. A creature from the other realm."

"Oh," I replied, without concern.

"Let's get back to the details of your ordeal, Livitha," Aunt Loveday said with the professionalism of a trained detective.

"You stated that the campers believed Agnes still had the book from which she read the spells?"

"Yes, and that she was at Blackwood Manor with the others."

"And you presume these 'others' are some other youngsters that were camping?"

"Yes, that's what I thought she meant. There was evidence at the campsite of other campers—flattened grass, tyre tracks ..."

"And they were scared?"

"Yes, there was no doubt that they were terrified, but I can't blame them, when all the light drained out of the woods it was intensely spooky!"

At this point, the effects of the tea began to wear off and some of the fear returned. "It was terrifying!"

"Now, now, calm down, Livitha. You've done exceptionally well. I'm proud of the way you handled yourself given it was your first experience with a creature from the other realm."

I shuddered recalling the stench and fetid breath of the creature as it brushed my cheek. "It was the other creature that saved me though! I tried the spells you taught me, but it wasn't enough. I wasn't powerful enough!"

"Never doubt your power, Livitha."

"Never!"

"It's time we began teaching her in earnest, Loveday," Aunt Euphemia said.

"Indeed," my aunt agreed.

"It was remiss of us not to begin sooner."

"We agreed to wait a while—until she had recovered from Pascal's betrayal and the Matthew Hopkins incident."

"Well, I think we have waited a little too long. Tomorrow-"

"Tomorrow is the fete, Loveday!" Aunt Beatrice blurted.

"Ah, yes, well after tomorrow then."

All four aunts agreed and then became silent and turned to watch me once more. I became a little uncomfortable under their intense stares of pity.

"Well!" said Aunt Thomasin, breaking the spell. "It's agreed, we begin to teach Livitha some real magick as soon as the fete is over."

"Indeed."

"Ooh, my turn first!" Aunt Beatrice's eyes sparkled.

"Agreed."

"But ... what about the creature in the forest? What about Arthur and Agnes?"

"Given that Arthur is on Blackwood land, it complicates the matter. It's late, and you're tired, time to turn in."

I knew that there was little point in pursuing the issue. Any questions I had would have to wait until after the fete. Aunt Beatrice poured another cup of her special tea into my cup. "It's not as strong as the last one, but it will help you sleep."

That night I slept well. It would be the last time for several days to come.

Chapter Sixteen

The morning of the fete arrived, and I was bemused at the level of importance it had attained in my aunts' eyes. Beatrice was particularly overexcited and during the early morning preparations her aura glowed and sometimes sparked with unruly energy. Bessy her whippet familiar was doing its best impression of a crazed dog, chasing her tail round and round as she played in the garden. The mood was infectious.

Lucifer wove in and out of my legs becoming increasingly annoying as I helped pack the aunts' ancient saloon car, a 1930 Humber Snipe complete with spare wheels mounted on the front wings. The car had been in their possession for as long as I could remember – I also remembered the stinging embarrassment of being dropped off at school in the ancient automobile – it was nothing like the modern cars my friends parents' had owned and was another marker of difference between us. When I complained about being taken to school in the 'old' car, Aunt Thomasin had never neglected to tell me that the Prince of Wales had used a fleet of them during his tour of India in 1931 and if it was 'good enough for him, then it is good enough for us, Livitha Winifred!'. Thankfully, looking at it now recalled none of those feelings; it was a truly beautiful car, a real classic, and its paintwork and chrome fittings shone as brightly as they had done on the day of its manufacture—a fact I now put down to magick; the car had never been serviced or even cleaned as far as I knew. I wasn't even sure it ran on petrol!

Chrome gleamed in the sunlight as I loaded the ancient saloon with the boxes of goods Aunts Beatrice and Thomasin had prepared for sale. Along with salves, ointments, and moisturising lotion there were carefully bound wands of mugwort, and others of sage and lavender. The mugwort wands carried a tag in Aunt Thomasin's beautiful copperplate hand and read 'Cleansing Stick. Use thyse to cleanse your dwellinge of troublesome ghasts and spirytes'. I realised then that I should have been more involved in the preparations and hoped that the archaic language and spellings would be taken as part of the branding for 'Haligern Cottage Apothecary' the shop my aunts were opening in the village and not as evidence of ignorance and illiteracy on their part. My concerns were unfounded in that regard; our presence at the fete had far greater repercussions.

Beside the box of jars filled with honey from Aunt Beatrice's hives, I placed another containing salve made from lavender and calendula, and various ointments infused with marsh mallow, basil, comfrey, nettle, or elder flower. There were bars of handmade soap, a creamy concoction of goats' milk and honey sprinkled with calendula petals. Unknown to the customers, the soaps, ointments, moisturisers, and lotions had a sprinkle of magick that worked wonders for clarity of complexion, easing painful joints, and sloughing off the negative energies that blocked their wellbeing. The aunts had a steady stream of regular clients who marvelled at their lotions and balms. My greatest concern was that the products would become too popular and bring trouble to our doorstep. However, I didn't want to dampen their spirits so continued to pack the car, savouring the scent, and hoping that some of the soaps had been saved to use in the cottage. Wrapped in homemade paper laced with petals and lavender, they were as good as any artisanal soaps sold in the bigger shops.

With one more box to collect, I returned to the kitchen. Lucifer was instantly at my feet, slinking past my ankles as I walked. "Lucifer!" I scolded as I quickstepped and lurched in an effort not to stand on him. "You're being just a little bit unhelpful!"

Ignoring my reprimand, he sauntered to my side, brushing himself up against my leg. This level of affection was unusual behaviour from my often acerbic feline familiar.

"Well," he whined. "I'm hungry."

Scratch the affection part. This was just cupboard-love. Typical.

And then it dawned on me.

In my efforts to help prepare for the fete, and my preoccupation with the events at Blackwood Manor yesterday, I had forgotten to feed Lucifer. Remorse flooded me, but we were running out of time. "Can't you go and catch something? I'm a little busy right now," I offered. It was the natural thing to do, after all, Lucifer was a cat.

I was unprepared for the onslaught of Lucifer's ire.

"How very dare you!" He swished his tail, giving an irritated flick against my leg. It whipped my calf. The pain was sharp.

"Ow!"

He flicked his tail again, this time catching my other leg, then stalked to the other side of the kitchen, and rounded on me.

"You think I'm nothing more than a ratter!" The last word was spat with venom.

Well, you are a cat! "No! I just thought that it would be nice for you to catch something ... fresh. We're a little busy this morning and-"

"Pah! How very dare you!" he repeated. "I am not a ratter!"

"I never said that you were. But you are a cat, and I just thought that it was kind of natural-"

"To catch a rat!" He finished.

"No! Yes! No, but I just thought maybe a-"

"What? A snake? A toad?"

"No, maybe a mouse?"

"A curse on you!"

I stared at him in disbelief. Laying a curse was a serious taboo. "Lucifer!"

"Lucifer!" Aunt Thomasin glided across the kitchen with a swish of energy. Her aura sparked as sharply as her words. "Take that back right now! Cursing your mistress is forbidden."

Lucifer merely tipped his nose to the ceiling.

Aunt Thomasin glared at the cat, hands on hips. "Lucifer ... I'm waiting. Take it back."

By now all the aunts had gathered.

"What's going on?"

"We'll be late to the fete."

"It's Lucifer. He just cursed Livitha."

"What? Lucifer. How could you!"

"It's her fault!" He said pointing a paw in my direction.

All eyes turned to me. "I only suggested that he catch his own breakfast," I shrugged and offered an apologetic grimace.

All eyes turned back to Lucifer. "It's true," he said haughtily, then widened his eyes until they resembled a doe's. Aunt Thomasin was the first to cave in.

"Poor Lou," she said and swept him into her arms. He allowed her to cradle him like a baby, tickling him under the chin.

I felt aggrieved; now I was the guilty party. "But he likes catching birds!" I offered in my defence. And it was true, Lucifer did enjoy hunting—a lot! "I had to rescue a blue tit from him last week."

Lucifer gave a pitiful meow. He was really laying it on thick. Aunt Euphemia bent in to pet him. "Oh, poor Lucifer."

Poor Lucifer!

"Apologise, Livitha Winifred Erikson," Aunt Beatrice demanded.

Lucifer gave a strangled meow. I knew that he was suppressing a snorting laugh.

"But he's the one that cursed me!" I protested, immediately a child again.

"Yes, but you insulted him, and I don't suppose he uttered a specific curse—one with an outcome?"

"Well no ... but I only suggested that he catch his own breakfast! We're so busy this morning."

"Apologise, Livitha."

"But-"

"Least said, soonest mended."

I huffed. Lucifer gloated.

With all eyes on me, I crumbled. "I suppose ... I'm sorry, Lucifer," I said with as much grace as I could muster which wasn't much. In my defeat I became petty. "What do you want for your breakfast, little kitty?" I threw this in to tweak him; he hated being called 'little kitty' just as much as I hated being called by my middle name of Winifred. "Smoked salmon and a bowl of port?" My sarcasm was barely hidden by my saccharine-sweet tones.

"That would be nice," he replied with genuine desire and jumped down from Aunt Thomasin's arms and was instantly at my feet.

"I was joking," I said.

"I wasn't." He fixed me with his huge green eyes.

Aunt Beatrice chuckled. "Oh, he is such a rascal!"

Aunt Loveday bent to tickle his chin and cajoled him into retracting his curse as I reached for a tin of cat food. He agreed to nullify the curse once he had eaten then eyed me with disdain as I pulled at the tab to open the tin. As I slipped my finger beneath the ring-pull, he placed his front paws on the side of my leg and extended his claws. His eyes said 'I dare you' whilst his claws left me in no doubt that the tin of cat food, even if it was from the supermarket's 'Deluxe' range, was not acceptable fodder. As the claws dug through my jeans and pricked at my skin, my aunts continued their preparations, and I submitted to the tiny tyrant and replaced the tin in the cupboard.

"You said salmon and port, Livitha," he complained.

"But it's not even nine o'clock in the morning, Lou!"

"Are you now attempting to oppress me?"

"Oppress you?"

"Yes, I am free to eat and drink when I desire, and what I desire."

I wasn't sure this was entirely true according to our law.

"I am not a servant!" He spat as though reading my mind. "I am not your lackey!"

"Oh, Lucifer!" I said with barely hidden frustration. "Fine! I'll get you something else to eat, and some port!"

"Good!"

Lucifer sat to attention beside the fridge and as soon as I opened the door it became obvious why he had behaved so badly. A full half side of salmon sat dressed and ready to eat beneath a layer of waxed paper on the shelf. Cooked last night by Aunt Euphemia, it had been prepared for a cold supper on our return from the fete. Despite my annoyance, I admired his audacity, and I couldn't blame him either; I wouldn't want to eat revolting lumps of congealed tuna and pollock when there was a beautifully prepared salmon waiting in the fridge. It was just another example of how I had to adjust to my new life. Discovering my cat was a familiar with an acerbic wit and curmudgeonly attitude, had been a shock. Learning to treat him less like a cat was taking time. After gaining Aunt Euphemia's permission I took a slice of the salmon and placed it on a prettily decorated saucer I knew Lucifer liked, then poured a dram of port into his drinking bowl hoping this offering would bring peace between us, at least for today.

Lucifer gloated and, by the sideways glance he threw at me, I knew that he was laughing, but he purred loudly as he bent his head to eat. I would make friends again with him later, I decided. Despite his arrogance, he loved nothing more than sitting on my lap as I read a book or watched a little television and demand that his chin and belly be rubbed.

With the curse nullified by Lucifer after his final mouthful of salmon, we finished packing the car and made our way to the village green where the fete was being held.

The day had not started well. It wasn't going to get any better.

Chapter Seventeen

The village green was a generous space that had once been almost central to the village. Ringed by stone cottages dating from the eighteenth century it retained much of its archaic rural charm. The village was listed in the Domesday Book, William the Conqueror's 1066 survey of England, but its roots went back much further than that date. Protective of their home, the villagers, many of whose families had lived here for generations, if not centuries, took great care of the green. Back in the 1990s, a developer had attempted to purchase it and two members on the parish council had been swayed by large bribes and convinced to push for de-registering the land and applying for planning permission for fifteen houses. One even had plans drawn up by a local architect. There had been uproar in the village, the plan had been thwarted, and the parish councillors voted out of office. Eventually both had moved out of the village. I shuddered at the thought as we approached the green; fifteen houses would have been a desecration of the ancient site of communal pastureland that had been in use from the time of the first settlements.

Despite the warmth from the sun, the grass still held onto the morning dew and my feet were soon wet. I regretted not following my aunts' advice to wear wellington boots, at least while setting up. Being centre stage at the fete, helping to sell the Haligern produce and promoting the new apothecary shop, wasn't within my comfort zone, and I'd given plenty of thought to my appearance. Over the years, with each pound that had added to my frame, my confidence had slipped. If only I were slim, I would often tell myself, then everything would be alright; I'd be that strong and confident woman I wanted to be.

For the fete I had wanted to appear approachable and friendly but also light and summery so had chosen a pair of capri pants in white stretch-denim and a forgiving navy and white striped top that skimmed my thighs and was cut a little longer over my bottom. White canvas loafers with navy detail completed the look. Mud encrusted wellies from my efforts at milking Olde Mawde just wouldn't work. Now, as I helped set up the table with wet feet, I wished Vanity hadn't seduced me again!

Aunt Beatrice looked quaint, perfectly matching the stone cottages that surrounded us. She had chosen to wear a full-length skirt in a dark mauve fabric and fitted blouse in lilac cotton and now topped it with a red pinafore. Both the pinafore and blouse had ruffles. The hem of her skirt was damp from the dew, but black wellingtons kept her feet dry. When she had appeared in the kitchen fully dressed for the day ahead, I had questioned her choice of attire. For a modern-day fete, she looked a little odd. Wise through centuries of life, a flicker of understanding had shown in her eyes, and I had felt an instant wave of shame; she knew that I felt a little embarrassed. Much as I loved my aunts, their eccentricities didn't go unnoticed and, as a child, I had often borne the brunt; school had been a nightmare at times. On one occasion a girl had cornered me in the playground, poking sharp fingers into my arms and chest, 'Is your mum a witch?' she had asked with spite, in full knowledge that both my parents had died. The taunts had been daily until a teacher had stepped in. Now, at the fete, my aunts would be on show for all to see. As the morning wore on, the warming sun drying the grass, Marjorie Babcock's taunt of 'fat little mouse' repeated in my mind and as we arranged the tinctures, lotions, potions, and soaps on the trestle table, I began to dread the arrival of the villagers and their stares of curiosity.

However, later in the morning, when the other stalls had been set up, and before the fete was opened, several of the stallholders came over to chat and admire our stall. One woman purchased several items and a man, entranced by the sparkling amber liquid, a jar of honey. None of them seemed to think my aunts weird or gave them sideways glances. Quite the opposite; they were friendly and enthusiastic. A stallholder who was selling his home-crafted woodwork bowls and platters bought a salve and thanked Aunt Thomasin for helping clear up his son's acne. A woman selling homemade preserves and bunches of freshly cut flowers thanked Aunt Loveday for blessing her garden; the crop of vegetables had been so much better this year she enthused. By the time the fete opened, and the ribbon cut with much excitement among the female populace by the village's newest celebrity, the very handsome, Dr. John Cotta, I was feeling increasingly at ease, and more than a little ashamed by my earlier thoughts. As it turned out, being considered a little fat and kooky was the very least of my worries.

The fete was buzzing and there was a lot of interest in 'Haligern Cottage Apothecary' produce. The pile of fliers we'd had designed and printed promoting the new shop was diminishing and I had even remembered to invite each customer to

our open day. Half of the produce had been sold by the time
Dr. Cotta arrived at the stall. I'd watched him cut the ribbon
then drink a glass of champagne with the parish councillors
and the owner of the local stately home, Lady Annabelle Hes-
kitt. Along with the house, Lady Annabelle owned a substan-
tial amount of land in the area that she herself farmed or rented
out to tenant farmers. From her laughter, Dr. Cotta was obviously entertaining his audience and, after mixing with the hoi
polloi, he made his way around the stalls where his charisma also worked its charm on more than one female stallholder. As I
watched his progress, Mike, the builder working on the shop,
arrived with a younger woman, her arm slipped through his.
As she picked up a jar of honey and peered at the label, Mike
squeezed beside a customer to stand directly in front of me.
"Liv!" he said and locked his eyes to mine.

"Liv!" Shock registered on the woman's face and was
quickly replaced by a scowl. "You are joking me!" She spat and
slammed the jar of honey back down on the table. "This is the
Liv you've been banging on about?" She threw me a disdainful
glance.

"Yeah!" Mike seemed oblivious to her anger and his attention remained on me. "You look ... lovely, Liv."

I made an effort to reply without seeming to encourage
him, but the woman's shrill voice drowned out my answer. As
she continued to harangue Mike he seemed to come to his senses. "Shut it, Nancy!" he said casting a glance around. "People
can hear you."

"I don't care who hears me."

Mike cast me a look of apology but as our eyes met a smile of besotted joy broadened across his face. "Liv," he said ignoring the scowl from his girlfriend. "You look ... lovely."

The woman's annoyance hurtled to anger, and she turned on him with hands on hips. "You're joking me!" she spat. "I'm stood right next to you, Mike! What the hell is going on?" He opened his mouth to reply, but she held up a palm to stop him. "No! Don't bother. I know what's going on. You're cheating on me, with *her*!" Again, a perfectly polished and pointed nail was jabbed in my direction.

"No! Of course, he isn't!" I protested, acutely aware that she was making a scene that was drawing more than a little attention. "Please, keep your voice down. People can hear!"

"I don't care if they can hear," she continued. "They should know exactly what kind of woman you are! Stealing my man!"

"Now stop right there!" I blurted, mortified at the humiliation of being slandered as a homewrecker. "I have no idea what you're talking about. Mike has done some building work for us at the shop and that is all."

"He does nothing but talk about you. Even dreams about you. Isn't that right, Mike."

Mike nodded and threw me a guilty smile then a wink.

The heat in my cheeks flushed to my hairline. "Please, I honestly have no idea what is going on. Mike and I-"

"See! See! Mika and I!"

"No! Listen! There is nothing between me and Mike!" I insisted. "Nothing."

Aunt Thomasin coughed, and I knew then that this had something to do with her. She had been enthusiastic about the builder and had prepared him a cup of tea at the shop. That must have been the moment she added one of her love potions to the brew. I twisted to look at her—to let her know that I knew, but she already had her back to me, and was hunched, delving into a box beneath the trestle table. That was enough to confirm her guilt. I gave an inward groan. My aunts meant well, but their meddling in my love life was becoming a serious liability.

As the woman continued to accuse me of 'snatching' her man – she even used the word 'bewitched' to describe his mooning, lovestruck gaze as he watched me – people began to crowd around the table. I had to do something to stop her. But how? Although my fingers were fizzing and beginning to itch irresistibly, I couldn't allow a display of magical powers in front of the whole village, but as she continued to harangue Mike and call me a 'conniving, fat old hag', my resistance broke down. Thankfully, the words that spilled from my mouth came in a whisper and the air around them sparked unnoticed.

"Whingeing, whining, moaning hag,
Your lying words are wrong and bad,
Your tongue will lock, your throat inflame,
No more will I receive your blame!"
The air between us vibrated.

"I won't stand for it. You've got to decide. Me or her, Mi-" Her eyes widened as she clasped her throat and pain contorted her face. "Burning!" she rasped. "Burning!"

Dr. Cotta was only a few stalls away as I offered the harridan a drink of water. She drank greedily then held out the beaker for more. As she drank, and the doctor moved to the neighbouring stall, I suggested that Mike take her to the hospitality tent and gave him a jar of honey to help soothe her throat. The woman was only a few feet away when the doctor arrived and stood in the exact spot Mike had just vacated.

"Livitha, you're looking bonza – I mean, lovely - today," he smiled.

Alarmed at his compliment I thanked him whilst desperately trying to remain composed then checked on Aunt Thomasin to pick up on any sign that she may have cast a spell on the doctor too. There were no tell-tale smirks or rosy cheeks that hinted at her guilt and she began to chat with the doctor with ease, explaining about each lotion he picked up. He purchased a jar of honey, holding it up to the sun, marvelling at how the amber liquid sparkled.

"We have happy bees at Haligern Cottage, Dr. Cotta," Aunt Thomasin said. "They love our meadows. We grow red clover and thyme just for them."

Dr. Cotta nodded his approval then fixed his gaze on me.

"So, Liv, do you think ..." His Adam's apple bobbed as he swallowed, "that ... would you join me for a coffee, tomorrow? I hear the village café serves wonderful cheesecakes and one of the best carrot cakes in the county."

I was staggered and threw Aunt Thomasin a glance to check again for signs of interference. She was standing with her jaw dropped open, watching the doctor as he asked me out. She raised her brows as though to say, 'Say yes, then!'

"I ... erm ..."

"The Reverend Parsival says that their coffee and walnut cake is the best ..."

"I ... I love coffee and walnut, and carrot cake is my favourite!" I heard myself say.

"Bonza! We'll have both then. Shall I pick you up, say at ten? Surgery doesn't open until twelve tomorrow, so I have some time to spare. Perhaps I can bring those books you were so interested in?"

"Oh ... yes! Erm ... - gather yourself together, twit! - I have some errands to run in the morning, so I'll meet you there?"

"Perfect!"

As he left the stall and I watched him walk towards the hospitality tent, movement across the green caught my eye. I couldn't repress a groan, for heading towards us, with a belligerent stride, was the group of children that had taunted my aunt at the shop.

Chapter Eighteen

As the children arrived at the stall, Aunt Beatrice bristled, her aura crackling. The children inspected the few remaining jars and bottles.

"I can't even read this!" said a gangly boy of about thirteen with the hood of his jacket pulled up around his head. Childish freckles dotted his cheeks, but a dark fuzz of hair covered his top lip.

The girl who had been the rudest at the shop picked up a jar and frowned at the label. "They can't even spell!" she scoffed, noticing the archaic spellings. After the incident at the shop she seemed intent on taking revenge and turned the jar to check the ingredients. "Bet this is poisonous," she muttered, and dropped the jar back onto the table.

"Please be gentle with the jars," Aunt Thomasin requested. Her voice was calm and without an edge to it, but I could feel her anger brewing.

The freckle-faced boy picked up a flier from the much-dwindled pile. "Haligern Cottage Ap ... Apothc ..."

Annoyed by his inability to read, the girl snatched the paper, glanced at the title then threw it back down on the table.

"It says 'Haligern Cottage Apothecary'," Aunt Beatrice said. She made a great effort to appear calm and friendly, although the flicker in her eyes told a different story. I had never really seen Aunt Beatrice lose her temper, but I had the suspicion she was about to do so.

"More like Haligern Cottage Coven!" the girl spat. "You're just dirty witches! My dad says it's true." The girl bent across the table. "And he says that he'll come and give you a kicking if you talk bad to me again."

Aunt Thomasin gasped and slipped an arm around Aunt Beatrice's shoulder as she quivered. Violet eyes sparked with rage as my aunt stood to her full height of five-foot nothing. "How dare you talk to me in such a fashion!"

The girl, already heavy-set with flesh bulging through the rips in her jeans towered over her. "'Coz I dare, you old hag!"

The girl had gone too far, and I quickly stepped to Aunt Beatrice's side. Heat building at my core, my patience already pushed beyond endurance, I made enormous efforts to keep my magick in check as the crowd's attention transferred to this new drama.

"What's in the potions, witch?" she taunted. "Eye of newt? Boiled frog's spawn?"

"That's enough!" I said in my most authoritarian voice. "I'd like you to leave this area." My fingers fizzed and I itched to throw out a blast of energy at the girl. In my imagination I had already thrown a shot that blasted her to the edge of the green.

"Make me, fattie Pattie!" The girl threw at me.

"Fat witch!" A younger girl with hot pants hugging her chunky thighs and vest top cut to show her bulging midriff, screeched with laughter. "Fat witch! Fat witch!" she sang.

I bit back my desire to tell her that she wasn't exactly a lightweight herself. Instead, in my calmest voice, I again asked them to leave.

"They're witches!" the older girl shouted. "Don't buy their rubbish potions!" She turned to Aunt Beatrice, eyes brimming with malice, and hissed. "It's poison!"

"How dare you!" Aunt Thomasin retaliated. "We are not selling poison! Our lotions are only made from natural ingredients—flowers and herbs from our garden."

"You're a witch," she hissed. "And witches should burn."

I gasped at her malicious words, shocked that someone so young could be so rude and vicious. Aunt Beatrice's aura pulsed, the brilliant light at its outer edge darkening to a dark purple as it hugged her outline. The energy radiating crackled and sparked. Like a charge of electricity, her power was gathering, and I knew that at any moment she would betray her magick and use it against the girl.

From behind my shoulder came hoarse and psychotic laughter.

The stench of sulphuric breath tickled my nostrils.

Startled, I turned.

My heart jumped into my throat.

Squatting on top of our car was the same creature I had seen running alongside us when I took Aunt Beatrice to the shop. It was entirely different to the one in the Black Woods. Far skinnier, it stood on two legs and had long, lean limbs that were sinewy with muscle. Completely naked, but without any indication whether it was male or female, flaxen hair hung in rat-tail strands, clinging in greasy lumps to the side of its face and hanging down its back to its skinny bottom. Dark green eyes boggled in its head, the central goat-like pupil flitting about as it chittered. Thin lips were pulled back into a lopsided grin that showed jaws filled with double rows of point-

ed teeth. With its leering grin, it looked quite insane. As it
caught my gaze it gave a hysterical screech then vanished only
to reappear perched on the shoulders of one of the men watching the scene at the table. He didn't notice the beast and it
disappeared once more before standing behind Aunt Beatrice.
Bending in as though to listen, its greasy yellow hair brushed
hers. Caught up in the argument, she didn't notice, and no one
in the crowd made any indication that they could see the peculiar and hideous goblin.

Mesmerised by the creature, and with no idea of how to
deal with it in this public space, I was paralysed by uncertainty.
I couldn't use my magick as I had done in the forest and although it looked hideous, the creature wasn't making any attempt to harm the crowd or my aunts. After failing to get
Aunt Thomasin and Aunt Beatrice's attention, I scoured the
green for Aunt Loveday or Euphemia. The creature continued
to shadow Aunt Beatrice and the girl continued to taunt my
aunts. To my relief, some of the locals had come to their defence.

"You're all witches!" the young girl shouted as one of the
other stall holders grasped her arm and attempted to pull her
away. Her face was flushed, and her eyes glittered as she tugged
against the restraining hand.

With panic rising, and not wanting to leave my aunts, I
continued to scout the green and noticed Dr. Cotta watching
the argument with interest. Alongside him stood the Reverend
Parsival. Mike's girlfriend listened as he spoke, bending close to
her ear as though sharing a secret.

I waved to Dr. Cotta and beckoned for him to come over,
hoping that he could help, then turned my attention back to

Aunt Beatrice. The creature, obviously visible only to me, re-mained behind her shoulder. Her face was set with grim deter-mination. She was holding her temper quite well and her aura wasn't sparking as much as it had; she knew just how impor-tant it was to keep control of her powers in mixed company. Just this morning, as we were unpacking the jars and bottles, she had mentioned that we all had to appear as normal as the other stall holders. She spoke with a hint of dismay about ap-pearing like 'any other group of geriatric women' and I won-dered how easy it was for my aunts to exist as elderly women. It was a choice they had made to support Aunt Loveday as she lived her life alongside Uncle Raif. Thanks to her magick, age crept upon him very, very slowly, and the coven sisters had kept pace with his ageing process. Their sacrifice over the centuries was quite incredible. I was unsure if I could ever be that selfless.

The vile taunting from the children reached a peak.

"You're witches," the girl shot at Aunt Beatrice. "Evil stink-ing witches!" For a moment, the girl's form wavered and in-stead of a teenager in ripped jeans and bright pink t-shirt she appeared in dun brown skirt with dirt-stained hem, bare feet, a less than white blouse and grey-white bonnet. Hair in pigtails, she screamed "Th'art a witch! And thou shalt burn!" The vision disappeared just as quickly as it had appeared, but the spiteful words continued to flow. "Burned at the stake. That's what they did to women like you."

The creature snickered behind my aunt and picked up a lock of her hair letting it slide through its gnarled fingers. I watched in horror as it eyed me, held a crooked finger to its lips, then fingered the ruffle at her neck. Aunt Beatrice seemed completely unaware of its presence although she grimaced then shivered.

"Now, that is enough!" I shouted both at the grotesque beast and the vile girl.

"Why? What you gonna do?" the spiteful girl mocked and cast me a look of such disdain that I felt my core begin to charge. My fingers began to fizz, ancient voices filled the back of my skull, and a hex began to form on my tongue. I was close to losing my self-control. "You're being intolerably rude-"

"Ooh! I'm being intolerably rude," she mimicked.

I took a deep breath, feeling myself tipping over into chaos. "You are, and you need to leave."

"Make me!"

My fingers crackled.

"Livitha!" Aunt Thomasin warned.

Heat coursed through my body, the anger welling inside me fuelling the energy. Ancient words began to slip from my mouth.

Ignoring the children, Aunt Thomasin placed a cardboard box on the table. She could sense the imminent eruption of my power. "Liv, why don't we just pack up?" she suggested with determination and picked up a jar. "We've sold most of our stock already."

"That's right! Go home, witch!" the girl spat.

Ancient words continued to fill my mouth and spill out. I wanted to roar the hex but could only whisper.

The girl leaned into Aunt Beatrice, easily towering above her diminutive figure. "You're a witch. You should be burned at the stake."

The creature stroked the girl's hair and snickered.

Aunt Beatrice's temper flared.

"I wish you would just disappear and go back to where you came from! All of you. You are ill-mannered recreants. And you," she said to the girl, "are full of spite. I wish that housing estate had never been built!" Her voice became shrill. "In fact, I wish it would just disappear into a hole!"

The creature cackled in triumph then vanished.

A low vibration passed beneath my feet and my hex fell silent.

Aunt Beatrice was visibly trembling.

The girl sensed the change in my aunt, mistaking her desperate efforts to restrain her power for weakness, and began to chant, "Witch! Witch! Witch!" The other children joined in.

The situation was intolerable. Heat supercharged at my fingertips as another tremble, this one noticed by the crowd, shook the green.

A hand clamped down on my shoulder, then Dr. Cotta pushed to my side and stood between me and the girl.

"We'll have no such talk here, young lady," his voice boomed. To my surprise, the girl clamped her mouth shut. "Go home." His voice was stern. "All of you. I shall be speaking to your parents later this evening."

She made a weak effort to refuse, "But-"

"Go home, Kayla Wick. You have outstayed your welcome here."

At that moment, Benny swooped down from the tree, so low that it clipped the top of the girl's hair. She screamed. He swooped again and she jumped away from the table. Then, arms protecting her head, she pushed her way through the crowd and ran to the hospitality tent. Benny returned and made the unfortunate decision to perch on Aunt Thomasin's shoulder. A hiss went around the crowd and they immediately stepped back.

"They must be witches," I heard a woman say.

"No, he's just a pet," Aunt Thomasin said then offered her finger to Benny. He hopped there then took flight, catapulting over the crowds.

Another vibration was followed by a thunderous rumble.

"Did you feel that?"

"Yes! That's twice. Is it an earthquake?"

"Must have been an earthquake."

"We had one a couple of years ago."

"It woke me up in the middle of the night!"

"The whole house shook."

Concerned chatter continued but Dr Cotta turned to me with concern. "I hope those children didn't upset you."

"Well, they were very rude, but they're just kids."

"Who should know better."

"Dr. Cotta-"

"You're not my patient, Liv," he smiled. "Please call me, John."

"John," I repeated. "Well, thank you. Those children were becoming very nasty. I couldn't get them to stop."

"They're not village children," a woman who had watched the entire spectacle explained. "They're newcomers from the new estate." She reached for a jar of ointment and placed a ten-pound note on the table. "They don't understand how much we appreciate the ladies from Haligern Cottage." She said this with a friendly smile to both aunts.

Aunt Beatrice's eyes glistened with tears. "Thank you!" Her hands trembled as she reached for the money. "I'll get your change."

"No!" The woman placed a hand over my aunt's. "What is in this jar is worth far more than you charge. Please, keep the change."

The crowd began to disperse, the vibrations in the earth stopped, the girl and her friends left the green, and the day held the promise of continuing as normal.

Dr. Cotta remained at the stall, picking up jars and bottles and reading the labels. He made no effort to ask questions but seemed interested, murmuring and 'aahing' as he picked up one and then another. Mike the builder returned to the stall without his girlfriend and stood uncomfortably close. I flashed Aunt Thomasin a frustrated glance and she turned to a customer whilst suppressing a laugh. I did not find it funny.

Several minutes passed, another grateful customer was served, and then a loud rumble was accompanied by intense vibrations beneath our feet.

The table wobbled.

The rumbling seemed to be coming from the area where the village had begun to spread up a low-rising hill—the new estate.

Another vibration, felt through my feet, was followed by a loud crack then a quake that jolted the stall. Several bottles toppled over, and Aunt Thomasin grabbed the corner of the table to keep her balance. I knocked against the builder. He took this as an opportunity to place an arm around my shoulder.

"I've got you Liv. Don't worry, I'm here."

Dr. Cotta grasped my elbow. Mike scowled at the doctor.

I unpeeled Mike's hand from my shoulder but another, more intense, quake threw me into his side. This time his arm slipped around my ample waist, and his fingers squished into my flesh. I cringed at him touching my fat as panicked screams rose across the crowd and the earth continued to shudder. A crack appeared in the grass. Glass jars chinked.

The vibrations blurred my vision, but the hillside seemed to undulate.

The vibration stopped and silence fell upon the crowd.

"Is it over?" A young woman asked, grasping the forearm of a man at her side.

"I think so," he replied.

"No!" she shouted. "Look!" She jabbed a finger at the hillside. "It's moving!"

On the hillside where arable farmland had been stripped and a housing estate built, the houses shifted against the skyline. Another vibration was followed by a deep rumble and several houses visibly leaned.

"It's collapsing!"

The crowd grew silent and mobile phones were switched on and raised to the spectacle. I watched in helpless awe as the houses yawed to the right and then began to sink.

"She said she wanted the housing estate to disappear!" A couple close to me cast disbelieving frowns at Aunt Beatrice. "Maybe she really is a witch!"

Rumbling thunder intensified until it filled the air. The ground shuddered, and the new estate disappeared into a yawning hole.

Chapter Nineteen

Back at the cottage, Aunt Loveday closed the door then sank against it as though shutting out the world. Our journey back had been silent, but the kitchen filled with chatter at the click of the latch.

"What on earth happened?"

"The houses just sank into the earth!"

"It's a sinkhole," I offered. "I've seen videos of them before."

"Terrifying!"

"I hope no one was in them?"

The room filled with a communal groan of horror.

"That would be terrible!"

"It's all my fault!" Aunt Beatrice gave a doom-laden sigh.

"How? Did you cast a spell?"

"I don't think so, but I did tell that girl that I wanted the houses to disappear into a hole!"

Aunt Loveday gasped. "You cast a spell then?"

"No! But ... oh, maybe I did!"

The image of the creature standing behind my aunt at the fete was bright in my mind. "There was something at the fete. It was hideous – like you'd imagine a goblin to be, I think – and it was standing behind Aunt Beatrice laughing – well, it was more of an evil cackle."

"Why didn't you say?"

"I couldn't. The crowd was there, and that girl was being vile—everyone was watching. To be honest, I wasn't sure if I was hallucinating. I saw it running beside the car the other day, but it was there and then gone within seconds and I convinced myself I'd imagined it. I didn't know what to do when it reappeared at the fete and no idea how to deal with it. I didn't want to betray our magick, especially with that girl accusing us of being witches."

Silence fell for a few seconds and then Aunt Loveday said, "Tell me exactly what you saw. Do not leave out a single detail."

I described my sighting of the creature as I drove Aunt Beatrice to the shop and then went through the entire incident at the fete, from the moment the children arrived at the table until the creature disappeared. Aunt Loveday's face became increasingly dour as I recounted the story and described the creature and explained how it had reacted to Aunt Beatrice's response to the vile girl.

"So, when she said, 'I wish it would just disappear into a hole!', it cackled?"

"Yes, it was like it had won something, as though it were delighted, and then it disappeared, and then the ground started to vibrate."

Aunt Loveday's hands gripped the back of the chair, knuckles whitening with the pressure. "It is a Gewyscan púca; a type of puck that grants wishes—but only harmful ones. It is entirely disruptive. They can be extremely dangerous and bring calamity upon those they imprint upon." She threw a pitying glance at Aunt Beatrice. "And I believe that it has imprinted upon you, Beatrice."

"Oh, for Odin's mercy!"

"How has it ... imprinted on her?"

"They imprint on the first person they light upon once conjured."

"I've never heard of a Gewyscan púca."

"That's because our knowledge is found in books like Arthur, books kept hidden and protected by the covens and the Varðlokkurs."

"And you really think that this gewyscan púca was conjured and has imprinted on Aunt Beatrice?"

"Yes, I do."

"So, if she was the first person it lighted upon, then it must have been conjured locally!"

"Indeed, I think you are correct, Livitha."

"But Loveday, who locally would know how to conjure that creature?

"I don't think that finding a murderous imp in the Black Woods and this puck are coincidental."

"You think the same person conjured them both?"

"Very probably and ... and I believe they used Arthur to do so."

"No!"

Chapter Twenty

The mood at Haligern the next morning was off kilter and a cloud seemed to hover above us all. Aunt Beatrice was particularly frustrated, her vibrant energy turned fractious as she struggled with the self-imposed vow of silence after discovering that a puck had imprinted upon her. Such was her horror at having caused the sinkhole she dared not speak a word in case the wish-granting puck, the Gewyscan púca, should be listening and twist her words to cause more calamity.

However, despite yesterday's disaster, after a series of misunderstood gestures, then an irritably scrawled note, she insisted we go back to the shop. I was keen to help assuage her anxiety, and so by nine-thirty am Aunts Beatrice, Thomasin, and I were motoring to the village. Aunt Beatrice's aura held the faintest tinge of purple that darkened to black at its core. Aunt Thomasin was less frustrated but the events of yesterday had left their mark on her too and she was unusually quiet. Both aunts were on edge, checking the passing trees and hedgerows for any sign of the Gewyscan púca.

"I don't think it's here," I placated. "I'm sure you could talk. Just choose your words carefully ... perhaps." Mirroring Aunt Loveday's favourite reprimand only deepened the furrow between Aunt Beatrice's brow, and I slunk down a little in my seat. The last thing I wanted was to upset her further, but it pained me to see her so het up at not being able to speak.

"Don't worry, Beatrice," Aunt Thomasin added whilst craning her neck to peer into the sky through the window. "We will find it and send it back home."

Aunt Beatrice grunted in response, sat back in her seat, and closed her eyes.

"We will!" I reiterated. "I promise." I felt a sudden need to soothe her soul. "I'll do my best to find it and send it home – wherever that is."

"You have to find Arthur first!" The words blurted from her mouth and she slapped a hand across her lips, her eyes wide with fear.

"It's not your fault ... the sinkhole." I caught her gaze through the rear-view mirror. "It's not." She shook her head in disagreement and slumped back against the seat. "And I will find Arthur! I promise."

"She will," Aunt Thomasin agreed. "You will, won't you." Her voice held a seed of doubt.

"Yes, of course I will. Arthur will be back where he belongs before you know it and we'll send this pesky puck back to where it belongs."

"I do hope so, my dear girl," she managed then pressed her lips together once more.

We arrived at the shop by ten o'clock and this time, despite Aunt Beatrice's grunted protestations and jabbing finger, I parked directly outside, and we entered by the front door.

"Livitha is correct, Beatrice; we can't show any sign of fear. They smell it, you know. I'm convinced of that."

"They're not dogs, Aunt Thomasin," I replied.

"Certainly, they're not, but humans pick up on weakness and fear just like dogs do. We can even smell illness—once we're tuned into it. The problem is that over the decades - centuries actually - people have become less and less in tune with the earth and each other, despite all the advances in communications that have been made. They rely more on others and technology to solve their problems; they no longer till the earth, or care for livestock, or grow healing herbs." The door closed behind us as Aunt Thomasin continued to bemoan the loss of the natural, earthly sensitivities we were all born with. "And do you know that I believe even natural witches are on the decline because of it. In my day we were in tune with Mother earth, the moon, and the sun. We felt their power. Now there seems to be so much noise in people's lives that fewer are realising their true nature."

Aunt Beatrice made mumbling noises of agreement and I filled the kettle for a cup of tea then returned to the car to retrieve the first box of tinctures that were to line the newly waxed shelves behind the glass fronted counter. The place already smelled of lavender and comfrey with undertones of smooth honey. There was also the bitterness that pervaded the kitchen at home. It wasn't unpleasant, far from it, it just wasn't sweet like the other smells that arose from the tinctures.

The kettle boiled and Aunt Thomasin made tea whilst Aunt Beatrice dusted down the immaculate shelves and placed each bottle of tincture upon them with reverence. I turned my attention to the shop windows. Ugly, slug-like smears marked the panes where noses and tongues had been wiped across the glass. I spritzed each pane with a mixture of water and vinegar and polished the glass until all traces of their malice had gone.

The last pane cleaned, I dropped the cloth into my bucket and squealed.

Behind me a tall figure blocked the light.

"Liv!"

My body tensed as the builder's arm slipped around my waist and hot breath stroked my cheek. He stood uncomfortably close and I took a step to the side and peeled his hand away from my middle. I couldn't escape that easily though and, as I took his huge hand to move it from my waist, his fingers grasped mine as though we were taking a turn on the dancefloor. I was twizzled to face him.

"Liv!" he repeated.

My heart beat hammer-like, the flush of unease already spreading along my neck.

"Mike." I stumbled for something sensible to say. My startled brain wouldn't co-operate and unhelpfully offered, 'Good to see you. I'm just cleaning the window."

His smile broadened. "It's good to see you too!" He gazed down at me, locking my eyes to his. They were glazed. I groaned inwardly. Mike's girlfriend had been right; he was bewitched. This had to be Aunt Thomasin's work!

I prized my fingers from his grip and quickly stepped into the shop. He followed me, his grin broad, then stood beside me at the counter. Aunt Beatrice, caught by surprise at our entrance, stared for a moment, gestured to her throat, then scurried out of the shop and into the backrooms. Seconds later Aunt Thomasin returned and, noticing my unease, looked sheepish and began to distract Mike.

"So ... quite a day yesterday," she said, struggling for something to say. However, it seemed to do the trick and their con-

versation picked up as Mike recounted the events from his per-
spective. I took the opportunity of moving across the shop
and placed several stoneware pestle and mortars on the shelves.
These were one of Aunt Euphemia's contributions to the shop
as she had managed to source some very robust sets from a
local maker as well as some vintage sets. All had been cleaned,
cleansed, then blessed and were ready for use whether for magical purposes or purely culinary.

"You should have seen them houses go! It were like thunder
but without the lightning! Rolling thunder. You could feel it
beneath your feet ... like an earthquake!" I wanted to add that
we had seen it but didn't want to divert attention back to myself. He continued to chat then shook his head. "And that's why
I'm here today—to check on the shop ... and you ... ladies." He
winked at me. I continued to arrange the shelves.

"Well that's most kind," Aunt Thomasin replied. "We're
very grateful."

"Aye, well, after yesterday ... After Nancy ..."

He left the sentence hanging. I was unsure whether he
wanted my Aunt to ask about Nancy or if he had genuinely
lost himself to introspection. The door opened and a customer
walked in. I stepped forward to explain that the shop wasn't
quite open yet, then Mike blurted, "She thinks you're all witches! She said as it was all you who had made the houses crash
into that hole. Can you believe it? She said as she'd heard you
curse those kids and wish that a hole would open up and swallow them down!"

"Oh, well that's-"

"Preposterous!"

He threw my aunt a confused look.

"Fantastical!"

Mike's face clouded over. "Fantastic?" You think those kiddies' houses being swallowed into a three hundred-foot pit was fantastic?"

"I'm sorry, we're not open yet," I said to the man who had entered the shop. With his attention focused on Mike and my Aunt, the man ignored me. Through the window I noticed that Doctor Cotta and Reverend Parsival were in deep conversation as they passed by on the other side of the road.

"No! No, what I said was 'fantastical'. It is a fantastical notion that we should be witches. I mean, it is just fantasy."

The customer held his mobile phone at my aunt and took a photograph.

"I'm sorry," I said as the man proceeded to photograph the bottles and jars on the shelves. "We're not open yet." A flash blinded me as he took a photograph only inches from my face.

"No photographs!" Aunt Thomasin's voice had an edge of anxiety. "If you don't mind."

"Sorry!" The customer lowered his mobile phone, but it remained in his hand. A red light glowed against his palm. "It's just so quaint in here. I wanted to show it to my wife. She's loves old shops like this."

"Well, it's a new shop."

"Yes, I built it."

The customer turned to Mike. "It looks the business, mister … ?"

"Saxby. Mike Saxby. I'm a carpenter by trade and specialise in restoration projects. This building is over two hundred years old."

"It looks it," the man said scanning the room.

Mike bristled, taking the man's words literally. "I've worked my butt off to get it looking right."

"And it does," the man replied, oblivious to the offence he had caused. He threw Aunt Thomasin a smile. For a moment, his eyes narrowed, and his face took on a weasel-like slyness. The energy he exuded gave me a queasy sensation and I disliked him from that moment.

"I'm sorry, but we're not open to the public yet." I opened the door. He made no effort to leave. I continued to hold the door open for excruciating seconds.

"Actually, I have a confession," he said with a smile that matched his weasel face. "I'm here on business."

I let the door close shut, expecting him to announce that he was a supplier looking for distributors; we'd had several companies contact us since the opening of the shop had been announced.

"What business is that?" Aunt Thomasin asked.

"I'm a reporter, for the Liarton Caller. I've heard several rumours that you were involved in yesterday's disaster."

Aunt Beatrice squeaked then disappeared into the storeroom. The room fell silent.

Aunt Thomasin was the first to come to her senses. "We were at the fete, Mister ..."

"Keith Cleghorn, Investigative Reporter at the Liarton Caller."

"We had a stall at the fete. We saw the houses collapse into the hole. That is the extent of our involvement."

He took out a pad and leafed through it. "Are you sure about that? I have several eye-witnesses who are prepared to go

on record - and one who has made a statement to the local police – that you were overheard plotting to cause an explosion."

"Ridiculous!"

"That's not true. All she said was that-"

Aunt Thomasin elbowed me, and I immediately clamped
my lips together.

"All she said was what?"

I remained silent, furious with myself for giving as much
away as I had. An air of unease and threat had descended in the
room.

"Are you saying people think they set off a bomb under
those houses? That's just ridiculous! Just about as stupid as my
Nancy thinking they're witches and casting a spell to open that
sinkhole."

"Oh?" The man's eyes glittered. "Nancy thinks they're
witches, does she?" He said this as though the statement were
ridiculous.

"Yeah, she's got a right bee in her bonnet about it."

"She does?"

"Yeah. And she reckons they've put a spell on me too. She
reckons they've made me fall in love with Liv." Mike's dewy
eyes returned to me.

Keith snorted as he cast me a disbelieving glance.

Heat began to fizz at my fingertips.

"But it's not a spell. It's real. I can't help it if she's the
woman of my dreams. Just look at her Rubenesque beauty.
What man could resist?"

"Rubenesque?" Keith said in a mocking tone. "You're right.
What man could resist?"

His sarcasm went unnoticed by Mike and, taking the quip at face value, his demeanour changed. With a threatening scowl, he said, "You'd better resist, Mister. No one touches my Liv. Got it?"

Mike towered above the scrawny reporter, and the mirth slipped from his face as he took a step back from the builder. Aunt Thomasin moved from behind the counter and opened the door. Keith stepped onto the path. On the other side of the road Doctor Cotta waved. I waved back despite the commotion now taking place at the shop's entrance.

"Be off with you. No one steals my woman!"

"Mike, I don't think he was interested in me that way," I said in an attempt to calm the situation. Mike closed the door against the reporter and a bemused smile spread across Dr. Cotta's face. The embarrassment that had crept along my neck now suffused my cheeks. It burnt there along with a rising anger. "And I am not your woman!"

Mike turned on me then, his eyes full of pain that quickly gave way to hardened obsession.

"I just can't help it, Liv! I'm overcome when I see you." He tried to grasp my hand as he talked. I quickly placed both behind my back and instantly regretted it as my chest pushed out. Appalled that this may be taken as some sign of encouragement, I took a step back and folded my arms to lessen my ample bosom.

Mike took a step forward. "It's odd, you see, I'm just overcome by your curves …" Glassy eyes coveted my body.

"Aunt Thomasin!" I squeaked as he raised his hands in a grasping gesture, and then my toes curled with embarrassment as he sculpted waves in an imaginary hourglass sweep of my body.

Mike towered over me, gazing with lovelorn eyes into mine. I swallowed, hysteria rising, my fingers beginning to spark. The bell above the door tinkled as it opened.

"Aunt Thomasin!" I pleaded, catching her eye as she stared like a rabbit caught in headlights from the newcomer to me.

"You're a real-life Venus de Milo." Mike's voice was rapturous and even Aunt Thomasin had the good grace to look embarrassed.

The new customer coughed just as Mike's lovelorn sigh became a groan of desire. Mortification swirled at my core. Noticing the cough, Mike swung round, revealing the man.

In that second, I would have given anything for a hole to open beneath my feet and swallow me down.

"Garrett!" I managed to squeak as my childhood sweetheart stared at me with deep confusion.

"Liv," Garrett said by way of greeting then forced a smile.

The sight of the ex-boyfriend I had been yearning to talk to since he had appeared at the cottage to question me about the murder of my husband's mistress, coupled with the overblown and fawning attentions of the spellbound builder were too much and I couldn't think of a sensible thing to say. "What are you doing here?" I blurted.

The builder slipped an arm around my waist in a possessive clasp. I flinched, nearly jumping out of my skin. "Can we help you, mate?" Whatever potion Thomasin had brewed was alarmingly potent. I uncurled his fingers from my waist, intensely aware of him pressing against my side. Garrett's smile dropped and his eyes grew cold.

"I've ..." He stared at the builder, then at me, then addressed Aunt Thomasin. "There have been reports of ... I heard about the sinkhole ... I was worried about you ... all. This is an old mining area and I know that some of the newer houses were built over the old mines."

"No need for you to worry, mate! I'll take care of the worrying."

Garrett threw Mike a deep frown then his eyes flicked to me and then away as though scalded. "So, I wasn't sure which part of the village was built over the old mines. I wanted to check the old drawings—I know there are some up at the house ... Blackwood Manor."

At this Aunt Thomasin said, "It's as Mike said, PC Blackwood-"

"It's DCI, Aunt Thomasin. Garrett is a Detective Chief Inspector," I corrected as Garrett flinched.

"So that's why he's snooping!"

"There's nothing to worry about here, DCI Blackwood," Aunt Thomasin said with an uncharacteristic terseness in her tone. "The shop was built hundreds of years ago, as was Haligern, so it is unlikely that a mining shaft will be underneath them."

"Well-"

Aunt Thomasin pulled open the door. "We're closed DCI Blackwood." Her eyes glittered with an anger I had never seen before. "I shall have to ask you to leave."

A flicker of pain flashed in Garrett's eyes and he left the shop without another word, and I wished that I had sunk into the hole along with the houses.

Ten minutes later, alone in the shop with Aunt Thomasin, I begged her to reverse whatever spell she had cast upon Mike.

"Aunt Thomasin, you've got to do something about this love potion!"

"Love potion?" she asked with innocent eyes.

"Yes, the love potion that you have given Mike. There must be an antidote."

"I didn't give him a love potion."

"Aunt Thomasin, please! It's so obvious that you did – the glazed eyes, the look of stupor on his face when he looks at me, the obsession with my figure."

"Well, you are rather Rubenesque, darling. He's not lying."

I huffed. "Please! Just give him the antidote."

Aunt Beatrice chuckled then opened her mouth to speak but quickly clamped her lips together. A pained expression came over her face.

"I'll find it soon, Aunt Bea. I promise!"

She returned to dusting the shelves.

"So," I said, turning back to Aunt Thomasin. "You'll do it?"

"Do what? Oh, the potion."

"Yes, the potion!"

"Well ... there is an antidote, but Livitha, are you sure? He's a very handsome man!"

I huffed with exasperation. "I'm not ready for another man in my life. My marriage has only just ended!" My marriage to Pascal, my husband of over twenty-six years had ended with spectacular humiliation on my fiftieth birthday only four weeks ago. Aunt Beatrice made a muffled mewl behind closed lips. I knew exactly what she wanted to say and threw her a warning glare. So, okay, there was one other man I would consider, the one man I should have married, but Garrett Blackwood had just walked off in a strop after Mike staked his claim over me and Aunt Thomasin threw him out of the shop.

Mike returned.

"Aunt Thomasin!" I demanded, as he made a beeline for me.

"Oh, alright. If you insist!" She stepped towards the kitchenette. "Mike, would you like a cup of tea?"

"Don't mind if I do," he replied, his eyes firmly on me.

Chapter Twenty-One

O nce again, Haligern's kitchen bristled with energy. Aunt Beatrice was fit to burst in her efforts to hold her tongue. I had been on the verge of suggesting she run into the garden and shout some nondescript, inoffensive word that couldn't be misconstrued as any kind of wish when Aunt Loveday strode into the kitchen like a maelstrom of dark energy. Today she had chosen to wear a floor length dress with a bodice that nipped in her already slender waist, and full skirt that rustled as she walked. The ruffle on the collar finished just beneath her chin. "There is absolutely one thing that I must do today!" Shining white hair was piled on her head, and a pair of pearl drop earrings finished the ensemble.

"One thing, Loveday?"

"Yes, one thing."

"Well?"

"I shall tell you. My head is whirling with thoughts."

"Tread carefully, dear," Aunt Euphemia said. "You know what happens when your thoughts whirl."

"Indeed," agreed Aunt Thomasin.

Aunt Beatrice opened her mouth to speak, the struggle of not joining her sisters' conversation unbearable. Aunt Loveday instantly drew a finger to her lips. "Not a word, Beatrice."

Sorry squashed A spider

Aunt Beatrice grunted her disapproval and turned to the counter to chop at the smelly-feet cheese and mix it with a little elixir. She made kissing sounds to call our tiny but chaotic visitors whilst Aunts Euphemia and Thomasin continued to question Aunt Loveday.

"Arthur!" was her monosyllabic response. "I must keep my thoughts focused. I can't use too much energy now. I need it. Oh, I desperately need it for the journey."

"You're going to her?"

"Yes, I am. It is time."

Again, I was left attempting to interpret their conversation, excluded by my inexperience and their shared history. One day, I too would be part of the inner circle, but my fifty years with the sisters was nothing compared to the centuries through which they had been companions.

"Are you going somewhere special, Aunt Loveday?" I ventured.

"Yes, I am! Or rather *we're* going somewhere special, Livitha. Get dressed. We are leaving in five minutes."

It was at that point I noticed the heavy walking boots that completed my aunt's ensemble. It could only mean that we were to traipse through the woods, across some difficult terrain—walking boots were not what she wore to visit the village or work in the garden. At any other time I would have been more than happy to stroll among the trees or climb hills, but his morning, after the stress of the past few days, my energy was low. Added to that, I had endured yet another night of uncomfortably hot sweats and sparking fingers. I was entirely sure that at some point in the near future I would wake to a bed ablaze with flames, the fire sparked by my unruly magical energy. I had already imagined the newspaper column exclaiming the bizarre incident of spontaneous human combustion. The policeman would turn up on Pascal's doorstep, explaining just how I had met my end. 'It's a rare event, sir,' he would say. 'But it burnt her to a crisp.' My imagination in overdrive, I had only managed to fall into a fitful sleep after wiping myself over with a cold flannel and placing the fire extinguisher at my bedside.

Dressed in my fluffy pink dressing gown, first cup of morning coffee in hand, I wilted in the face of my aunt's declaration and her exuberant energy. "In five minutes?" I barely managed to hide a pained expression.

"Yes, dear," she replied ignoring my lack of enthusiasm. "And wear something smart, but comfortable. It is quite a journey we will be taking."

I sighed. I couldn't refuse. "So where is it that we're going?"

"Ah," exclaimed Aunt Euphemia. "A place you will never forget."

Aunt Beatrice made mumbled sounds of excited agreement and the gold flecks in her irises sparkled.

"Can I come?" Aunt Thomasin asked.

"Not this time, Thomasin, if you don't mind. I need Livitha's absolute focus."

"But it has been such a long time since I went," she complained.

"Well, that's a blessing really, sister."

"But we really should visit more often—for purely social reasons."

"I suppose," Aunt Loveday said, her eye distracted by something beyond the kitchen window. Raif passed by pushing a wheelbarrow and her face softened. Love gleamed in her eyes as she waved. Uncle Raif stopped for a moment, blew her a kiss, then continued to the corner of the house and disappeared from view. The moment was tender and I felt a prick of jealousy, instantly regretted, at the strong bond of mutual love and affection they shared—if only I could have a man like Uncle Raif to love, if only a man like that could love me too. I kept the thoughts very much to myself, making a special effort to think as loudly as possible, 'not with the help of love potions though' just in case Aunt Beatrice was eavesdropping but, consumed by her own problems, she made no sign that she was listening in to me today.

"Five minutes, Livitha," Aunt Loveday repeated.

I made a supreme effort to gather my energy, smile, and appear more enthusiastic, then left to dress for the mysterious journey. Downstairs my aunts continued to chatter in their almost incomprehensible way.

Returning to the kitchen, dressed in comfortable jeans and cerise fleece, four pairs of eyes scanned me.

"Is that what you're wearing?"

"Well, yes. I like to be comfortable."

Aunt Thomasin picked a piece of lint from my sleeve then pulled at some pilled bobbles of micro-fibre fleece. "It's a striking colour," she said pulling at another bright pink bobble. She gave my face a once over. I almost expected her to lick her finger and smooth my hair. Once again, I was a child being dressed and made presentable. The feeling wasn't entirely comfortable and my discomfort increased tenfold as she pulled a pair of tweezers from her apron pocket, said, 'Keep still' then proceeded to clamp my chin between her fingers and pluck a rogue hair from my top lip before I realised what was happening.

"Ow!"

"Hah!" she crowed. "Look at that one!" She held up the tweezers for my aunts to see the thick hair trapped between its silver pincers.

"I can't believe you just did that!" I complained, a flush rising instantly to my cheeks.

Aunt Euphemia snorted into her teacup.

Aunt Beatrice giggled at the sink.

Lucifer, who had appeared just as Aunt Thomasin ambushed me, snorted from the doorway. I threw him a glare, mortified that he should have witnessed the embarrassing scene, knowing that he would revel in reminding me for years to come.

Aunt Loveday looked at the offending black hair, lips pulled into a grimace.

"Oh, for goodness sake! It's not that bad," I blurted, finger pressed to my lip, the skin still smarting.

"It's very wiry," Aunt Thomasin said as she inspected it closely. "I couldn't let you go out with it sprouting from your top lip, darling. It really looked like the beginning of a moustache, and you don't want to end up like Old Mawde now do you."

Lucifer chortled at this in a rather unpleasant way. "I think Old Mawde has a spare pipe, Livitha. If you'd like me to ask, I can."

I batted the air in his direction in a gesture for him to be quiet. I didn't appreciate his humour.

"Now, Lucifer, don't be spiteful," Aunt Euphemia reprimanded. "This is a difficult time in Livitha's life. Her body is undergoing profound changes. We have to be supportive."

He snorted his derision and I wondered once again why I had any fondness for the feline at all. "I was only joking," he said with an irritated flick of his tail but a broad smile across his face. Long, vampirish incisors gleamed against silken fur black as pitch.

"Ignore him Livitha, he's just jealous," Aunt Thomasin said.

"Hah!" he huffed in disagreement.

"Jealous of what?"

"Of your powers. He has always had a chip on his shoulder about his position as servant. Isn't that right Lucifer?"

Lucifer only made a snuffling noise through his nose, flicked his tail, and returned to the darkness of the hallway. I felt a pang of guilt then. I knew he resented the serfdom that being my familiar entailed, which was why I always tried to treat him with respect and didn't insist that he carry out any domestic duties as was my right. My aunts weren't quite so sensitive, insisting that their familiars carry out their fair share of duties. Given Lucifer's superior and insulting attitude, I wasn't sure I was doing the right thing. Perhaps I was spoiling him?

"I'm sorry if I caught you unawares," Aunt Thomasin apologised, "but I couldn't let you go out with that protruding from your top lip, now could I."

"No, but ... you could have just told me and let me fix it myself."

I could tell she wanted to say something else in her defence, but instead she merely said, "She's ready now, Loveday."

Chapter Twenty-Two

A heavy mist hung over the grass as Aunt Loveday led me to the end of the vegetable garden and then to the orchard beyond. As we came to the stone wall that marked the garden boundary, she took my hand. Her energy sparked against my own, but she tightened her grip before I had a chance to pull my hand away. The remains of an archway sat within the wall, but it had long since been filled in with bricks to become a solid wall. A little further along the wall was an archway that led to the meadow beyond the garden. The woodland lay just beyond the meadow.

"Shall we go around?"

She responded by holding my hand a little tighter and then began to recite a charm. The mist thickened around us, rising to hide the wall and when it cleared the brick infill had gone and a heavy oak door with a huge wrought iron handle and massive hinges was in its place. Aunt Loveday raised a hand and the door opened. I stepped through in awe. This was the first time I had witnessed my aunt's magick but as I stepped through the doorway, I was disappointed; the space wasn't another realm, it was just the meadow with the woodlands beyond. However, I kept my disappointment to myself and when Aunt Loveday slipped her arm through mine, walked with her through the meadow. It was then that I noticed the differences.

The meadow flowers seemed taller and more vibrant shades of red, blue, yellow, and purple. The sun seemed warmer, and its glow softer. Birdcall was abundant, its song sweet. Beyond the grass and flowers, where the meadow met the woodlands, the trees seemed greener, the black spaces between their trunks, darker. A group of deer, three adult females and two fawns, stood within the tall meadow grass and watched our progress. A cloud of what I thought to be small birds flew as a murmuration in the sky, but as it rose, twisted, then flew close, I saw that it was a battalion of tiny fairies. Excited chittering filled my ears as they swooped down. It faded to buzzing as they rose high into the air. I flinched as they came close but, with Aunt Loveday holding my hand, my usual reflex of panic stayed under control.

We entered the woods and walked until we reached a clearing that I didn't recognise. At its centre was an old woman. In her arms she carried a bundle of sticks. She carried these to a fire above which a cauldron hung on a blackened tripod. Steam rose from the vessel. With a shock, I recognised her as the woman from my dream where I held Garrett's hand and we looked on as she collected firewood.

As Aunt Loveday and I approached, she laid the sticks on a pile. A mist rose around us until the woodlands disappeared and we were alone in the clearing with the woman. At least ninety years old, she wore a long and full skirt in a heavily woven brown fabric, a linen blouse in a creamy shade, and a black woollen shawl crossed at the front and held in place by a worn leather belt. A headscarf was tied at the nape of her neck from beneath which silver-white hair hung in thin plaits. Her face was kindly, but she didn't speak.

"Greetings Gunhild, Protector of Realms. We have come to call on Ragnhild."

The old crone nodded then turned her attention to the fire, adding more sticks to the flames. The newly added sticks sparked and fizzed.

From a pocket in her skirt, Aunt Loveday withdrew a leather pouch. She passed it to the woman. Without thanks, the woman took the bag and withdrew a handful of powder then threw it on the fire. Sparks erupted as the powder fizzed. The woman began to chant and delved again into the bag. This time she brought out a small square of parchment covered in runes and symbols. She read the parchment, whispering the words in a voice far stronger than I expected, then threw it into the fire. After this, the entire pouch was tossed on the fire. As the leather began to scorch, she withdrew a knife from her pocket. The blade glinted in the sunlight as she held it to the sun. For the first time a sense of danger fell upon me and I hoped that a blood sacrifice, or worse, a sample of our blood, wouldn't be needed.

"Stay calm, Liv," Aunt Loveday soothed, picking up on my fear. "Gunhild must do her work."

I took courage from Loveday as the woman held the knife high and began to chant once more. I listened to her song as her voice rose in a demanding tone then fell to a whisper. Words were hissed at the knife and then with arms held aloft and her face to the sky, she invoked the power of the sun, the moon, and the goddess of foresight and wisdom, Frigg.

Stepping up close, she reached for my hair, grabbing a lock between her gnarled fingers. Too surprised to move, I caught a glimpse of the knife; the blade was sharp, the handle wooden and carved with intertwined dragons. I flinched as she chopped off a length of hair, but she quickly moved on to Loveday and pulled a lock free. I could barely watch as at least six inches of Loveday's beautiful hair was hacked off.

The crone dropped the hair at our feet then squatted, stabbed the blade into the ground, and began to scratch a circle around us. I watched with fascination as the circle was completed and she began to scratch runes around the circumference. My knowledge of runes was rudimentary, but from what I could understand she was invoking the power of Frigg to open a gateway before signing herself off as the author.

As the last rune was written, the woman picked up our hair and threw it in the fire. Sparks flew and sunlight was replaced by darkness. I began to panic as I remembered my horrifying experience in the Black Woods.

"Stay calm, Liv." Aunt Loveday's voice seemed to come from the far distance but as rapidly as it had disappeared the light returned, and we were at the edge of the clearing beside a great oak. The woman and her cauldron were gone.

Loveday's aura shone violet with specks of pure silver, a perfect midnight sky speckled with stars. I could see mine reflected in her eyes and watched it wax and wane, in awe at the aurora borealis of pure energy.

"Beyond this gateway is Ragnhild," Aunt Loveday said.

"The Warlock?" I asked in surprise.

"Yes, the Varðlokkur, the keeper of our secrets. It is she who will show us the way to Arthur. To enter we must send out our desire for help from the gods, the first gods, the gods of our forefathers, of our people. She gripped my hand and, as she began to recite the supplication, a golden mist shimmered around her figure. It waxed, waned, and was replaced by a silver one. The air pressure around me intensified and I felt as though every particle of skin, and every fibre of muscle, were being squeezed. A great weight was upon me and, enveloped by a shimmering mist, I was blinded by a flash of light. My ears popped as the air pressure around me changed. The weight lifted and we were no longer beside the great oak, but within a circular room. Dark wood lined the domed wall. Hovering globes of bright mist, illuminated the space. A woman stepped from the unlit space between two globes.

I gasped.

Ragnhild was the most beautiful woman I had ever seen. Statuesque, with long and slender limbs, her alabaster skin glowed bright, and her tresses of silken hair were so blonde they were almost white. Her aura shimmered with pure gold. Fern-green eyes settled on me, and I felt foolish in my supermarket 'mum' jeans and cerise hooded fleece, wishing I had listened to my aunts and dressed a little less casually whilst taking at least some time to style my hair. Unconsciously I combed my fingers through my hair. It was a wasted effort; I was gauche in the extreme compared to Ragnhild. I shrivelled a little under her gaze, but the smile she offered held no hint of judgement.

"So," she said to Loveday at my side. "This is the daughter of Soren Erikson, son of Steinthor Erikson?"

"It is Ragnhild. Forgive me for bringing her before the Summoning."

"There must be great trouble brewing for Haligern if you are breaking with tradition, sister. Tell me your woes."

Surely, she should know, I thought. Green eyes flashed at me and I pressed my lips together, sure that Ragnhild shared the same gift as Aunt Beatrice. I tried to think only flattering thoughts, focusing on the décor. 'Don't think so loud!' Aunt Beatrice's words repeated in my mind.

"You are young," Ragnhild said with a gentle tone. "Self-control is something you will master—one day."

Aunt Loveday threw me a quizzical frown. I gave a weak, apologetic smile, certain I was letting her down. A flush crept to my cheeks but she returned a reassuring smile before turning her attention back to Ragnhild.

Washed out by the diffused light of the floating globes, nothing in the room could be discerned. The space felt warm, devoid of drafts, and there was the distinct odour of applewood smoke. Somewhere in the distance burning wood crackled. Ragnhild stared directly at Aunt Loveday.

"So, sister, you have lost him."

Aunt Loveday's aura fragmented then reassembled as a tremble ran through her body. "Oh, sister Ragnhild, Varðlokkur of our people, I have!"

"He was taken," Ragnhild stated.

"We believe so."

"And you want me to find him."

"Oh, Ragnhild, sister through the centuries, Keeper of Secrets, Gate Maiden of the Realms, he is lost to us, trapped. His call for help blocked from me."

"Sit," Ragnhild commanded.

Suddenly a fire appeared between us and the domed roof gave way to an indigo sky glittering with a billion stars. Beneath my feet were fur rugs. Loveday sat as instructed. I followed her lead. Ragnhild appeared on the other side of the fire, her arms held aloft as she sat cross-legged. Her soft voice drifted across the space, a singsong of ancient words. Enveloped by her voice, pure magical energy rose through the earth. She faded from sight to reappear between us, and light shone down on the wolfskins where we sat. From within her cloak she pulled a bag and placed it in Loveday's palm. Made of soft leather it was tied with leather thongs decorated with silver beads like the ones Loveday had described as part of Arthur's binding. Runes were branded into the leather. Ragnhild removed the bag from Loveday's palm then raised it high and whispered words I could not understand.

Untying the thongs, Ragnhild then drew the bag to her cheek and whispered, 'Where is the Book of Haligern? Tell us of the lost magick. Let it speak.'

I expected her to reach in and pull out the individual runes, but instead Ragnhild poured the contents of the bag onto the skins. Pale squares littered the fur, but only three held runic inscriptions. Ragnhild muttered, her words indecipherable to me, then took each of the shown runes and placed them close to Loveday.

"Tell me what you see."

Loveday took a deep breath, closed her eyes, and wiped a hand above the runes. "A journey alone to a dark room. A life … a young life to be taken … great magick, dark magick has been summoned … Arthur! I see you Arthur!" Loveday's eyes snapped open and she stared directly at me. "He is being held in a dark room. There are antlers on the wall. A man with bright and curling hair – I can't see his face, but his hands are wrinkled. A girl sits in the corner—she is afraid—full of re-gret—he has Arthur, reciting from his pages." Loveday closed her eyes again. "I see. I hear. He is reading from the page … a conjuring spell!" She shuddered. "His pronunciation is wrong. He is struggling to understand. A ring. I see a ring. A black tree! The wind howls ... something howls ... outside the windows." She gasped. "Blackwood! The signet ring of the Blackwoods. It is he that is blocking Arthur." She stood, facing Ragnhild. "A Blackwood has him, Ragnhild!"

My heart seemed to shrivel; she couldn't be talking about Garrett!

Ragnhild's face was dour. "Only his incompetence is saving Haligern, Loveday," she said with foreboding. "If he masters the words of that spell, then he will summon the demon."

"He has already summoned a creature from the dark realm."

"That is true, it roams the forests," Ragnhild agreed.

"If he is successful in his spell craft ... Oh, it is all my fault!"

"You must take better care of your knowledge, Loveday. You have become complacent."

Loveday nodded.

"Blackwood cannot be allowed to use your knowledge to his own ends. Only Arthur's power stops him being successful, but his energy is waning—I feel that."

"The girl in my vision was full of regrets," Loveday continued. "Her face wasn't clear, but I am certain it was Agnes. She summoned the puck, Livitha, I'm sure of that. It is an easy spell to cast, but the summoning of a demon—that takes more practice and a stronger magic. And the demon, the one I saw Blackwood trying to summon, is an altogether different creature to the Gewyscan púca or the imp that chased you through the woods. It is a demon of great power. If it is unleashed, I am not sure we could return it to its proper place. It would cause absolute carnage!"

As our eyes locked in mutual horror, the fire and the lights receded. Ragnhild's figure became obscure and, as the darkness grew, a new light began to brighten in the distance.

"He is here, Loveday," Ragnhild's voice called from the darkness as the distant light grew in brightness and size.

Wind whipped at my hair and a chariot pulled by stallions galloped in an indigo sky, the light behind it casting their forms in silhouette. Loveday clasped my hand.

"He calls for you, sister."

"Arthur?" I asked in a whisper as I watched the chariot approach.

"No!" Loveday whispered. "It is Erik."

The chariot and its magnificent horses faded. Light brightened the space once more, but mist diffused the light. Loveday stepped forward and a cloud of white and shimmering mist rose to envelope her. As it thinned, I saw her as though looking through a lens and I realised that we were no longer in the same realm. I reached for her, but my fingers only touched the shimmering mist and it rippled as though I had dipped my finger in a pool of water.

"Hist!" Ragnhild's hiss of disapproval scorched me and I withdrew my hand as though burned.

"Watch!" she commanded. "Loveday has waited centuries for Erik to return to her. Watch and let them reunite."

The mist evaporated, and the air filled with noise. Men roared. Metal scraped against metal. And two figures became apparent. A young woman with flaxen waist-length hair, and narrow braids held by silver beads at the side of her face, knelt on the ground. A headdress of antlers circled her head, a skin of fur was held across her shoulders by a golden broach. On her wrist was the same band of decorated silver my aunt always wore. Head bowed, she whispered to the man cradled in her arms. "Erik! Don't leave me. Erik! Be strong."

The injured man gazed into her eyes. His words were whispered too low to hear. The woman rocked, stroking his bearded face. Blood bloomed across his tunic, the chain mail glistened red. He scrabbled at the ground, his fingers inches from the sword at his side. The woman reached for it and placed it in his hand, clasping hers around his to hold it in place. "Erik," she repeated. "Yfel ferhþlufu, Erik." She stroked his beard and bent to kiss his forehead. "I love you. On ecnesse, Erik. For eternity. Go, my beloved warrior. Join thy brother. Sit with thy father in the Great Hall."

Minutes passed as she whispered to the dying man until, finally, as his eyes glazed, dead to this world, she tipped her head back and roared her grief to the sky.

The scene faded and two figures stood facing one another. The young woman and the slain warrior alive again. He reached a hand behind her head and pulled her to him until their lips met. They kissed for long moments and then she laid her head against his chest. His form began to evaporate, and she grabbed at the thinning air. "Erik!" she called. "Erik! Yfel ferhþlufu." His form thinned then disappeared. She sagged. "On ecnesse, Erik, on ecnesse." As I watched, tears streaming down my cheeks, the young woman caught my gaze and began to change. Her flaxen hair became white, her face aged, her wolfskin shawl disappeared and before me stood Aunt Loveday, her face stricken with grief. Tears ran freely down her cheeks and, as she stepped towards me, she staggered. I wrapped my arms around her slender form, holding her as she sobbed. "It was him, Livitha." Her cheeks were wet with tears, but her eyes glittered with joy. "It was Erik. My Erik."

She allowed me to hold her, then dried her tears.

I had no idea what to say without sounding crass. I opted for a pathetic, "Are you ... alright?" whilst offering her a crumpled tissue from my pocket. She took it with a sniff and a smile then nodded. Still unable to think of anything suitable to say I slipped an arm around her waist and waited for her to take the lead.

She sighed, then turned to Ragnhild who had reappeared from the shadows and stood illuminated by the floating globes of light. With a sad smile on her face she said, "He has waited many centuries, Loveday."

"And I too," Loveday replied.

"One day you will be together again."

I couldn't help wondering where Uncle Raif fitted into that scenario.

"But now is the time to find your book, Loveday. The future of Haligern depends on it."

In the next moment, the space darkened, and we were transported to the forest behind Haligern Cottage. Twilight had fallen. Although the time spent in Ragnhild's realm had seemed only minutes, in ours, hours had passed.

We were back in familiar territory, and I walked with hurried steps to the edge of the forest and into the meadow where Haligern sat in silhouette against the last band of colour in the sky.

Chapter Twenty-Three

At the back of the house, Aunt Euphemia drew heavy curtains against the dark as we made our way across the lawn. With a flick of fabric at the drawing room window she was gone and, as her face disappeared, the carriage lamp fixed to the side of the back door flickered on. The candlewick burned a rich orange then filled the carriage lamp with soft light, the flame dancing behind thick glass.

There was a story behind the old Georgian carriage lamp that had fascinated me as a child. As a teenager I dismissed the tragic tale of forbidden love as fantasy told to entertain. Hand clasped in Aunt Euphemia's after an evening walk beneath the full moon, I would listen to the story of a highway man and a beautiful lady. Against her will, the lady was to be betrothed to another and, as she journeyed to her wedding, the highwayman rescued her, taking the carriage lamp to light their way across the moor. They were happy for a while, but the couple were betrayed, and the highwayman captured, forced to stand trial, and hung at Tyburn gallows.

"The lady in the story was Aunt Thomasin," Aunt Loveday said as I gazed at the lamp.

"How did you know what I was thinking?"

"I didn't, but you always asked the question as a child. We never told you the truth, obviously, but you're one of us now; it's important to understand our history."

"You have all lived such amazing lives!" I said. "Mine is pathetic in comparison—twenty-six years of boring domesticity."

"Well," she said laying a gentle hand on my shoulder, "you are making up for it now."

"Aunt Loveday," I said, faltering as she placed a hand on the door handle. "Erik ... I don't understand. I mean, you love Uncle Raif, don't you?"

"Oh, yes! With all my heart. Your Uncle is one of the finest men I have ever met. I cannot imagine my life without him."

"Then why have you been waiting for Erik? How does that ... work? Isn't it kind of ... cheating."

She cupped a hand to my cheek. "Ah, Livitha, I understand your concern, but please understand that I would never do anything to hurt your uncle. He understands. We have lived together through the centuries, sharing our most intimate secrets. He knows about my life before I met him." She was quiet for a moment then said, "Livitha. Raif is my soulmate—we are entwined forever, but the love I have for Erik is burned into my soul. One cannot live as long as I, and not be torn by love. Raif is a good man and he has room in his heart to accept my love for Erik. I would never hurt him—never! Erik died so, so long ago, but I will never stop loving him, just as I will never stop loving Raif ... once he passes." Sadness enveloped her and tears welled in her eyes as her aura waxed and waned. "Although quite how I shall survive without him, I cannot countenance." She wiped away the tear that had fallen on her cheek and opened the door. "Come along, we must tell your aunts exactly what we discovered today."

We entered the house, hanging our coats on the pegs in the hallway and removed our now muddy boots. Our evening meal, a rich lamb stew, was cooking on the stove and the aroma filled the kitchen. My belly grumbled in greeting and I was suddenly ravenous. The large kitchen table had been cleared of bottles, jars, and boxes, scrubbed clean and six places laid. Silver forks, knives, and spoons glinted in the soft light that glowed from the lamps dotted about the room. A spoon at the top of the setting could mean only one thing—Aunt Beatrice had made one of her famous crumbles.

"You're treating us tonight, Aunt Beatrice," I said as she appeared from the pantry.

She nodded vociferously, opened her mouth to speak, then pursed her lips in irritation.

"Crumble?"

She nodded.

"Apple and bramble?"

Again, a nod and she gestured to the table for me to sit.

Within the next minute the kitchen filled with chatter as my aunts and Uncle Raif joined me at the table. The lamb stew was cooked to perfection and we waited for everyone to finish before sharing our news.

"So, Arthur *is* at Blackwood Manor, just as Livitha said?"

"Yes!" She turned to me. "I had to be sure, Liv. We can't proceed unless we are absolutely certain Arthur is there."

"I understand and I'm glad we went to Ragnhild—it was ... incredible."

"It was." A tear was quickly wiped from her eye. "Now," Aunt Loveday continued, "what Ragnhild helped me to see was that whoever has him is attempting to conjure an El-lengæst—an immensely powerful and malicious demon. I saw it quite clearly. The only thing that is stopping him is his lack of knowledge."

"A novice, then?"

"A younger member of the family?"

"I can't be sure. The hand I saw in my vision, with the signet ring, was wrinkled with age."

"The Blackwoods have been excluded for a number of years now; their knowledge could have slipped."

"I know that Editha Blackwood turned her back on magick after they were cursed. She said that it had brought about too much tragedy."

"But obviously someone is still practicing."

"Yes, or rediscovering their roots perhaps?"

"Who lives at Blackwood Manor now? To my knowledge, the family moved out decades ago and the house was rented out."

"I'm surprised that it hasn't been sold to a developer and made into apartments. It is far too big for one family."

Uncle Raif disappeared into the pantry and returned with a bottle of red wine.

"I think this will lighten the mood; a 2012 Rioja Reserva. Is that an acceptable vintage, ladies?"

"Perfect, darling," Aunt Loveday agreed.

As Uncle Raif uncorked the bottle a thud was followed by the shriek of shattering glass and the bottle was knocked out of his hand as a large rock was thrown through the window. It landed on the table, shattering glass across our plates before it rolled onto the floor. Shards spiked the crumble.

I retrieved the rock. "What on earth!" A note was tied to it with string.

"What is it?"

"It must be a message," I said as I fumbled with the string.

"Read it!"

Printed in capitals it read, 'We know about you! Witch!' Beneath the blocky script was a stick figure in pointed witch hat, fitted bodice, and long skirt. The skirt and hat had been coloured in black. The flames at her feet had been coloured a vibrant orange and red—the only colour on the page. Beneath the picture was simply stated, 'We burn witches.'

"It's happening again!" Aunt Thomasin said.

"I'm sure it can't be that!" Aunt Euphemia soothed though her glance to me was filled with fear.

Incensed that anyone dared to break our window and threaten us, I ran outside. Torchlight bobbed in the distance.

"Who's there!" I shouted. "Show yourself!" The light continued to bob about in the dark then disappeared. Gravel crunched on the driveway. I took a step to follow them, but Uncle Raif's hand slapped down on my shoulder.

"Come back inside, Livitha. It's a dangerous thing that you intend to do."

"But they threw a rock into our home!"

"They did, but it is not safe to follow them."

"Them? Do you know who they are?"

"No, but this is not the first time we have faced threats of this kind. Come inside."

Angry, but unwilling to be rude to my uncle, I returned to the kitchen. Aunt Euphemia was sweeping the glass shards into a pile whilst Aunts Thomasin and Beatrice were clearing the table. A breeze blew through the broken pane.

The rock had been placed on the windowsill and Aunt Loveday stood with the note in her hand reading the black print scrawled across the paper.

"It is horrible!"

"After all this time! Why now?"

"Calm yourselves, sisters. We must think."

"We must stop the gossip before it spreads."

"It may be too late for that."

The next half an hour was spent in examining the note and discussing just who might have sent it. A hammering knock at the door startled us all and Aunt Beatrice, already on hyper alert, squealed.

"I'll go," Aunt Loveday said and disappeared into the hallway.

I followed quickly behind. The lights in the hallway grew bright as she strode towards the door. Another insistent knock made the heavy door vibrate in its frame and as she opened the door, brilliant light and demanding voices flooded the hallway. Aunt Loveday staggered back under the barrage of noise and blinding light. Pushing past my aunt, I slammed the door shut and a muffled peace returned.

"Who is it?"

"It's them! The mob!"

"Don't be preposterous, Euphemia," Aunt Loveday scolded, her vision now recovered. "I think it's a newsman."

"A newsman!"

"Why on earth would a newsman be here?"

I remembered the protective magick that enveloped the cottage and its grounds. "Can't we use the shield against him? Stop him coming to the door?"

"This isn't an episode of Star Trek, dear," Aunt Loveday said. "I'm not Captain Kirk. I can't just press a button and have a defensive shield pop up. And anyway, it's not there to keep the humans out."

I was impressed that she remembered the episode of Star Trek I'd forced her to watch with me as a child.

The knocking continued.

"Should we answer?"

"No!"

"But they're very insistent!"

"Just ignore them."

The knocking and calling continued for at least twenty minutes but eventually the noise stopped, and I returned to the kitchen with my aunts. When the knocking started again, I was unable to hold my temper and stormed to the door.

Chapter Twenty-Four

I expected to be met by a barrage of flashing lights and an angry horde. Instead a single figure stood beneath the porch, fist raised to knock once more.

"Dr. Cotta!" I blurted. "But it can't be you!"

His face broke into a smile. "Well, it certainly is!"

I pushed past him to peer into the driveway. There was no sign of the angry mob and their flashing camera.

"Liv ... Miss. Erikson, are you alright? I've dropped by to see your uncle."

"Where are they?" I demanded, my anger still swirling.

"Oh, the reporter? I sent him packing. It's a nasty business. It's not every day a sinkhole swallows an entire housing estate. From what I hear, the builder is in real trouble. Something about building over mineshafts."

"You see! It wasn't me," Aunt Beatrice blurted from the kitchen doorway. As soon as she spoke, she clapped a hand to her mouth and disappeared back into the kitchen. Dr. Cotta narrowed his eyes momentarily then turned his attention back to me.

"That hack reporter is doing the rounds and bothering everyone who witnessed the houses collapsing. He was making a nuisance of himself at my office today."

I breathed a sigh of relief. "He almost hammered the door down."

"Yeah," Dr. Cotta drawled. "I had to get tough with him. I told him I'd call the police if he didn't leave as he was trespassing and obviously harassing your family."

"Thankyou!" Blue eyes gazed down into mine and I stood dwarfed by his huge frame. Time disappeared.

"So," he said as Aunt Euphemia coughed behind us. "Can I see him? Your uncle."

"Yes! Yes, of course!"

Thankfully, Aunt Loveday's senses were still intact, and she invited the doctor in, ushering him into the drawing room where Uncle Raif was already waiting. "Make the doctor a cup of tea, please Livitha." The door closed behind them.

"I wish that puck was here now," Aunt Beatrice said. "I could wish for something for you, Livitha!" Aunt Beatrice said this with a twinkle in her eyes and a nod towards the drawing room door.

"Don't you dare!" I scolded. "Don't you very dare!"

With a gentle, cackling laugh, Aunt Beatrice placed the kettle on the stovetop and handed me the empty teapot. "Make yourself useful, Liv, or I may just have to make a wish!" She snorted at her own humour.

"I think I preferred you when you were silent!"

I made the tea with burning cheeks and managed to persuade Aunt Thomasin to take the tray through to the drawing room whilst I waited in the kitchen. I was becoming quite agitated. The assault on the cottage, and now the visit from Dr. Cotta, had thrown our focus away from what we really needed to discuss—rescuing Arthur from Blackwood Manor.

Chapter Twenty-Five

Waiting for Dr. Cotta to leave took far longer than expected. Unlike most modern doctors who made only the fleetest of home visits, Dr. Cotta was happy to sit and chat with Uncle Raif and Aunt Loveday. I couldn't blame him; both were charismatic and could carry a conversation well, so when Aunt Loveday emerged from the drawing room and asked me to make another pot of tea, and bring biscuits too, I was both dismayed but unsurprised.

"But we have to go!" I hissed. I had made up my mind to visit Blackwood manor that evening.

"Go?" Aunt Loveday asked.

"Yes, go—to Blackwood Manor." I said this in the quietest tones despite both the drawing room and kitchen doors being closed.

"Tsk, Livitha. Don't act rashly. You can't go there tonight."

"But ... Arth-"

She held a finger to her lips. "We mustn't speak of it now. Bide your time."

Frustrated, I agreed and returned to the kitchen table to wait.

Another half an hour passed before Dr. Cotta said his goodbyes and left Haligern Cottage.

"Such a nice man," Uncle Raif said as he took the first riser upstairs. "A true gentleman, despite his origins."

"Indeed," Aunt Loveday agreed. "We can't all be related to royalty, my love." She offered him an indulgent smile and watched as he ascended the stairs then returned to the kitchen.

"Despite his origins?"

"Yes, Dr. Cotta comes from a troubled background. He had a tough time growing up."

"Oh, I see."

"But ... and I say this without prejudice, but there is something troubling about him."

"He seemed so nice though, Loveday."

"Exactly that. He seemed a little too good to be true, and far too interested in Uncle Raif. He asked about you too, Livitha."

"Me!"

Aunt Euphemia dug me in the ribs. "See, you are still attractive, despite ... erm, ... your age!" She beamed at this, but I knew that what she meant was despite my spreading waist and hormonally induced hair growth. I instinctively put a hand to my face. "Don't worry, it's fuzz-free!"

"You can go off people you know!"

"Liv thinks he's an Adonis," Aunt Beatrice stated. "I wish I could-"

"No!" all three aunts shouted in unison.

"Don't say another word, Beatrice. You've done enough damage already."

"But Dr. Cotta said that it was the builder's fault for building over a mineshaft."

"That's as may be, but I doubt it would have opened up in his lifetime without your meddling."

"Meddling!"

The air crackled around Aunt Beatrice, her indignation growing by the second. My Aunts rarely argued, and I had never witnessed them freeing their energies the way they did in that moment. Sparks flew, popping overhead in a rainbow of colours.

"Now, sisters, stop this! Obviously, it is not Beatrice's fault that the sinkhole opened up. She wasn't to know that the puck had imprinted upon her."

"But she knows now, and she was about to wish that Dr. Cotta and Liv-"

"Shh!" I hissed, terrified. The last thing I wanted was for the errant puck to meddle in my love life. Having my aunts tinker with love potions was damaging enough. "We have to make plans! To get Arthur." The room quieted and all eyes turned to me.

"What do you suggest, Livitha?"

"That we forget about Dr. Cotta and focus on Arthur. Finding him is the key to restoring calm in the cottage. When we find Arthur, we find Agnes and the fairy and the spell to send the puck and the imp back to where they came from. Without him this chaos is going to continue, and I feel sure that the villagers will become more and more resentful towards us."

"But Dr. Cotta said it wasn't our fault," Aunt Beatrice repeated.

"Perhaps he did, but whoever threw that rock with its poisonous message doesn't believe that."

Gloom descended but at least the sparking, combative energies had been quelled. We returned to the table. Aunt Beatrice made a fresh pot of tea, and we discussed the problem in earnest. Freshly brewed tea, particularly one with a few drops of Aunt Euphemia's favourite elixir, always helped to clear our thinking.

"We must go to Blackwood Manor." I said with finality. "It's the only way."

Aunt Beatrice shuddered. Aunt Euphemia made a slight mewling noise that was neither assent nor dissent. Aunt Thomasin sat in brooding silence. There was no enthusiasm for my suggestion.

"I don't think that would be the best option."

"No, indeed."

"A meeting of the covens is perhaps the best solution."

"The curse ..."

Bottles clinked. "Oh, for goodness sake," I said in exasperation as the fairies began to stir. "Do they need more cheese?"

"They've had enough for today. We can't give them an overdose, Livitha."

"But I cannot stand another night with them sneaking into my room. I barely slept last night. Every noise wakes me."

"Once we find Arthur ..."

"We've found him. We know where he is. Let us go to collect him."

"It's not that easy, Livitha."

It seemed quite simple to me—we could either knock on the door and demand his return, or we could break into the house and snatch him back.

"That's a wonderful idea for the movies, Livitha, but we have to deal with real life and breaking into the Blackwood's ancestral home, well ... it goes against coven policy."

"Coven policy!"

A frown fell across my aunt's face, and her reply was curt. "We have our standards, Livitha. We cannot break our code."

"It's a code of honour among our people that we must abide by. Chaos is the result if we do not."

"Or war."

"Yes, or war, and that is something to be avoided at all costs."

"But Arthur was stolen!"

"Yes, but not by one of our people."

"A pseudo-witch."

"A girl with fantastical ideas."

"A girl who stole our most precious possession and passed it on to someone unscrupulous," I insisted.

"Yes, all of that is true, but it wasn't stolen by one of our own."

"Are we agreed then sisters?"

My aunts nodded whilst I sat dumbfounded.

"Livitha? Do you agree?"

"I'm not sure what I'm agreeing to," I explained having lost the thread of the conversation.

"That we must call a Council of the Covens in order to take the next step forward and retrieve Arthur."

"Well," I said with growing frustration, "If it is the only way ..."

"It is."

"Then yes, I suppose so."

The sisters clasped hands and placed them at the centre of the table. I reluctantly extended my own. "Agreed." The aunts said in unison.

Chapter Twenty-Six

I turned the bedside light off that night in a state of perturbation. Aunt Loveday had insisted on calling a Council of the Covens in order to seek permission to question the inhabitants of Blackwood Manor. I found not being able to simply drive to the house and knock on the door frustrating, but etiquette and Council Law apparently dictated that first the Council Elders must meet to discuss the situation and then either grant permission for us to seek Arthur, or create a plan of action. We simply could not act unilaterally Aunt Loveday had explained when I had questioned her over our evening mug of cocoa. That was how wars began. My response had been a huffed sigh of resignation—I knew I could retrieve Arthur if I was given the chance to enter the house. Afterall, I had solved the case of the murdered mistress and discovered exactly why the woman had been killed and how! I had fantasised about becoming a private investigator on more than one occasion in the past few weeks and was itching to solve this case too. Working in my aunts shop was an honour, and I was delighted that they had enough belief in me to want me to manage it, but after being released from my previous humdrum existence, I was greedy for a little more excitement in my life. Perhaps, I thought as I turned once more in bed, I could do a little investigative work on the side; the shop didn't have to be my only interest.

"Ouf!" Lucifer grumbled as my foot kicked him from beneath the duvet.

I restrained myself from saying sorry. He had been grumbling the entire evening—pawing at my duvet and pulling out the cotton threads with his long talons whilst complaining about how uncomfortable my bed was and how stuffy the room.

"Huh!"

Oh, for goodness sake! "What's wrong, Lou?" I asked with forced patience.

"Well, it is customary to apologize for kicking a man in the teeth!"

I couldn't help tweaking him. "But you're a cat ... Ow!" Claws pierced deep into the soft arch of my foot.

"Oh, sorry!" he said with complete insincerity. "I was just stretching, and you know how I love to extend my claws when I stretch."

It was true, he did love to stretch, and his claws would extend to their full and hooked magnificence, but that was generally on an armchair or a tree in the garden. This was pure malice. "You know very well that you stabbed me with your claws out of spite."

"Why ... absolutely not and I am quite offended that you would even think such a thing. I'm uncomfortable. I needed to stretch. That is all." He said this as he slowly retracted his claws.

I quickly moved my foot out of his way. "Just go to sleep, Lucifer." I was truly irritated at this point and beginning to overheat. I threw the bedclothes aside and lay spread-eagled, hoping for a draft to cool me down. Sweat accumulated at my breastbone as a sudden wave of hormonal heat engulfed me.

Accustomed to my now nightly sauna-like sweats Lucifer emitted a disdainful meow and jumped off my bed. "I'd rather not," he said with disgust in his voice. "It's far too hot in here and ... sweaty. If you ask me-"

"Which I'm not!"

"It's rather disgusting having to sleep in your room when you make it so damp and muggy!"

I ignored his jibes. The room was neither damp nor muggy. "Lucifer, if you're just going to insult me, I'd rather you left."

"I will and I don't need your permission to go."

His attitude was making my temper boil. "Actually, you do!" I said with irritation, knowing that this was exactly the kind of remark that would tweak him.

"Well!" He spat. "I absolutely do not! I am not your skivvy, Livitha Winifred Erikson!"

He knew how much I hated my middle name. "Actually, you are," I said in defiance. "You're my familiar and that means you are not only my spy, but my domestic too."

He growled with anger—definitely triggered. "I shall no longer sleep in this room ... Winifred. You're on your own. I hope that the fairies don't bite you tonight!" The chuckle that followed was purely evil, but he had hit the mark with the mention of fairies.

Panic fizzed along with the pain in my fingers, but I made a superhuman effort not to show it. "I'm sure they won't. And anyway, once I've found Arthur, they will no longer be a problem."

He snorted. "Good luck with *that*!" With a pad of paws and flick of his tail against the carpet, he clawed at the bedroom door then disappeared through the gap. I listened as he padded along the hall and down the stairs, no doubt to curl up with Bess beside the fire in the kitchen. As the noise of his footsteps disappeared, I tuned into my bedroom, listening for any sign of the tiny demons that had tormented me over the past weeks. All was silent and, after a few minutes, sleep dragged me down to its depths.

I woke with a start to noise outside. Sitting up, drenched in sweat, heart palpitating, I listened. Somewhere in the distance a car door slammed. It was quickly followed by a second. After checking through my window and seeing nothing, I returned to bed and pulled the duvet up. The fairies were absent. Lucifer was not within striking distance. I could sleep without worry.

Two minutes later I sat bolt upright. Someone was walking down the driveway. More than one person, at least three or four. I realised then that my new witchy powers came with better hearing. This was a revelation and a boon as before my fiftieth my hearing had begun to dull a little and Pascal had been able to walk up behind me without me realising—not a great development for a woman who never saw the funny side of being startled and would jump at her own shadow if spooked.

Several lights bobbed in the dark. I dressed and made my way downstairs. From the window I could see figures at the head of the drive where the trees gave way to the turning circle. Illuminated by a bright moon, they stood in a huddle, torches pointing to the ground. I felt certain that one would be the reporter, come back to harass us. In the hallway, I pulled on my jacket, grasped the walking stick propped against the wall, then opened the door. Lucifer jumped through the doorway just as I took a step over the threshold and I had to take quick steps to avoid stepping on him. I stumbled down the steps. The long stick caught against the ground and I fell, landing with a thud on the gravel. "Lucifer!" I hissed as he disappeared uninjured into the shadows. I gripped the stick and noticed its ridged plastic surface. Instead of Uncle Raif's hazel walking stick, I had picked up Mrs Driscoll's broom. Not the traditional besom broom with wooden handle and birch twig brush that my aunts favoured - and had quite a collection of - but a plastic affair with a bar of soft nylon bristles and plastic-coated aluminium handle. The huddle of figures watched in silence as I pulled myself up using the broom to help.

"It's the witch!" I heard one hiss.

Chapter Twenty-Seven

"This is private land!" I heard myself shout. "You're trespassing."

"Witch!" one of the men shouted back.

It was true, I couldn't deny it so instead I said, "You have no right to be on this property." Adrenaline coursed through my body and the familiar heat was stirring at my core. Trembling, and with an attempt at a commandeering voice, I followed it with, "I demand that you leave."

"What did she say?"

"Dunno. Couldn't hear her."

My voice did that thing where it seemed to split and warble. My throat had become dry, my efforts a damp squib.

I raised the broom, coughed to clear my voice, then said. "Leave!" My voice had suddenly become hoarse.

"Tell them, Livitha!" Lucifer demanded as he slinked around my ankles.

"I'm trying," I retorted still annoyed with him for nearly breaking my neck on the steps. "Will you stop doing that!" I said irritably as he continued to hover around my feet. He did a final turn around my left leg then sat beside me, imperious and full of bristling indignation.

"She's talking to that cat!"

"Look how its eyes glow."

"It's her familiar."

Light shone directly at us, blinding me, and making Lucifer hiss.

"Turn off the light, imbecile!" He yowled.

"That is creepy as hell!" one of the men said. "Did you hear it yowl. It was like it was talking."

"It was talking to her, like she could understand, and she talked back."

I began to feel as though we were specimens being observed in a laboratory.

"If you don't leave," I tried again. "I'll call the police."

One of the men took a step forward. Now the light shone so that I could see his face. I didn't recognise him, but the look on his face was familiar; just like the girl at the fete, it was full of obsession and hate. His brows knitted together in a scowl. "You're a witch. It was you who destroyed my houses. I was there at the fete and heard you all talking about the estate—how you wanted a sinkhole to swallow it up."

"And it did!" A man shouted from behind.

"Shut up, Carl." The man held my gaze. "And it did," he repeated. "You've ruined my business. I'd only sold three of those houses." As it dawned on me that this was the developer who had built the new estate, he took a step closer to me. I held my ground although my heart beat fiercely in my chest. "I can't sell a hole in the ground ... I'm ruined, and it's all thanks to you, witch!"

"Weren't you insured?" I asked.

"Well, yes, but ... that's not the point! You destroyed my houses with your dark magic!"

"No!" I managed and bit down on my words. I couldn't get drawn into admitting that we were witches.

"Witches should burn!" A voice thick with menace leaked from the darkness.

"An eye for an eye, Trevor! Sink her house."

"Shut up, idiot! I told you no names," he hissed. "And how the hell am I supposed to sink her house? Idiot!"

"Burn it down, then!"

"Yeah, burn it down."

"Burn the witch with it!"

His eyes narrowed as he considered this suggestion. "I think you may have a point."

"You're insane! You can't burn down my house!"

"You destroyed mine."

"Burn the witch!" Carl hissed.

"This is madness! It wasn't our fault the houses fell into that hole!" I countered. "You shouldn't have built over an old mine shaft."

He growled at my words. "There weren't no mine shaft."

"Yes, there was. Dr. Cotta said there was, so it's your fault that the houses fell into the sinkhole."

"No, it's not. It's yours. Carl, light the torch."

"No!"

A glug of lighter fuel was followed by the scratching of metal as Carl lit rags tied to the end of a pole. Carl jabbed the lit torch at mc. Flames danced only inches from my nose. "Listen, please! The ground beneath the houses was a warren of mining shafts. It's the planning office you need to take this up with. How can four elderly women be the cause of a sinkhole opening up?"

"Because they're witches!"

"We make herbal remedies. The villagers come to my aunts when they have skin complaints or trouble sleeping." This was true.

"Sally in the village says you can see into the future."

"My aunt sometimes reads runes. That doesn't make her a witch." It wasn't a lie; runes could be divined by someone other than a witch.

"Nancy said that you cast a spell on her boyfriend to make him fancy you."

My cheeks burned at the memory of Mike's attention. I almost felt his hands stroking my waist. The accusation was true. Aunt Thomasin had given him one of her love potions. "I can't help it if he ... likes me." Again, this wasn't a lie.

"Yeah, well, you're not exactly his type. Why would he ditch Nancy for you? She's fit."

"Hey!" I countered, heat searing my cheeks. "That's rude."

Lucifer snorted at my feet.

"True though. His bird's fit and you're ... well you're pretty enough, but you're a bit old *and* on the heavy side."

"I'm only five years older than Mike!"

"Well, still ... his bird said he was besotted, like he was bewitched. Couldn't stop talking about you, dreamed about you, then told her you were the only woman he could ever be with."

My cheeks burned. "I can't help that, and it doesn't mean I cast a spell on him."

"Did you?"

"No!"

He scowled at me. I returned his scowl with a hard stare. "I'd like you to leave," I tried. He made no effort to move.

"Very authoritative, Winifred!"

"Lucifer! That's enough." The words to the cat were out of my mouth before I could stop them.

"You are a witch!" the developer said. The crazed look in his eyes had returned. "Get her!"

Chapter Twenty-Eight

It took less than a second for me to realise I was being at-tacked. Stumbling over the broom, I ran for the house, but one of the men had pre-empted me and blocked my path.

I panicked!

Broom in hand, I darted to the bank of trees that edged the driveway and crashed into the undergrowth between two mas-sive yews. Footsteps pounded behind me. Barely able to see, I ran into the woods. At any second the angry pack would be on me; I was a fox hunted by hounds but without the fox's guile and knowledge of the woods.

"Faster!" Lucifer called. "This way."

Heart pounding, I tried to run and caught my arm against a tree trunk. Unbalanced by the impact, I fell heavily.

"Get up! This way!"

Luminous eyes guided me from the darkness.

I scrabbled to my feet, broom in hand, and followed Lu-cifer. Behind me branches snapped. Laboured breath and pounding feet meant the men were close. They had several ad-vantages over me—they were younger, and they had torchlight. I only had Lucifer. Glowing eyes appeared to the right. "This way! And duck." I made the turn and ran straight into a low branch. I stifled a yelp of pain as bark scratched across my fore-head. "Now squat," Lucifer hissed.

I squatted. The men lumbered past only inches from my side.

Lucifer's glowing eyes stared straight at me. "I told you to duck!" He said after they had passed.

"I tried!"

The footsteps stopped. Torchlight swung in my direction, illuminating my hiding spot. "She's here!"

"They heard you!" Lucifer hissed.

"Or you!"

I stood, knocked my head on the overhanging branch, then stumbled away from the shining torch. A hand grabbed my jacket. The grip was enough to yank me back, but I pulled forward and the fabric slipped through his fingers. Released, I sprinted forward. Undergrowth scratched at my legs and I stumbled into yet another tree. Without light to guide me, I was blind. Breathless and unable to escape the men, I slowed.

"Keep running, Livitha. Those are bad men. They'll hurt you if they catch you."

Fear ripped through me, urging me on, but the chemicals of defeat were also running through my blood. "I can't get away, Lucifer! Whichever way I go, they follow."

"Broom!" Lucifer shouted.

Despite it being clutched in my hand, I had forgotten about the broom. I could use it to fend them off when they finally caught up with me. I took a fighting stance, broom handle thrust forward.

"No, you must fly on the broom."

"Are you crazy?" I hissed. "This is Mrs. Driscoll's broom. It's not magic!"

"No, but you are! Liv, you must fly. There's no other way."

"But it's just a plastic broom. Probably made in China."

"We don't have time to discuss its provenance. Just use it."

The tramping of feet grew louder. Torchlight flashed through the branches, illuminating Lucifer's eyes. He hissed and jumped back. "Just believe and say the spell," he commanded as he slipped into the undergrowth.

"You're hiding!" I hissed. "Where can I hide?"

"Turn yourself into something small," he said and squeaked.

"I can't," I said with a shudder. "And don't turn into a mouse!"

"I'm not hanging around to be caught by those men. They'll have my guts for garters!"

"No one uses garters these days."

"Well, they'll do unspeakable things to me. Skin me alive!"

"You're overreacting, Lucifer!"

"You've obviously never participated in a witch hunt before. What they do to us familiars, is so much worse than what they do to your type."

"My type?"

"Yes, a witch. They do far worse to us!"

"Worse than torturing, hanging, drowning, and burning?"

"Absolutely! The things I've seen ..." He shuddered.

The men's voices grew loud. "She's this way."

"How do they know where we are?"

"Perhaps because you keep talking?"

I held back my retort and listened. The men were close. I clutched the broom a little tighter. Perhaps Lucifer was right about the broom. "What spell do I use, Lucifer?"

"The spell for flying—obviously!"

"I haven't been taught a spell for flying!"

"Tsk! Very tardy. What have the aunts been teaching you? Never mind. Listen to your inner witch."

Panic began to overwhelm me. "My inner witch?"

"Yes, just listen. Focus on the broom. Imagine yourself flying."

I clutched the broom, staring at its dark outline in the moonlight.

I tried to tune in to my inner witch but all I could hear was the pounding of my heart. It beat a steady, painful, booming rhythm.

A twig snapped nearby. The men whispered, but each word was audible to me and I realised that they would not give up easily.

Listen to your inner witch!

I focused again on the broom. *Fly!* I squeezed the handle. *Fly!*

"When I get her," a deep voice whispered. "I'm going to throttle her."

"String her up in the tree, feet first. See if she can cast spells then!"

The man with the deeper voice grunted in response.

Their venomous words shocked me. Lucifer was right; these were very bad men!

Fly! I thought with all my effort as I straddled the broom and held the handle tight.

Ancient words began to form.

This is the broom who travels through the land. "Þis is seo besma ðe geond lond fereþ."

The voice whispered to me, coming from somewhere deep inside my mind.

Fly broom! "Beflīeheþ besma."

This is the broom that fought against the loathsome one. "Þis is seo besma seo wiþ laðan gefeaht."

I felt my core heating, the familiar painful tingle in my fingers returned.

So you withstand against anger and rage. "Swa ðu wiðstonde hatheort."

It avails against capture. "Heo mæg wið ræpan."

The ember sparking from my thumb was so intense that I shook my hand to dissipate the pain. It was all very well having the gift to cast spells, but when the energy started to gather it became supercharged pins and needles.

Fly broom! "Beflīeheþ besma."

It avails against the loathsome one who hunts through the land. "Heo mæg wið ðam laþan ðe geond lond huntoþ."

"Hanging's too good for a witch. They should rip out their innards like they used to—with a cawl hook!"

"Gross!"

"It's what they deserve. 'Tis the law. Do you hear me witchy? When we get you, we're gonna have you tried and then your innards'll be spilt all over the floor. Tis what we do to witches in these parts."

The man's voice had changed. Its cadence subtly different. Gone were the modern intonations and a far older dialect had emerged. Beneath the hate in his voice was fear, and fear, I knew, was the father of cruelty.

Adrenaline surged, my hands trembled, and the sparks became fireworks.

Fly now, broom! "Fleoh þu nu, besma."

"Look at that!"

"It's the witch! Get her!"

The broom juddered.

Sparks, fiery red, and orange, illuminated the broom and undergrowth. An angry face loomed out of the darkness.

Fly broom! Fly!" I screamed.

The broom shot forward just as enormous hands grabbed for me.

"Hold on Livitha!" Lucifer shouted. "Fly high, Livitha! Fly high!"

The broom rocketed upwards.

"Grab her!"

Leaves brushed my hair and twigs snagged my clothes as the broom throttled skyward. It rose vertically through the branches until it broke through the canopy. Stars glittered. At any second, I felt sure that my hands would slip and I would crash to the earth and die in a crumpled heap but, as it continued to climb, I realised that my hands were stuck. Magick held me fast to the broomstick, and my palms glowed with lava-like intensity. By some miracle, I managed to sit astride the handle and remained upright. The plastic bar, with its nylon bristles, stuck out from my behind.

"Well done!"

Startled by Lucifer's voice, I screamed, and the broom began to plummet.

"Pull it up!" Lucifer shouted digging his claws into my shoulders. "We're going to crash!"

With Lucifer's talons anchoring him to my shoulder, I pulled back on the handle and we began to ascend.

"Level off!"

I levelled off then crouched over the broom. It shot forward. Lucifer mewled and his talons dug a little deeper into my shoulder. I eased back and the broom slowed.

"Talons!" I shouted as the pain spiked my shoulder. "Get them out!"

The talons retracted, but Lucifer remained pinned to my jacket. "I have to say, you're not very good at this!"

"You scared me half to death," I scolded, ignoring his jibe.

"Well, where did you expect me to sit?"

"I didn't expect you to sit anywhere! I thought you would hide in the bushes."

"Tsk! It is a familiar's duty to accompany his witch when out on the broom. Haven't you read the handbook?"

"There isn't a handbook!"

"There is. It's in my cupboard."

Distracted by the knowledge that the cat had a handbook of familiar etiquette the broom began to waver.

"Steady! You must focus, Livitha."

Without any idea of where we were headed, I focused again on remaining in the air. The broom steadied and I became a touch more confident.

"I can't believe I'm flying!" I said as we continued over the treetops.

"Neither can I," was Lucifer's sardonic reply.

"Your confidence in me is touching, Lou!"

"You're being sarcastic ... Well ... I guess it is your first time."

I took his words as an apology, unable to keep the grin from my face. Nothing was going to sap my joy at flying through the starlit sky.

Lights shone in the distance. "We're approaching the village."

"Skirt round it. We cannot be seen. There's enough damage limitation to be done once we return to the coven as it is!"

"Damage limitation?"

"Yes, you don't imagine that we can allow those men to spread the word about your powers, do you?"

"Well ... no! Oh, Lucifer, we can't let them spread the word!"

"Indeed. So, turn back to the coven. Mistress Loveday will have the answers."

However, I was in no mood to return home quite yet. "I'd rather practice a little more, Lou. This is fun!"

"How childish!"

Again, I ignored the jibe—flying was joyous!

I skirted the village as suggested and we travelled miles over open farmland until the land became thick with trees.

"We should turn back!" Lucifer's voice was querulous.

"Not yet," I said. I had relaxed enough to attempt a 'manoeuvre' and banked to the right. The broom tipped a little too far and Lucifer yowled with fright as he hung from my shoulder.

"Livitha!"

I rolled back, heart pounding. "Perhaps that is a little too advanced right now!"

"Just point it straight. On second thoughts, just gently circle until we're facing Haligern again. I want to get off."

Whoosh!

A blast of air buffeted against my side and once again the broom tipped. We were cast in shadow as the moon's light was blocked by a vast object flying overhead. Instinctively, I ducked. Berating myself for misjudging our height and hitting a flight path, I expected to see a plane overhead. Instead, what I saw made my innards curdle and a mewl of distress leak from my mouth. A huge gargoyle-like creature hovered above us. As I noticed a change in air pressure, the stars disappeared beneath a black veil of smog.

Chapter Twenty-Nine

I recognised the monster instantly. It was the gargoyle-like imp that had attacked me in the Black Woods.

The broom stalled as panic flooded my veins. We lost altitude and were suddenly free-falling through the sky. My mind was focused on the absence of light and the huge monster above me. All thoughts of flying were gone. The singsong of ancestral voices in my mind blocked.

"Livitha!" Lucifer screamed as we plummeted towards the earth.

Treetops loomed.

The creature dived beneath us then looped to hover over us. A foul stench of sulphuric rot filled my nostrils.

The top branches scratched against my hands and then we were crashing down, my body jarring and bouncing against the branches of an ancient fir.

I landed on a pile of pine needles that was surprisingly soft, but every bone in my body hurt and I lay stupefied by pain and shock, the beast temporarily forgotten. Rustling in the trees alerted me to something coming through the branches. I gasped with fright as Lucifer bounded from a branch and landed on my belly.

"Soft landing!" he panted and jumped down. "Surprisingly springy!"

I lay spreadeagled, amazed that I wasn't dead, mentally checking each limb. I curled my fingers with trepidation. They curled without a problem, apart from the usual stiffness of fifty-year-old joints. Next, I tried my toes. They wiggled. I hadn't broken my spine! My confidence grew as the seconds passed.

"You might want to hurry it up a bit, Livitha. Generally, people get up and run when they are being chased by an over-sized imp."

"Generally, people aren't expected to get up and run after they've just crashed to earth!" I retorted.

"Well, you might want to make the effort!" There was an insistent tone to Lucifer's voice I couldn't ignore. Nearby, branches cracked and split as the imp crashed through the trees. Darkness pushed away the moonlight that filtered into the woods.

I scrambled to my feet, crawling on all fours until I could push myself up. Breathless and with dull pain wracking my body, I followed Lucifer through the trees.

Light!

"Yes, that would be great!" I replied to the voice whispering in my mind.

Light the way.

Inspiration struck as the word was repeated. My hands had illuminated the forest when I had panicked as the men approached me. I could use the same energy to light my way through the forest. As I hobbled after Lucifer, I flicked my fingers, wincing at the ache in my joints. Sparks sputtered then my palm began to glow. White sparks fizzed and popped, and a ball of light formed.

"Hah!" I said in delight as the light hovered above my palm; this was a new trick I could show the aunts when I returned—if I returned! Light forced back the darkness and Lucifer's tail flicked in the distance as he followed a track. Behind me the imp thundered. I ran faster, expecting it to dig its claws into my back at any moment.

Breathless and with a stitch stabbing at my side, branches cracked and snapped as the creature thundered through the trees. Given the speed with which it could move, I was certain it was toying with me, much like I had seen Lucifer toy with a mouse. With the tiny creature caught, he would begin his game. The poor mouse would be slapped and thrown in the air. It would fall to the ground stunned, and Lucifer would watch as it regained its senses then pounce when it made a dash for freedom. He was a stone-cold killer and I had never seen him lose his quarry. Now I was the mouse - a 'little fat mouse' - hunted by the imp—its entertainment for the night.

There was no way I could outrun it.

I had to slow it down.

Inspiration struck.

I turned and threw the ball of light as though lobbing a Molotov cocktail. As it illuminated the forest, I saw two things: the imp and the huge wolf-like creature. Both stood on two legs, had mouths filled with dangerously sharp incisors, and both were staring directly at me.

Werewolf!

My mind refused to process the image—it was far too much like a scene from a horror movie to be real. My mind had detached from reality.

It's a bona-fide werewolf! Run!

In the next second, the imp sprang at me and the wolf launched an attack. Paralysed, I watched in horror as the wolf bit down into the demon's fur and fell with it to the ground. Shrieks and growls filled the air as the enemies fought again.

Werewolf! The word repeated in my disbelieving mind.

"Liv! This way!"

I followed Lucifer to a set of iron gates. Beyond them was a turreted gothic mansion—Blackwood Manor.

The main entrance to the house was through a large stone-built porch, but although light shone from the stone mullioned window to the left, its door was hidden in shadow. Only two more rooms had lights on, one on the second floor and another in one of the turrets. To the front of the house a large turning circle was laid to gravel with a circular lawn at its centre. A statue stood on a pedestal within the lawn, but in the poor light I couldn't discern its shape. Most of the house and grounds was hidden in the night, but I imagined a large formal garden to the rear hedged in by the Black Woods. Like the woodlands around Haligern, the Black Woods stretched for miles, but unlike Haligern these were dangerous, infested with imps and – it felt ridiculous to think the word – werewolves! A low growl that sank into my bones reminded me of their presence. I had to get to the house!

A padlock secured the gates and despite my efforts to push them open, the gap allowed by the chain was far too narrow for me to squeeze through. Lucifer stood beside me watching my efforts with impatience. "Come on, Livitha! They'll be here any minute!" Lucifer was right, whichever beast was defeated we were sure to be hunted by the victor. My life depended on getting into Blackwood Manor. I had only one option—to go over the top of the gates. As I stepped on an iron cross bar and pulled myself up, the gate clinked, and Lucifer sauntered to stand opposite me on the other side of the gate. "How did you get through?"

"I walked. There's a gate to the side." He gestured to an opening, a smaller gate within the larger one. With the snapping of branches and thunder of paws growing louder, I jumped through the open gate and sprinted to the house. As I reached the door a howl pierced the night. Behind the gates, with its claws wrapped around the iron rods, stood the werewolf. Glowing amber eyes seemed to be watching me! I turned to the door and rapped on it harder than I had ever done in my life.

"Help!"

Chapter Thirty

E xcruciating minutes passed before the door began to open and, as a young man's face appeared, I squeezed through the gap and threw myself into the lobby.

"Close the door!" I panted. "Close the door! There's a ... something chasing me!"

Without any hint of surprise, the man closed the door, asked me to wait, then disappeared.

I bolted the door for security as he left the reception hall. "Well, he must be an incredibly professional butler, or ... or a braindead zombie!" I quipped, astounded by his lack of curiosity. Lucifer didn't reply and I quickly scanned the room; he wasn't in the lobby! "Lucifer!" I hesitated for a second, then unbolted the door. "Lucifer!" I called, but he didn't appear and when I heard footsteps approaching, I quietly shut the door and took my place at the centre of the lobby. The young man reappeared.

"Follow me. The Professor would like to speak to you."

I felt as though I were being summoned to the headmaster's office and followed meekly. The professor sat dwarfed by an enormous desk piled with books that rose above his head. A lower pile of books at its centre was illuminated by a bright desk lamp. On the wall behind me was a hunting trophy—the stuffed and mounted head of a stag with magnificent antlers.

He held an oversized magnifying glass in one hand and raised his head to greet me as I was shown into his office. He threw me a questioning but friendly smile.

"Patrick tells me that you've had some problems."

I barely heard him as I noticed the book he was reading. Its leaves were thick, its leather binding a wraparound style. Thongs tipped with silver beads were laid across the desk. On the open pages were runic inscriptions and outline drawings of strange animals. It was Arthur!

"Miss? Are you alright?"

The professor's voice broke through my thoughts. Kindly eyes peered out from behind horn-rimmed glasses, but a deep scar puckered the skin along his left cheek giving him a slightly lopsided appearance. The scar, faded with time, ran into the abundant white whiskers of enormous lambchop sideburns and a moustache to match.

It was then that I noticed his peculiar hands – slender fingers wrinkled with time, ended in long, slightly hooked nails. There was more than a passing resemblance to claws. A gold ring with a black tree on its square face sat on the small finger of his right hand.

He coughed. "My dear, are you alright?" He repeated.

"I- ... Yes! Sorry! I didn't mean to be rude. It has been quite a night!"

"So Patrick informs me."

"I'm so sorry to barge in! So sorry, but there was something chasing me through the woods. I saw the lights ..."

He chuckled.

Was he insane? "Well," he said placing the magnifying glass on the table and rising from his seat. "We shall have to investigate then."

"No! We can't! It was vicious!"

"But if there's someone in the woods, we should call the police!"

His reaction confused me; he made no indication of concern. "It wasn't someone, but some *thing*!"

"Did it by any chance stand on two legs—this beast?"

"Yes! Yes, it did!" So, he knew about the werewolf!

"And did it have eyes that glowed orange?"

"It did! So, you've seen it too?"

"Indeed, I have."

"So, you know how dangerous it is!"

He chuckled again and removed his glasses, peered at me, then replaced them. "I'm sorry, I didn't catch your name. I'm Professor Fenicke, but you can call me Toby."

Not Blackwood? I hid my confusion. "Hi, Toby," I stumbled. "I'm Livitha Carl- ... Erikson." It seemed odd to introduce myself using my maiden name, but also satisfying. It was also a mistake.

A flicker of more than surprise flitted over his eyes and the kindliness dimmed. "Of the Haligern Erikson's."

It was my turn to be surprised. "... I guess so."

"So, you are Soren's daughter?"

"Yes! Did you know him?"

"Only by reputation."

By reputation? What did that mean? I knew so little about my parents and wanted to ask this man everything he knew about my father, but he brushed at the air as though fobbing off my thoughts and instead of clarifying his statement offered me a broad smile. The sight of his teeth was enough to dislodge my train of thought. Like his nails, his teeth were overly long, and the canines slightly pointed. I began to wonder if I had wandered into a den, and the follicles at the nape of my neck prickled as the hairs stood on end.

"Well, Livitha. I have a confession to make."

Oh, heck! Was he going to admit to being some supernatural being, perhaps even a werewolf! He certainly looked like he could transmogrify into one.

"The dog-like creature that you saw was a werewolf."

He was! My heart pounded. *Maybe a pack lived here!* My entire scalp shifted. Was I in even more danger inside the house than out? My mind flooded with questions as he watched me react to his statement. I think I staggered a little because Patrick grabbed my elbow. I flinched at his touch. Did the forest hide a pack of werewolves? Was that the Blackwood curse? But this man wasn't a Blackwood, so-

"Now, don't be shocked. It was Hector that you saw."

"Is he cursed?" I tugged my elbow free.

"Cursed?" He laughed. "Oh, you mean does he carry the werewolf curse?"

I nodded.

"No, no. I think that is only for the cinema. Hector is one of my staff. He was wearing a suit."

"The werewolf didn't have a suit on!"

"No, no! Hector was dressed up as a werewolf."

"Dressed up?"

"Yes, he was wearing a costume; a werewolf costume."

I had a vague recollection of Pascal laughing at my absolute confusion when he told me about people he'd called 'furries' who liked to wear costumes and participate in *adult* activities and I mean 'adult' in the context you wouldn't want to type into your browser! My confusion increased. "Why was he ... dressed up?" I asked tentatively, bracing myself for the answer.

"You didn't think it was a real werewolf, did you?"

"Well ..."

"Oh, my dear girl!" The chuckle deepened to a laugh and tears pricked his eyes. I had obviously amused him. "It's my turn to apologise, then."

"But what on earth is he doing out at night dressed as a werewolf?"

"It was his idea. We've had some trouble recently – several attempted break-ins – and he thought that if he patrolled the perimeter dressed as a werewolf then he would protect the property and scare the trespassers half to death so that they wouldn't return. We're very isolated here. It is both a blessing and a curse."

"Well, that's a relief!"

He threw me a frown. "A relief that we're being targeted by thieves?"

"No! No, of course not. I meant ... I meant that it was a relief that he dresses up to scare people."

"Yes, it is. We had a wonderful Hallowe'en party last year and Hector said he wanted to get his money's worth out of the costume, so I agreed to the prank."

The werewolf had looked so real! It had fought with the imp!

"So, as I said ... there's really nothing to worry about. Just Hector, being Hector ..."

I struggled with the story Professor Fenicke was telling me and the vicious fight I had seen in the woods. My mind whirled. Did it mean that the demon was a fake too? When I didn't respond immediately, the professor narrowed his eyes.

"So, what exactly are you doing in the woods at this time of night?"

Trespassing!

"How did you get here? We're quite a way from the road."

Well, you won't believe it, but I flew here—on a plastic broom! "I ... my car broke down and I thought I'd take a short-cut through the woods."

"You don't have a telephone to call for assistance?" He watched me closely.

Heart tripping as the professor's suspicion began to show itself, I was impressed with how fluidly I came up with an explanation. I was becoming quicker at dodging difficult questions and, with this one, I could verify the claim. "Flat! The battery's dead. I should have charged it up this morning, but I forgot." I pulled the mobile from my pocket as I rambled on about what a dinosaur I was with technology. Holding up the mobile, I pressed the on switch to prove that the battery was dead, thankful for the first time that I had forgotten to put it on charge.

He chuckled again. "It seems that we have that in common, Livitha Erikson. I have only just caught up with the facsimile."

My confusion cleared as I realized he meant a fax machine. In the early years of my marriage, Pascal had purchased one for the home office and it would spew out typed messages from various colleagues across the world but, like our early stereo system that played cassettes, and the next one that played CDs, it now sat gathering dust in the garage. Technology moved so quickly these days it was hard to keep up and I empathised with the elderly man.

Somewhere in the house a door closed, and footsteps could be heard walking along a corridor.

"Now," the professor said turning off the table lamp. "I think some refreshments are in order and then we must find you a room for the night."

"That's very kind, but-"

"No, no. I won't hear it." He flapped his hand at me. "We have plenty of room here. You're more than welcome to stay."

"Well … I really don't want to inconvenience you any further!" In part I was elated to be invited to stay the night as it gave me an opportunity to rescue Arthur and search for Agnes. On the other hand, I was terrified; there was something deeply peculiar and rather ominous about the professor.

"You can't go out into the woods at this time of night, my dear. It's much too late."

"Perhaps Hector could see me to my car?" The suggestion was a gamble; there was no car!

"I doubt you'd find it in the dark. No," he said with confidence. "You shall stay here as my guest tonight. In the morning, we'll find your car and then call for assistance."

"I don't want to put you out …"

"You won't be."

"Perhaps I should go."

"I think you should stay."

There was an edge of menace in the coldness of his eyes despite an indulgent smile.

"Now, Patrick will show you to a comfortable sitting room whilst Mathilda prepares your room."

Patrick showed me into a room with sofas and an open fire and then I was left alone. A huge marble fireplace sat beneath an enormous gilt mirror. Pieces of elaborately crafted, flower-adorned Rococo vases, which I was sure were Dresden, sat either side of the mirror. An enormous Persian rug was laid over wide oak floorboards. Armchairs deep enough to keep out the draft, and hide their inhabitants, sat either side of the fire whilst a long, cushion-scattered sofa sat before the fire. The overall effect was of faded opulence, the room warm and inviting. However, unable to shake my unease, I perched on the edge of the sofa and waited for the professor to return.

When the door finally opened, I was surprised to see a young woman. I felt a tinge of guilt at her appearance: a forced smile didn't reach her eyes and her ponytail was less than smooth. It was obvious she had been woken and forced to serve me. As she placed the tray of teacup, teapot, milk jug, and plate of biscuits on the table at my side, I scrutinised her face and compared it with the photograph of Agnes. There were similarities, but it wasn't Agnes. She left without speaking and I noticed the time on the clock; five minutes past one—no wonder she seemed annoyed!

More uncomfortable than ever, my imagination took flight and in my mind the professor morphed into the werewolf in the woods, albeit with white hair and horn-rimmed spectacles! I took a chocolate digestive from the plate and ate it in two bites. Minutes passed. The ticking grew louder and, sure that

Blackwood Manor wasn't the refuge I had hoped, my unease grew.

Noise from outside caught my attention and I turned with another biscuit caught between my teeth to see Lucifer's face pushed up against the window just as the door opened and Patrick stepped back into the room. The biscuit broke, landing with a plop into my teacup.

"Your room is ready. Follow me, please."

Chapter Thirty-One

I waited half an hour in the guest bedroom before deciding to return to the professor's study and rescue Arthur and had begun to open the door when Lucifer scratched on the bedroom window. He darted through the gap as I opened the window and paced the room, tail swishing.

"Well!" he exclaimed.

"Well?"

"I've had to wait outside for more than an hour!"

"But you're used to being outside."

"I am not in the habit of being made to wait!"

"You're not in the habit of being patient more like."

"Pshht!"

"Oh, Lou. Don't be so grumpy."

He huffed then said, "So, Miss Marple, what's the plan?"

I ignored his jibe. "Arthur is here, and I think Agnes is too. We have to get them out."

"We?"

"Yes, Lucifer, we!"

I tiptoed to the door.

"There's no one there!"

"There might be!"

"There isn't. I can hear a mouse breathing ..."

I ignored Lucifer's arrogance and restrained myself from reminding him of when Mrs. Babcock had managed to startle him into becoming a mouse and hiding in my pocket.

"Let's go," I whispered and opened the door. Dim light shone in the long corridor from a lamp at the far end. Most of the space was cast in shadow and, after a quick check either side, I stepped out of the bedroom. Lucifer trotted beside me.

"Is there anything I can help you with?"

I leapt three feet from the hot breath at my neck.

"I'm sorry, I didn't mean to startle you." The young man from the foyer stood beside my door.

"Where did you come from?" I gasped. So much for Lucifer hearing a mouse breathe!

"Can I help you?"

Yes, you can disappear and let me get on with searching the house! "I was thirsty and was hoping I could get a glass of water."

"I'll bring you one."

"I don't want to put you out!"

"This is an old house with many corridors. It's a labyrinth. Professor Fenicke doesn't like us roaming around at night. Some of the staircases are a little rickety and if you should have an accident ..."

"I'm sure I'll be fine."

"Just wait in your room ... please."

It took more than twenty minutes for the man to return with a glass of water and when he did it was with a suggestion that I stay in my room as there had been intruders recently and one of the staff had been hurt when he had discovered them in a downstairs room. I wasn't convinced he was telling the truth.

Like the rotten staircase, it was just a convenient story to keep me in my room.

Determined to get back into the professor's study and rescue Arthur, I waited another half an hour then made a second attempt to leave. The man sat in a chair a little further down the corridor. His head was nodding but he flinched as I opened the door. I closed the door and paced the room.

"Can't you just go to sleep. Everything will look better in the morning."

"I can't just go to sleep, Lou. I have to get Arthur back and find Agnes! For one thing, Arthur is the coven's most important possession and in the wrong hands it is dangerous. And, if I can't get that baby fairy back then my life will be hellish! Those fairies will taunt me for the rest of my life!"

"Pooh! I doubt it."

"Well, I can't stand another night of them filming me whilst I sleep. Did you know that they sent the video to Pascal?"

Lucifer emitted a joyous snort. "Indeed, I do," he said. "You've whinged about it enough times."

I huffed then sat down on the bed, irked by his attitude. "You could be a little more supportive, Lucifer. Afterall, you are my familiar. It's your job!"

"Indeed."

He curled up beside my thigh. "Wake me at daylight. It's time for a nap."

"Lou!"

"Daylight, Livitha!"

With that I picked him up and placed him on the floor. He made an irritated yowl. "This is no time for being difficult.

What am I supposed to do? I have to get Arthur back and there's a man standing guard outside my room."

"He's sitting."

"Okay, he's sitting, but he's still there guarding me."

"He was asleep."

"He woke up when I opened the door."

"Well, Livitha, make sure he doesn't wake up when you open the door."

"And just how am I supposed to do that?"

He let out a sigh of resignation. "You're the witch, Livitha. Do something witchy!"

"Something witchy?"

"Yes, something witchy such as ... oh, I don't know ... a sleeping spell perhaps?"

"But I don't know sleeping spells. I haven't been taught any yet."

"Tsk! Your education is certainly lacking ... Listen, it pains me to say this, but you have within you great powers and sometimes knowing an exact spell isn't necessary. You must draw the magick from within yourself. For heaven's sake woman, you wake most mornings with your fingers sparking and your bedclothes ruined by stray embers! You're a powerful witch, Livitha – it's the only reason I bother to stick around as one day the kudos of being your familiar will be worth it! Step up to the mark and be the witch you are meant to be!"

"Well ..."

"No 'wells'. Go out into that corridor and make that guard sleep until daylight. Cast a spell so strong that he couldn't wake if an earthquake hit the place."

"That would be a little dangerous! I mean, he couldn't escape."

"Oh, for Thor's sake!" With that, Lucifer disappeared, and the door opened. "Out here now!" he demanded from the corridor.

I stared in surprise. "You can disappear and reappear?"

"Of course! How else do I get to the other realm?"

Another layer of the onion of my new life was prising open and I marvelled at the mysteries and secrets I had yet to be allowed to have knowledge of.

"When we get back to Haligern, you have to tell me all about the other realm."

"Just focus, Livitha! He's waking up."

I stumbled out into the corridor, pushed by an invisible force, and faced the man.

"Up again?" the man said with a less than friendly voice.

I channelled my inner witch and as green light filled the corridor, he staggered backwards, his eyelids drooping. As they closed, his head lolled, and an invisible force lifted him to his chair and sat him down. The green light faded, and a loud snore filled the space.

"He's out cold!"

"What did you expect?"

How about well done? "Okay," I said, ignoring Lucifer's lack of praise. "Let's go!"

With Lucifer at my heels, I retraced my steps to the lobby then made my way to the professor's study.

Chapter Thirty-Two

Light shone from the lamp illuminating the books on the professor's desk and my hope failed. "It's gone, Lou! It's not here." The book that I was certain was Arthur was nowhere on the desk and a search on the shelves and in the drawers had drawn a blank too.

"What did you expect?"

"I had hoped Arthur would still be here."

"Because thieves generally leave out their stolen goods for all to see!"

"What did you say?"

"Thieves-"

"That's it! Someone else is after Arthur! The professor and the man upstairs mentioned that they'd had trouble with intruders recently. He even had someone dress up as a werewolf to scare them off."

"That's a lie."

"Pardon?"

"That he dressed up as a werewolf. That's a lie."

I had thought so too, so was interested in what Lucifer had to say. "I didn't believe it either. What makes you certain?"

"The smell. It was definitely a werewolf. They have a certain pungent ... aroma."

"I did notice a whiff."

"They're smelly beasts, that's for certain. The imp also stinks!"

"I noticed the imp—sulphuric," I grimaced.

"Brimstone."

"Brimstone?"

"Yes, any creature conjured from the dark realm stinks of brimstone."

"But the werewolf ... he didn't stink of brimstone. It was a different smell."

"It was," Lucifer agreed without elaboration.

"So, you don't think that the man - Hector - dressed up as a werewolf?"

"Well, I suppose it is possible that he did, although the werewolf we encountered was genuine—a bona fide lycanthrope of the cursed variety."

"A lycanthrope of the cursed variety?"

"Tsk! So *many* questions." He sighed. "Yes, a shapeshifter. A human with the ability to transmogrify into a wolf-like creature although likening them to wolves isn't really fair on the wolf—they are majestic beasts. A lycanthrope is something else—a vicious, often wasteful, hunter. Often, the lycanthrope will hunt to kill and not just eat, although they do acquire a ravenous appetite after the process of transmogrification. It is a very energy-greedy process."

I turned to Lucifer in surprise, fascinated by his knowledge. "You know an awful lot about werewolves."

"I do." His eyes glowed and he sat in majesty on the professor's desk. "So, Livitha, you believe that someone else is searching for Arthur? Someone who doesn't consider this manor their abode?"

"Yes, I do."

"And do you think that they have already found him, hence his disappearance from this room?"

I searched the room. Nothing was out of place. No windows were open. "There's no evidence that anyone has broken in—at least not tonight, so I would say that the professor has put the book away."

"Under lock and key, perhaps?" Lucifer remained on the desk, licked a paw, rubbed it behind his ear, then returned his gaze to me. "Hmm?"

"Yes, I'm sure you're right. Under lock and key." I scanned the room. One wall was filled from floor to ceiling with books. Another wall was dominated by a stone mullioned window. On either side of this were cupboards each with keys. I quickly checked through them. Arthur was not among the possessions inside. Lucifer remained on the table watching my efforts. "Aren't you going to help?" I asked as he remained sat.

"I've already helped enough."

"Oh, really?"

"Yes, you wouldn't have thought to look in the cupboards if I hadn't suggested it."

I shook my head and bit my tongue and spent the next minutes checking each cupboard and possible space that the book could be.

"I can't find him!"

"There is another way."

"Oh?" I turned to Lucifer.

"Yes. Arthur is more than a book. He is a grimoire."

I nodded. He was indeed a grimoire.

"He is full of ancient spells, charms, hexes, and witchy knowledge."

"He is ... but how is that going to help me find him."

"Well, he has a voice. Mistress Loveday couldn't hear him call because he was too far away, or because he was being blocked by a sinister force. It's just a theory, but perhaps you can hear him—now that we're so close?"

Hear Arthur? "Well ... I'm not sure how to 'talk' to him."

"You don't have to talk to him, just listen."

"Like a tracking device."

"I'm not sure what a tracking device is, but when I'm hunting, I can follow a scent, perhaps you can follow the scent of his magick?"

"Hmm, I guess, although I have no idea what to sniff for."

"Not sniffing! Listening."

"Okay, but I have no idea what to listen for."

"I think you'll know when you hear it."

Outside, a wolf howled. I shivered. Moonlight glinted in Lucifer's eyes and then a shadow blocked out the light. Something had passed across the study window. I ducked below the desk. Lucifer sat as a statue. With his eyes closed he disappeared into the shadows.

"Has it gone?"

"No!" he hissed.

"Tell me when it has." I squatted beside the desk until my thighs began to burn and just as I could bear it no longer, moonlight brightened the room.

"What was it?"

"The werewolf."

"The fake one?"

"No, the real one."

Real fear washed through me then. The werewolf I had seen in the forest had been huge and vicious, its talons capable of ripping through doors. "What if it comes in?"

I expected Lucifer to offer soothing reassurance, instead he said, "Then it could eat us."

"That's it? That's your advice?"

"What did you expect?"

"I ... don't' say that again, Lou! You're being extremely annoying tonight. Please, help me find Arthur, and then let's get out of here."

"And Agnes."

"I'll settle for Arthur right now."

"I would advise waiting until daylight."

"Sure," I said, completely accepting this advice—there was no way I was stepping foot outside the house until dawn.

With frequent glances at the window and my ears tuned in to any untoward noise, I resumed my search of the study. I tried to tune into Arthur's magical soundwaves, but again came up with nothing. "I know he's in this house, Arthur—somewhere. We have to find him."

"If it were me, and I had a stolen possession someone else wanted to steal, particularly one with magical powers, then I'd keep it close—very close. In fact, I'd sleep on it."

"Sleep on it? Do you think the professor is actually sleeping on it?"

"I do. I bet he has it under his pillow."

"Under his pillow?"

"So many questions! Yes, Livitha, under his pillow. It's time for you to play tooth fairy!" He snorted at this joke but not without a nervous glance at the window. "Come along. When we find the professor, we will find Arthur, I am sure."

Chapter Thirty-Three

The house was vast with several wings adjoining the main building and I had no idea where to begin my search for the professor's bedroom. I remembered that one of the turrets had lights shining from the windows when we first arrived, so I decided to begin my search there. After several moments of orientating myself, I set off with a reasonable amount of certainty that the turret was through a door to the left.

The door led to a corridor which led to another set of stairs which took us to the second floor. A quick look out of the window on the landing confirmed that we were close to the turret and taking the next two returns on the staircase brought us out onto a landing and the entrance to the turreted wing of the house. In my memory, the floor with the lights had been the second. "This is it, Lucifer."

"Open the door then," he replied with impatience.

"I'm going to."

"Tooth fairies are as light as feathers. You may have trouble."

Ignoring his jibe at my overly generous figure, I placed a hand on the doorhandle.

"They're too light to make the floorboards creak, so ..."

"I can do this, Lucifer!"

"Just saying ..."

Shaking my head and again biting back a retort, I opened the door. A bed sat in central place, but it was unmade. I closed the door with a gentle click and moved across the floor to try the other door. Again, the room was dark and empty. "It must be the next floor," I said, gesturing to the stairs. We climbed again. The stairs hugged the side of the turret, spiralling to the next level. On this floor there was only one door. Moonlight brightened the space showing my footprints and Lucifer's paw-prints on the dusty floorboards. The door opened into a room lit only by moonlight. The floor was uncarpeted, the walls pan-elled in dark wood, and a bed with four massive bedposts dom-inated the room. To its side was a throne-like chair. Unlike a four-poster bed, the bedposts weren't topped by a curtain rail, nor were they intricately carved or pleasantly shaped. They were more like gateposts and stood at least six foot high.

I stepped inside, mesmerised.

With growing unease, I noticed the heavy rings bolted on-to the bed's posts. The chair was fitted with shackles. The shack-les were constructed of a padded leather band topped by a met-al cuff. Once strapped in, it would be impossible to escape. My guts gave a queasy flip. I had walked into a chamber of torture!

"I think we should leave." Lucifer's voice was uncharacter-istically fearful.

"What is this place?"

"I don't know, but I don't like it."

Neither did I. The place had an unnerving energy, not black, but dark. Rage and pain had festered here. I turned to scoop Lucifer into my arms, needing to feel the comfort of his being, and noticed the damaged panelling. The wainscotting had been scored in great arcs. In places it was splintered and in others gouged down to the bricks. The damage had been done with incredible and destructive force.

Outside, a howl pierced the night.

I left the room, closing the door fast behind me and hurried down the stairs with my lightest step, forcing myself not to run.

Back on the landing of the west wing, I stopped to gather my breath, horrified by the images that filled my mind. Someone had been hurt in that room!

Afraid of being in the house more than ever, I was no closer to finding Arthur.

I checked my watch. "We're going to run out of time," I said, forcing thoughts of the room out of my mind. "Come on!" Without waiting for a response, I focused my efforts on finding the professor, checking behind each door with caution. Half an hour later, I had discovered another two guests and, as my watch ticked over to three am, I found Agnes.

Before waking her, I drew the curtains to let in the moonlight, but there was no sign of the larval fairy.

"Agnes!" I hissed prodding the sleeping girl's shoulder. "Agnes!"

She woke slowly. This surprised me. If a stranger had prodded my shoulder in the middle of the night I would have flown out of bed in fright, and these days probably lit the room ablaze with sparks of energy. As I'd prowled the corridors, particularly after hearing the wolf's howl, it had taken enormous willpower to keep the fizzing in my fingers under any kind of control. Fear nibbled continually at my resilience. "Agnes!" I tried again. This time she rolled towards me.

"Mrs Carlton? Is that you?"

Impressed that she recognised my voice I agreed that it was
indeed I. "It is Agnes. I've come to ..." I had to choose my words
carefully, sure that if I said I'd come to take her home she would
resist. "You're in danger, Agnes. I've come to help."

"Help?" she said slowly. "Danger?"

She didn't seem to comprehend my words and I wondered
if she had been drugged. "Agnes, are you alright?"

"I'm not sure," she said dully. "I'm tired."

"Yes, I know, but you have to wake up. Agnes ... where is
the book?"

"Oh, for heaven's sake!" In the next moment Lucifer
jumped onto Agnes' belly. She yelped and I placed my hand
across her mouth before she had a chance to scream.

"Sorry!" I said as she squirmed. "Lucifer! Get off her. I'm
sorry, Agnes, but please be quiet!"

With my free hand I plucked Lucifer from the bed. With
claws extended he brought the bedclothes with him. Agnes immediately clutched at her belly.

"He stabbed me!"

"Did not!"

"Lucifer!"

"Well, it worked didn't it," he said without remorse.

And it had. Agnes now appeared fully awake, the shot of
adrenaline coursing through her veins had done the job. Lucifer's method was unorthodox, perhaps a little cruel, and I
didn't approve, but Agnes now gave us her full attention.

"What are you doing here?"

"You're in trouble, we've come to take you home."

At this she burst into tears. I was taken aback. I had expected the response of a sullen teenager refusing to leave a party. I

slipped an arm across her shoulder, guilt sliding across me as I noticed the tiny pinpricks of blood on her nightshirt. One of the cartoon-like sheep now had a blood-spotted fleece.

"But you can't! He won't let me leave! He won't let any of us leave."

"Who? The professor?"

She nodded her head vociferously, sniffed, then wiped her eyes with the bedclothes. "The book changed everything!"

Arthur! "Listen, I need you to get dressed. We have to find the book-"

At this she shook her head and pulled at the bedclothes. Why was she so afraid?

"What happened—with the book? Why did 'everything' change?"

"Mrs. Carlton, I'm so sorry! It's all my fault. I took the book. And now he won't let us leave." She began to sob again, and my patience thinned.

"Agnes, we can talk about who is at fault later. Right now, we have to find the book and take it back to Haligern. We can make everything right if we have the book. Do you understand?"

She nodded caught my gaze then shook her head. "He changed, Mrs. Carlton. The book changed him."

"How did the book change the professor?"

"He was so nice before. We had such great discussions. He's a history professor, well, a medievalist with a special interest in paganism and he was so full of knowledge—so interesting, and I wanted to know more ... and then I told him about the book in your aunts' house. He was really interested and asked me to take some photos of it, but ... but I took it instead and then ...

then I had it in the forest and we ... everything changed!" She sobbed into her blanket.

"Agnes, please ... you made a mistake but if we get the book back, we can fix it. You just need to tell me where it is."

Her sob intensified until she gasped for breath and said, "I can't! He'll turn the demon on us if we say a word!" She began to tremble.

"Oh, get some backbone, girl!"

"Lucifer! She's scared."

Agnes stared at me. "Did you just talk to the cat?"

"I guess. He's-"

"Your familiar!" She said this with the joy of revelation.

"Erm ..."

"I knew it! I told my mum you were all witches, but she wouldn't believe me. That book is a grimoire, isn't it! A real one!"

I remembered the sworn oath of my initiation. No one outside the coven was to be enlightened as to our witchy status. "Erm ... I'm not sure. It is valuable though, so we need to get it back and I do know someone who could help with the ... demon problem."

Agnes threw back the bedclothes and stood to face me. All fear seemed to have disappeared. "If you're a witch, then you can help me ... us, escape this place!"

I didn't want to burst her bubble so went along with her assumption. Perhaps there was a spell to cause memory loss. Could a wand do that? It would be useful to have a device like Will Smith's gizmo in 'Men in Black'—all memory of the incident completely forgotten and our witchy status secret yet again. At this point the entire village would need a dose of it though. It was something I would have to broach with my aunts as soon as possible.

"Do you know where the book is?"

She nodded. "Yes, it's in his bedroom."

"Hah! I told you so."

I ignored Lucifer.

"Why does it keep yowling like that. It's freaky."

"Huh!" Lucifer tapped his tail on the floor with annoyance. "How very dare she!"

Again, I ignored him. "Oh, it's just the way he meows. He's always been like that."

"He's talking to you!"

"No," I lied. "He probably just wants to go pee."

"How very dare you, Livitha Winifred-"

"Or catch a rat," I said picking him up. "He likes catching rats."

At this Lucifer hissed and sprang out of my arms. "Just wait until we get home and I have a chat with your fairy friends!" he threatened. "That will teach you some manners!"

"The fairy! Of course. Agnes, where is the ... creature you took from the house?"

"You know about it?"

"Yes. Your mother told us that you had a creature that you were convinced was a fairy."

"It is! It is exactly like the creature drawn in the book—your grimoire. It even has fairy written beside it in Anglo Saxon."

"You read Anglo Saxon?"

"Yes, well, a bit. And the professor confirmed it."

"So ... where is it?"

"He took that too."

"In his bedroom?" I asked with hope.

"Yes. I don't think he trusts us, and then there have been the break-ins, so he takes them with him to bed."

"Hah! I told you," Lucifer crowed. "He's keeping them close. Time to do your tooth fairy bit." He swished his tail then trotted to the door and began to scratch at the wood. "Let's go. I want to get out of this place. It's beginning to give me the creeps."

"Show me the way to the bedroom, Agnes."

Chapter Thirty-Four

Minutes later we stood outside the professor's bedroom. A light shone from beneath the heavy door.

"This is it," Agnes whispered. "What if he's awake!" She gripped my arm.

"I'll pretend I'm sleep-walking," I could think of no other excuse as to why I would be opening the professor's door in the dead of night.

"But you're fully dressed!" Agnes complained.

"I'll make sure he doesn't see me!" I whispered, unpeeling her fingers from my jacket. I held the doorhandle down and opened it slowly, listening intently for any sign that the professor was awake. The door eased open until a bedside table, and then the bed, along with the professor, came into view. A loud snort confirmed that he was fast asleep and to my joy a large, leatherbound, and ancient book, lay open across his belly. *Arthur!* On the bedside table, beside the lamp, was the hurricane lamp in which the professor now kept the larval fairy. I shut the door and stepped back.

"He's in there!" I said, in whispered triumph.

I relived the scene I had glimpsed. The professor's bed, a large and curtained four-poster, dominated the room and was flanked by bedside tables. Heavy curtains, hanging from an oversized pole, covered the window and reached the floor. If the professor awoke whilst I searched the room, I could hide behind them or drop to the floor beside the bed, which was exceptionally large and high. Somehow, the horror of the evening had boosted my courage. I now had no doubt that retrieving Arthur was crucial to the safety of Haligern coven and it was with absolute determination that I re-opened the door and stepped inside. If the professor awoke, he would be put back to sleep with a spell. My confidence buzzed and I felt the now familiar heat grow in my belly and the tingle in my fingers fizz.

I left the door ajar, focused on the professor, and stepped up to the bed. Glasses on the bedside table glinted beneath the lamp. One arm dangled over the side of the bed, the other lay at the edge of Arthur's open pages. A thumb rested on the leather flap and leather thongs with silver beads were threaded through the professor's fingers.

I debated whether I should cast a spell on him now but was unsure if it would work. The man outside my door had been conscious so could hear my voice, the professor was not. Instinct told me that my magick wouldn't work on someone who was deaf to me. I took another step forward and switched off the lamp. He snorted. I froze. He snuffled. I waited. Seconds past and I began to move Arthur, excruciatingly aware of the professor's rotund belly rising and falling beneath my fingers. There was no way I could explain away my presence if he awoke. Hands trembling, I lifted the book. It was surprisingly heavy, and I had to lower it again, making a second attempt using both hands. By now I was hovering over the professor's middle. As I lifted the book, the leather thongs began to slide through his fingers. He twitched, mumbled, then shifted in bed, rolling over to the side. To my horror the thongs pulled against the book. Pain began to spread through my lower back as I strained over the professor to keep the leather thongs loose against his hand. I gave a gentle tug. The thongs were stuck fast. The professor mumbled again, shouted 'Not her!', then began to grind his teeth. The pain in my back was becoming unbearable and I was about to lay the book back down and admit defeat when a tap at the window was followed by a howl. My heart thumped. The professor sat bolt upright. I dropped beside the bed. The thong came free and I clutched Arthur to my breast.

Throwing back the bedcovers the professor strode to the window, flung one curtain aside, pulled the window closed, locked the clasp, and returned to bed. To my immense relief he quickly fell into a deep sleep and I made a quiet, but triumphant, retreat from the room; I had Arthur and the fairy. Now all we had to do was get home!

Chapter Thirty-Five

We stayed in the house until dawn, waiting in the kitchen and plotting our escape, ready to slip into the pantry if anyone discovered us. Our route to freedom would not be easy. Leaving from the kitchen door, we would make our way to the front of the house where a generous turning circle joined a short driveway beyond which were the huge iron gates. Once through them we had to trek the long track that cut through the woodland and eventually joined the road back to civilisation. From the kitchen to the gates we would be easily seen, but with its psychotic gargoyles and vicious werewolves, I didn't want to risk going into the wider forest.

As Night gave way to grey light, and the shadows receded, we ran from Blackwood Manor. Lucifer sprinted ahead, easily reaching the gates with Agnes close behind holding the fairy in its jar. I was much slower and quickly breathless, but with Arthur tucked under my arm, I focused on the gate and ignored the growing stitch in my side.

As I reached midway, the front door slammed and a man's voice erupted in a tumble of angry, indecipherable, words. I refused to look back, but within seconds I stopped dead in my tracks.

A bank of dark and rolling clouds was smothering the woodland beyond the gate.

Agnes and Lucifer stared at the house. As sound became muffled and the air pressure around me intensified, I turned to look.

On the steps, his arms wide open as though in supplication, the professor bellowed an incantation. His face puce with effort, his words were unclear in the strange and oppressive atmosphere that surrounded us.

"Agnes, Lucifer!" I shouted as the charcoal bank of rolling fog swallowed the trees and gate. "Come to me! Run!" Both sprinted to my side and we stood together as the fog advanced.

"Is it smoke? Is the forest on fire?" Agnes stepped behind me as the fog rolled a little closer.

"I can't smell smoke."

As it billowed towards us a stench of sulphur seeped into the air and a solid mass became evident beneath the dark particles of smoke-like fog. It drew close and the fog thinned to reveal a membrane of glistening tissue. Veins crawled across the membrane, joining in an intricate web tracking across its surface, throbbing as though pumping blood, as they connected.

"That is revolting!"

Lucifer mewled and slinked between my ankles. "Do something, Liv!"

"But what? I don't even know what it is."

"This is the professor's work. He is conjuring a demon. A demon!" He mewled again and pushed up against my leg.

Agnes squealed and gripped my arm in a painful pinch as something hard and angular pushed from within the membrane.

The membrane stretched until a gnarled fist became visible.

Agnes screamed as a pig-like snout with long and bowed fangs appeared. "It's a monster! Save us, Liv!" She held me in front of her like a shield.

The membrane stretched and thinned.

I focused on my core, willing it to heat up, but a pair of red eyes stared directly at me from behind the thinning membrane, and malevolent energy pulsed from the creature, rolling over me in waves. Queasiness roiled in the pit of my stomach and I gagged as my energy sapped. Arthur began to slip from my grasp.

Behind me, the professor continued to chant.

The demon's growl became audible.

Behind the thinning membrane a thousand evil creatures waited.

I had a moment of clarity; this was the dark realm I had witnessed during my initiation, and I had only seconds to act before the fabric was rent and a gateway opened from that evil place into our world.

Ignoring the rising nausea in my belly, I turned my attention to the professor.

Face red with effort, his hands were pressed to his temples, his eyes tight shut in concentration. He continued to recite the conjuring spell. It was just as Loveday had seen in the runes, only this time it appeared to be working.

Without thought I ran towards him, raised my arm, and lobbed Arthur. The book hurtled through the air. Ancient words flowed through me and the book gathered speed on a trajectory to hit the professor. Like a heat-seeking missile it aligned itself for impact. I clapped my hands, and it went in for the kill, slamming into the professor's head. His glasses flew from his face. He staggered then dropped to the ground. Arthur swooped upwards and, with a flick of my finger, returned to me. I grabbed him as he hovered and tucked him back beneath my arm.

A growl erupted behind me and I turned to the fog. A claw had broken through the skin, but the fog and membrane were retracting. The thing inside squealed and the clawed hand disappeared.

The fog thinned, the bulbous membrane shrivelled, and headlights appeared unnoticed at the gates.

Within seconds the fog had evaporated taking the hideous monsters with it.

"Professor Fenicke!" Agnes ran back to the man sprawled across the steps. He made no effort to move and I grew concerned that he may be seriously hurt. I retrieved his horn-rimmed spectacles from the bottom of steps.

"You've killed him," Lucifer said as we stood over the professor.

"I can't have!" It had only been my intention to stop the professor conjuring the demon, not kill him! "Arthur clouted him, that's all."

"It knocked him out."

"Is he breathing?" In the thin light he seemed fragile, his face lined with age, just a vulnerable old man. A bruise was already forming, the side of his face swelling where a black eye would form. Blood trickled from his nose.

"We should call an ambulance," I suggested then flinched as someone pushed past me.

"Uncle!"

The man crouched beside the professor and then demanded to know what had happened. As he turned to Agnes, I recognised his profile. "Garrett!"

"Liv! What the hell is going on?"

Without waiting for my reply, he turned back to the professor, taking his wrist to feel for a pulse.

"He banged his head ..."

"His pulse is weak." Garrett stroked his forehead, gently brushing at stray hairs.

"He may have concussion," Agnes explained. "Liv threw a book at him."

I cringed at her words and shrivelled as Garrett turned to me with anger flickering in his eyes. "You did this?" he asked with an incredulous frown.

"Well, I ... He was ... He had my book!" I held Arthur up as evidence.

"That's the book she hit him with."

"Agnes! It wasn't quite like that."

Garrett took one look at the heavy book, threw me a disapproving glare, then returned to tending the professor. "Uncle ... Uncle Tobias, can you hear me?"

"Perhaps we should call an ambulance?" I added in a small voice.

Garrett turned with loathing to me. "What are you even doing here, Liv? And at this time in the morning?"

It was impossible to explain; Garrett would think I was mad if I started warbling on about demons, and goblins, and grimoires, and rents being torn in the fabric of dark realms that threatened our existence. "I ... the book!" I spluttered holding Arthur up again as evidence.

This time Garrett took note of the book and his face became stony.

The professor groaned.

"Uncle Tobias!"

"Uncle?"

"Yes, this is my uncle Tobias."

"But he said his name was Fenwicke."

Garrett ignored me, removed his jacket, and lay it across the injured man. After several minutes Uncle Tobias regained consciousness and began to speak.

"Garrett!" he exclaimed, though his voice was hoarse. "You're back!"

"Yes, I'm back, Uncle. What happened?" He glanced at Arthur. "What have you done?" he whispered.

"I just wanted it back, boy! I just wanted it back."

Garrett made a low groan then spent the next minutes tending to his uncle and checking for injuries. Satisfied there were no broken bones, he helped him to sit, then scooped him into his arms and, without another word or a backward glance, carried him into the house. The door slammed behind them and remained closed. I stood on the steps confused and bereft.

"Let's go, Livitha," Lucifer urged, nudging my leg. "We are trespassers on Blackwood land and definitely unwelcome."

As the iron gate clanked shut behind me, I was filled with a sense of dread anticipation, sure that my uninvited presence at the ancestral home of the cursed family had stirred up trouble for Haligern coven and perhaps destroyed any chance of happiness I had with Garrett! But more than that, I was riven with curiosity. There was a dark secret festering at Blackwood Manor, and I was determined to discover exactly what it was!

Chapter Thirty-Six

The sun was rising on another late summer day and all four aunts were in the kitchen when I finally staggered through the door. A pot of tea sat at the centre of the table and Aunt Euphemia was adding drops of elixir to four teacups. The aroma of ground coffee filled the room along with freshly baked bread. Lucifer jumped over the threshold and ran to his bowl, mewling in annoyance on finding it empty.

Four pairs of eyes turned to me with worry etched on each face.

"Liv!"

I staggered through the doorway, completely drained of energy. My feet and legs ached with the long walk and I felt emotionally battered. My head buzzed with questions and re-criminations; Garrett's accusing eyes were scorched onto my memory.

"Arthur!" Aunt Loveday exclaimed. "She *has* been to Blackwood Manor!"

I held up the hurricane lamp and placed it on the table. "And the baby fairy!"

"You found it! Oh, Liv, that's wonderful. Sit down, you look absolutely done in!"

"Take the lid off, let it free."

"No!" Aunt Loveday placed a hand over the hurricane lamp then instructed Aunt Beatrice to make some of the cheesy mash laced with elixir but before she had a chance to reach the pantry, excited chittering erupted from the hearth and a flock of winged fairies flew out of the chimney. They swarmed, flew up to the ceiling, then made their move, flying round the table in smaller and smaller circles until they created a moving shield around the lantern. Glass clinked and the door of the lantern opened. The buzz was joined by a high-pitched yowling and then they rose en-masse, a tiny and buzzing tornado, and disappeared back up the chimney.

"It was me that brought it back!" I shouted as the last fairy shot up the chimney. The fairy reunion had not gone the way I had planned. In my mind I had presented the baby to its mother, she had wept, eternally grateful to me for rescuing her child, and promises were made to leave me and my mobile phone alone! "They have to know it was me! I can't go through another night of them in my room!"

Fluttering and movement caught my attention as a fairy shot from the hearth at full pelt, aiming straight at me. For those seconds I froze, the old panic gripping me. Inches from my face, the creature hovered.

"Don't move, Liv."

My hand twitched, ready to swat the tiny monster the moment it attacked.

"Put your hand down!"

"But it's just staring at me!" For the first time I got a good look at the creature. It was quite stunning with long and slender limbs, and hair like a dandelion seed head, a fluffy halo of white. Large violet eyes rimmed by dark lashes stared at me from the face of a miniature china doll. Its wings vibrated and it hovered at eye-level like a hummingbird. "It's beautiful," I said.

The creature's face broke into a smile showing rows of miniscule teeth as sharp as pins. In the next second it shot forward, landing on my face. I made a terrified mewl, too scared to move; one false move and it would bite! It clung to my face with one hand anchored on the edge of my nostril. I waited for it to sink its teeth into my cheek.

"Aaw! It's giving you a kiss!"

"Bless!"

I sat as a statue until the tiny creature released its grip. It chittered at me then disappeared back up the chimney.

"Did you see that?" I said in disbelief, feeling for tell-tale drops of blood on my cheek. My fingers came away clean. "Did it really kiss me?"

"I think it did, Liv."

"It said thank you for rescuing its baby!"

"That is so sweet!"

"Delightful!"

"Perhaps they can be trained?"

I couldn't let that one past. "Nope! No, way Aunt Beatrice. They're devils! I risked my life to get Arthur back so that Aunt Loveday could find the spell to get rid of them!" This wasn't quite true, but my aversion to the little monsters was complete. I couldn't countenance sharing my home with them for a day longer.

"And I shall find a spell to rid us of them, Liv, just as soon as you tell us why the police were here this morning." She took a breath and then continued. "We have been so worried about you! We thought you were having a lie-in until the police arrived, but then we discovered that your bed was empty-"

"Stone cold and empty!"

"Yes, Euphemia! Stone cold and empty. And then we became very worried."

"And then a little angry."

"As soon as we discovered that you had not slept in your bed, we knew that you had gone against our agreement! We were to consult the Council, Livitha! We agreed!"

Her disappointment stung and my thoughts were scattered; had she mentioned the police? "It wasn't like that! I didn't mean to go."

"How can you not mean to go?"

"Men! There were men outside. They wanted to burn down the house."

My aunts grew silent. Aunt Loveday pulled up a chair to sit opposite me. "Tell us what happened."

"I will, but you just said that the police were here to question me." Dread had washed over me. "What did they want?"

"It was DCI Blackwood again," Aunt Thomasin said. "The one who came to the shop."

"Garrett? This morning?"

"Yes, DCI Garret Blackwood. He said he was on police business and wanted to speak to you. You've missed him by about forty minutes."

So, Garrett had been here after I'd left Blackwood Manor. No doubt to arrest me for assault, or grievous bodily harm, or actual—whichever was the worst. Had his uncle died? Light began to brighten in the room, and a dizzying sensation filled my head. I trembled. I was a murderer—again!

"She's gone as white as a ghost!"

"Is she going to pass out?"

"Have I killed him?"

"What?"

"Oh, my goodness! Livitha, whatever have you been do-ing?"

"Arthur," I managed. "I had to get Arthur."

"Yes, we've established that, Livitha. Go back to the men that wanted to burn down the house—tell us what happened from there. Blackwood didn't mention arresting you, in fact, he seemed more concerned for your welfare," Aunt Thomasin soothed. "Now, tell us exactly what happened."

Aunt Loveday took Arthur from my grip and hugged the book to her chest. "Let her recover a moment; she seems to be in shock."

A blanket was placed around my shoulders and Aunt Beat-rice poured me a coffee. Aunt Euphemia added a few drops of elixir 'for clarity of mind' and then they waited. As I sipped the coffee, I felt lifted, and after a few minutes I began to explain exactly what had happened, beginning with the mob who had come to the cottage on a witch hunt.

"I am so sorry!" I said realising just how selfish I had been. "I should have returned here, to make sure you were protected, but when I was in the air, it was so incredible, all I could think of was flying—the joy was so intense."

"We understand; the first time is overwhelming."

"You don't need to worry about us, Livitha. We are battle-hardened warriors when it comes to facing the mob!" Aunt Beatrice's face, pinched by worry, broke into a weary smile as our eyes met. "We're tough old birds, Liv," she said placing a bony hand over mine. "Don't underestimate us."

"I won't! I don't!"

"Beatrice is right, Livitha. We may appear geriatric, but we are far stronger than we appear. Centuries of adversity have taught us many lessons."

"Indeed, they have, Euphemia," agreed Aunt Loveday. "They have also taught us to tread very carefully were others fear to go."

"Blackwood Manor?"

"Indeed, Livitha. Blackwood Manor."

"I *am* sorry that I went there, but in my defence, I hadn't planned on it. I strayed into their territory and it wasn't until the imp was above me that I realised my mistake. Once we were in the forest, the house was the only safe place I could go—at least it seemed safe. But the woods are infested! Imps and ... and *werewolves*!" I blurted the word.

"Lucifer, is this correct?"

Lucifer looked up from his bowl of port, nodded, then continued to lick at the red liquid.

"Lucifer?"

He sighed, sauntered across to the table, and jumped up to face Aunt Loveday. "Livitha is correct. We did encounter a werewolf. Professor Fenicke aka Tobias Blackwood attempted to fob us off and declared that it was a member of his staff in fancy dress, but I wasn't fooled. It was a lycanthrope of the cursed variety, one that I haven't seen in these parts for more than a century."

"But you told me you were thirty-two years old, Lucifer!"

"I am."

I sighed. Pursuing the truth about his age right now was pointless.

"As I was saying, I haven't seen the type for many years."

"A werewolf at Blackwood Manor?"

"Yes! And there was a room with posts and shackles!" I said in a rush as I remembered the horrifying torture chamber. "The panelling had been scratched through to the bricks! It's the Blackwood curse, isn't it! Are they werewolves?"

"Well, they were cursed, but not with lycanthropy ... at least I don't think they were."

"The curse is shrouded in mystery, Livitha. None of the covens know the truth ... not really."

"Once you gained entrance to the manor, then what happened, Livitha?" Aunt Euphemia pushed.

I continued with the story, explaining how I'd found Agnes – who was now safe and well and back with her mother – and then Arthur and the fairy, and how Tobias Blackwood had attempted to conjure the demon just as the runes had shown.

"It's more serious that we thought," she said as I completed my story of how I had defeated the professor's attempt to conjure the demon.

"Will they arrest me?"

Aunt Loveday shook her head. "And risk being investigated? No, the Blackwoods will keep this to themselves, although we must inform the council of the attempt to conjure the demon. Tobias Blackwood was very nearly successful in tearing a rent in the fabric between our world and the dark realm; the consequences if he is successful next time will be dire—for us all."

"Do you think he will try again then, Loveday?"

"I hope not, but we can't take the chance."

"What do you suggest?"

"An immediate convening of the Council."

The room fell silent.

After a few moments, Aunt Thomasin said, "I agree Loveday. The Blackwoods must be confronted, but there is another issue we must address." She looked at each aunt in turn. "The mob who came to the house last night ... Livitha mentioned that they changed during the chase through the woods. What was it that you said, Liv? They seemed to talk in a different accent?"

"Yes, it seemed an older dialect."

"Please, can you recall their words?"

"Well, one of the men said, 'Tis what we do to witches in these parts.'"

"An unusual choice of words for a contemporary man to use."

"Indeed. Archaic, I have to agree."

"And I experienced a similar incident at the fete."

The aunts turned their attention to me as I explained about the vision I'd had at the fete as Aunt Beatrice was being verbally abused by the teenage girl. "... for a few seconds she changed. Her hair was in pigtails and she wore a bonnet. And her dress was long with a pinafore. She kind of looked medieval ... well early modern. And her language was different too."

"What did she say?"

"It went something like, 'Th'art a witch and thou shalt burn'. She was so vicious when she said it. I was shocked someone so young could be so full of hate."

"'Tis a pity, that is certain."

"It is peculiar, that you should experience a vision."

"It could just be the imprint of the past."

"Like a ghost, you mean?"

"Kind of. It's the imprint of energy, a scene replayed, its energy signature still here."

"After such a long time. If what Livitha says is correct, the imprints are hundreds of years old."

"It's possible. Afterall, ghostly sightings are often just the re-enactments of past events."

"Hmm."

"The men weren't ghosts, Aunt Loveday. They were real."

"I don't believe they acted alone. Witch hunts are unusual in these days. People are far more accustomed to reporting a crime to the police instead of becoming vigilantes," Aunt Thomasin pondered. "And the visions add to the peculiarity."

"She is correct about the men though," Lucifer added. "They were real, and the leader identified himself as the developer of the estate that Mistress Beatrice trashed."

"Lucifer!" Aunt Beatrice hissed. "That is not fair."

"Well, it has gone, all of it - the entire estate - down into a pit three hundred feet deep."

"Now, now! We've been through all of this. You know very well that the puck was responsible."

"Indeed, and he is still here."

Aunt Beatrice clapped a hand across her mouth only taking it away to beg Aunt Loveday to cast a spell to send the puck back to its own realm.

As Aunt Beatrice was placated, and a promise made to search Arthur for the spell Agnes had used to summon the puck and break it, a knock came at the door. Aunt Loveday answered it and when she returned her face was pale. "It's DCI Blackwood. I've asked him to wait in the garden, but he wants to talk to us all—together."

Chapter Thirty-Seven

T he sight of Garrett in our garden took my breath but I did my best to appear casual as we assembled beneath the great oak. He looked a little nervous, coughed, then began to speak.

"We were tipped off about an attempt to commit criminal damage last night. In particular, the threat was against your property. I'm glad to be able to inform you that we have three men in custody who have admitted intent. They were found with various tools and several jerry cans of fuel. We have them in the cells at the station in town." His brows knitted together. "They were raving ... about witches, and broomsticks, and talking cats! ... Anyway, drug tests came back positive, so the conclusion back at the station is that they were hallucinating, and the on-call psychologist is arranging a mental health evaluation ..." His face grew stern. "Ladies ... Liv ... I have an apology to make. This morning, when I discovered Liv at Blackwood Manor, I assumed that she had caused my uncle's injuries, and I reacted badly. But ... since talking to him, it has become clear that she was actually attempting to save him." He coughed. "... from a dog attack, so ... thank you and ... it may be best if we agree to leave the issue where it is, given that the situation which caused the dog to escape won't arise again. That is, if you're agreed, we can agree not to take the situation further ..."

Several moments of disbelieving silence followed until Aunt Loveday spoke. "DCI Blackwood, we are truly grateful for the bravery of your officers in apprehending the men who attacked Livitha last night. We were deeply concerned that they would attempt to return and burn the house down as they had promised." Aunts Euphemia, Thomasin, and Beatrice agreed that the men were indeed brave and that they now felt much safer knowing the men were in custody and then Aunt Loveday added, "Livitha expressed deep concern for your uncle this morning and we are glad to hear that he is well. We are also thankful that you have recognised Liv's ... bravery ... in saving your uncle from the dog that was attacking him."

Garrett nodded. "It was a beast, my uncle said."

"Vicious!" I agreed, playing along with the deceit.

Garrett offered me a weak smile. "The groundsmen have been instructed to keep a look out for it and shoot it on sight."

"Well, that's for the best," Aunt Loveday said and took a step forward. "And again, we thank you and the bravery of your colleagues. Now, I'll walk you to your car, DCI Blackwood."

His eyes caught mine. "Oh, I had hoped to have a few words with Liv ... just for our records ..."

"Of course." Aunt Loveday took a step backwards and gestured for me to join Garrett.

The aunts returned to the house and we were alone.

"Liv, I'm sorry about this morning. It was a shock seeing my uncle on the steps."

"I didn't mean to hurt him, Garrett! I hope you know that."

"I do."

He took my hands and, sure that we were going to share a 'moment' I waited for him to speak. He turned my hands over, scrutinising the palms and my fingers. "Well," he said with a broad smile. "Those fingers have healed up nicely!"

"Oh ... yes," I said, surprised at his matter of fact tone. The injuries inflicted by Matthew Hopkins, the Witchfinder General, had healed over the past weeks and now only faded bruises were visible on two fingers. "I've always healed well ..."

"Good!" he said with a slow nod of his head. He opened his mouth as though to speak and then snapped his jaw shut.

I wanted to throw my arms around him, and feel his lips pressing down on mine, but I only managed to mirror his 'good' and then walk with him to his car. Excruciating moments passed as we hovered at the car door. *Say it!* I willed him. *Ask me out!*

"Well ... I'm glad you're alright and that we've managed to ... iron things out with your aunts."

"Me too!"

Our eyes met as he slipped into the driver's seat then the door slammed, the engine started and, with a quick wave, he drove away.

The car slowed to a stop at the gate. *Here it was! The moment.* He was going to reverse and pledge his undying love, or at least ask me out for dinner.

Grief passed over me in a wave as the car picked up speed and rolled through the gates.

My phone rang and I answered it without checking the screen, sure it would be Pascal complaining about some other photo the fairies had sent.

"Hello," I answered without enthusiasm.

A man's voice said, "Livitha?" and my heart tripped.

"Hi, yes. It's me."

"G'day, Liv! It's your friendly neighbourhood doctor."

"Oh, hi!" I said with forced enthusiasm as Garrett's car disappeared.

"... I was just wondering if you wanted to go for that coffee. This afternoon would be good for me!"

Garrett's last chance to ask me out before I went for coffee with the doctor had just been and gone. My heart sank. "Yes, Dr. Cotta," I replied. "I would love to."

Epilogue

A week later Aunt Thomasin flew into the kitchen like an autumn leaf blown on the wind. "We've got to get the cottage ready." Breathless, she grasped a broom and began sweeping.

"Ready for what?" I asked as she motioned for me to lift my feet. I drank the last mouthful of coffee from my cup and moved out of her way.

"We have a houseguest. Loveday has just received confirmation. He will be here in two days. Quickly, there is so much to do."

"But the house is already clean. It's always clean."

"Well, it needs to be cleaner. We're entertaining royalty!"

Aunt Euphemia returned from the garden, pail of goat's milk in hand. "He's coming then?"

"He is. It is so exciting!"

"Can someone put me out of my misery, please? Who is coming to stay?"

"Why, Vlad, of course."

My heart missed a beat. They had to be kidding. "Vlad?"

"Yes, you know, "I vant yor blod!" Aunt Euphemia cackled. Milk splashed onto the floor.

I dry swallowed. "Vlad the Impaler is coming to our house?"

"Yes, darling. He's our summer guest. But just to note; he's not keen on being called Vlad the Impaler on account of one of his ex-wives."

She didn't elaborate. "And?"

"Oh, yes. She mocked him mercilessly and called him Vlad the Impala. We think it was her accent-"

"We think she was Australian."

"I thought she was South African?"

"Hmm, I'm not sure ..."

"Anyway, it enraged him, so, just a heads up, try not to mention it."

Aunt Thomasin cackled. "Just a heads up!" She snorted with laughter.

"What's so funny?"

"He beheaded her," Aunt Beatrice sighed as Aunt Thomasin continued to laugh. "Took a sword and just – swish! – head chopped clean off. At least that's the story."

"Oh!" A stone dropped to the pit of my stomach. I swallowed down my panic. At least the summer was nearly over. "So just a few weeks then?"

"He may stay a little longer. He did say something about having the castle renovated and needing somewhere else to stay."

"Oh, yes, it could be a little longer."

"A little longer? It's a castle!"

"Yes, it is."

"So, how much longer?"

"Oh, perhaps ... maybe until after All Hallows?"

"I bet he draws it out until the Winter Solstice!"

"You could be right, Thomasin."

I shuddered. The thought of having a vampire stalking the cottage's rooms and hallways was unnerving and I felt a sense of panic that was paralysing. I swallowed again. "So ... when does he arrive?"

"Oh, he's coming by ship. We have to pick him up from Whitby in two days."

"Whitby!" I almost yelped. "Are you sure it's Whitby?"

"Oh, yes, he's quite adamant about that. There are some boxes being delivered today. He's asked they be put down in the cellar."

I shuddered and felt the follicles at my temples contract.

"Just some essentials he's had sent beforehand. Livitha ... are you alright?"

"Yes!" I squeaked although nausea was swirling in my belly. Never in my wildest imagination did I ever think that I would be sharing a house with a vampire.

"Oh, my," Aunt Euphemia said staring directly at my head. "Sit her down. She's having a turn!"

I was walked backwards to a chair.

"She must really be terrified of old Vlad."

"Oh, poppet. He's harmless ... really."

Aunt Thomasin laughed. "I wouldn't say that. He's certainly bloodthirsty."

I squeaked.

"Oh, stop teasing the poor girl."

"Well, it's true. He's not harmless—at least not to humans."

"There you go! Nothing to worry about; we're witches."

"He has been known to-"

"Vlad has given me his solemn promise that he will behave," Aunt Loveday interrupted as she glided into the room. "There is really nothing to worry about."

"I can't believe that you've invited a vampire to stay for the summer. What's next? The Wolfman? Ted Bundy? Geoffrey Dahmer?"

"Oh, Livitha, don't exaggerate. Ted Bundy and Geoffrey Dahmer are both dead."

"So is Vlad!" Aunt Euphemia cackled then snorted and had to turn away and even Aunt Loveday burst out laughing.

"It is a tradition among us witches, that we give succour to Vlad-"

"And his wives."

"Yes, and his wives, although thankfully at the moment he's single so we won't have those ... ladies to accommodate."

"But you said before that there were problems in Salem when he was invited there!" My head swam, then buzzed, then began to throb.

"Listen, Livitha, Vlad is a pussycat if you handle him properly. He won't harm us. You must remember that it is important to have allies in this world. We have so many enemies. A man like Vlad is powerful. He has connections within the darker realm, and we need that influence to work for us. Think of it as diplomacy if you will."

I shuddered. Images of Nosferatu brushing his teeth in the guest bathroom wouldn't leave my mind.

"He's very handsome, Livitha. Not like that fiend at all. I'm sure you'll like him."

I threw Aunt Beatrice a disbelieving glance.

"It's true," Aunt Thomasin said. "You may really like him." She followed this statement with a wink.

"Pssht! Thomasin. Don't say such things," Aunt Loveday reprimanded. "Witches and vampires? It's not a good combination—too much fire!"

"At least he's single!" Aunt Thomasin giggled and threw me another knowing glance. My cheeks began to prickle.

"I can find a man on my own, thanks!"

"Well, your track record isn't that great."

I gave an exasperated sigh. Aunt Thomasin was determined to hook me up with a man and seemed to have learnt nothing from the carnage her last potion had caused. "I had coffee with Dr. Cotta last week, actually!"

"Dr. Cotton?"

"No, it's Dr. Cotta. John Cotta."

The room grew silent as my aunts exchanged glances.

"What?" I said as they remained mute. "I know I'm punching above my weight, but he's the one who asked me out!"

Aunt Beatrice gasped. Aunt Euphemia's eyes grew wide. Loveday squinted then looked out of the window whilst Aunt Thomasin stared directly at my head.

"What is it?" I began to feel like an insect beneath a magnifying glass.

"Well ... It's just that the name rings a bell, Liv," Aunt Euphemia said without taking her eyes from my head. She fidgeted. "Someone from long ago."

The atmosphere in the room became strained. "It's ... not a common name, I guess, and he does have ancestors in England, that's part of why he's here. He wants to do some research into his family's history."

"I'm sure he's absolutely lovely, Liv," Aunt Beatrice said without meeting my eyes. "And a doctor too! Quite a catch."

"He's gorgeous, Liv. Well done!" Aunt Thomasin's words were insincere.

"Well ... it's early days. We've only been out once—just for coffee, but we did get on. We had a laugh."

"Has he asked you out again?" Aunt Beatrice exchanged a look with Aunt Euphemia.

My cheeks began to redden. "Yes, for dinner, on Friday."

"Oh, you can't go on Friday!" There were sighs of relief from my aunts at this proclamation. "That's when you've got to pick up Vlad from Whitby."

"Me?"

"Well, you are the most experienced driver."

An awkward silence fell. All four aunts stared at my hair. "What is it?" I touched my head searching for whatever they were looking at. Did I have nits?

"Look! It's spreading!"

"What is it?" I patted my head but could feel nothing. "Is something in my hair?"

"No." Aunt Thomasin shook her head but continued to stare.

"For goodness sake! What is it? What's wrong with my hair?"

"Well, it's a little bit different from a few minutes ago."

"Different? What are you talking about?"

"I'll get a mirror."

"So," Aunt Thomasin said, changing the subject as Aunt Beatrice disappeared to find a mirror. "We're going to have the Count stopping with us. I can't wait to ask him about Salem"

I checked my reflection in the kitchen window, but the ancient glass only warped my appearance.

"I want to know all about the vampires in England," Aunt Euphemia added with enthusiasm. "I know they have pockets of them in France, but if they're here ..."

Aunt Beatrice returned with a mirror from the hall. "You may want to sit down," she said.

I took the mirror and checked my reflection and held back a gasp.

My hair, which this morning had been a little grey at the temples with a sprinkling of silver through the crown, now sported a streak of pure white at least three inches wide above my ear. It ran the full length of my hair. "What happened?"

"Your hair has gone white."

"I can see that!"

"It's a reaction-"

"Well, I did feel afraid when you told me about Vlad."

"Did you feel any tingling in your fingertips?"

"I didn't see any sparks."

"There weren't any."

"It's not unusual for it to appear without fireworks."

Once again, they were talking around me and not to me. "What are you talking about?"

"Your power Livitha, it just took a leap forward. Shock may have triggered it."

I fingered the strip of white hair as I considered my reflection. It felt a little wiry, but I liked it. "Maybe now I really will set my bed on fire!"

Aunt Beatrice slipped an arm around my waist. "No need to worry, darling girl. I'll put a pail of water beside the fire extinguisher."

I groaned.

Aunt Thomasin resumed sweeping the already clean floor. "There is a silver lining, Liv," she said. "At least the Count won't be interested in you—far too old!"

Lucifer sniggered. "I think I *shall* ask Old Mawde if she has a spare pipe, seeing as how you're entering your 'cronedom' now Winifred!" Amused by himself, he continued to laugh.

I threw him a glare, but he only laughed harder.

And then inspiration struck. I whispered ancient words and clicked my fingers. As my fingertips sparked, a cluster of white hairs appeared on Lucifer's ear. It quickly spread the entire length of his body to the tip of his tail.

"Lou," I said with saccharine sweetness, "would you like some salmon?"

"Don't mind if I do," he replied, instantly serious.

"My pleasure," I replied, reaching for the supermarket pouch of salmon in jelly.

He scowled.

"It is from their 'Deluxe' range, Lou. I'm sure it'll be delicious!"

THE END

DEAR WITCHY MYSTERY fan!

There is no pre-order for the next 'Menopause, Magick, & Mystery' novel, 'Night Sweats, Necromancy, & Love Bites', but don't despair! It will be available very soon. To receive an email straight to your inbox on publication day with a link to the book on Amazon in both ebook and paperback form, please sign up to my reader group. Once you join please download my gift to you. Click here to join[1]

WEBSITE[2]
FACEBOOK[3]

Other Books by the Author
If you love your mysteries with a touch of the supernatural then join ghost hunting team Peter Marshall, Meredith Blaylock, & Frankie D'Angelo in:
Marshall & Blaylock Investigations
When the Dead Weep[4]
Where Dead Men Hide[5]

Menopause, Magick, & Mystery
Hormones, Hexes, & Exes[6]
Hot Flashes, Sorcery, & Soulmates
Night Sweats, Necromancy, & Love Bites (forthcoming)

---

1.   https://dl.bookfunnel.com/pgh4acj6f8

2. https://www.jcblake.com

3. https://www.facebook.com/JCBlakeAuthor/?

4. https://books2read.com/u/bwdyA0

5. https://books2read.com/u/3GdV7L

6. https://books2read.com/u/4A7pJe

Printed in Great Britain
by Amazon

78302495R00161